TROUBLEMAKER

Brian Pera

St. Martin's Press ☙ New York

www.stmartins.com

Library of Congress Cataloging-in-Publication Data

Pera, Brian.
    Troublemaker / by Brian Pera.
        p. cm.
    ISBN 0-312-25232-3 (hc)
    ISBN 0-312-27708-3 (pbk)
    1. Gay youth—Fiction. 2. Rejection (Psychology)—Fiction.
3. Memphis (Tenn.)—Fiction. 4. New York (N.Y.)—Fiction.
5. Omaha (Neb.)—Fiction. 6. Carnivals—Fiction. I. Title.

PS3566.E672 T76 2000
813'.6—dc21   00-027122

First Stonewall Inn Edition: November 2001

10 9 8 7 6 5 4 3 2 1

For Dennis Cooper

Colorado Springs

Nothing else in the world to do, and nowheres else to go's how I ended up at the carnie. And that's how I met Red; got the fire hair, freckles scattershot all across his face. Said he was running, said he didn't know where he'd be tomorrow but sure as hell not there in Nebraska. I couldn't of said it better myself.

It was the last time I seen my ma. I come all the way from New York to Omaha, gone to her house and—what's new—she wouldn't let me in. Peeked out the window and mouthed the words I knowed so well by then.

. . . Go . . . away . . .

Just to bug her, or cause I come all that way for nothing and now what, I stood there, not a budge—stared her down. Her eyes skirted every which way over the windowpane, without she'd look me in the face. The more she done it the harder I stared. How'd we get to this place's what I's thinking. It was all in my head but not put together.

Red. I followed him around and for the most part he didn't mind. He even told me some about his self. Said he come to Omaha from a rinky-dink neighbor city. Got sent to Boystown, where Pappy Flanagan's supposed to save the souls. ("There's no such thing as a bad boy," says Pappy. "Yeh right," said Red, "just good and better.") He ain't got a ma or pa, or so he much as said. Somebody-or-other sent him there, and the second he was in he was trying to figure how to bust out. Made two tries and got caught both times—they dragged his ass back. And cause they knowed he wanted out they put the pressure on even harder, more than on the other guys what just sat around and did the "yes sir" "no sir."

Wouldn't you know he finally got out without he even had to try.

Some man, some bigwig or other, come to Boystown, made an act like *I's 'a gonna take care of this boy myself, gonna be my pet project, my special ward.* Told them he'd put Red to work in his yard, make a man out of him. And cause the guy got money what fooled all the soul-savers, he took Red's hand and waltzed him right out of there.

Sure he took care of Red, give him everything a guy could want and more. But there's always a few small hitches for the price of room and board. Not just do this and do that but favors traded plain and simple. Strip down and dough-si-dough: Red was the man's private boy. But the guy liked to share. There was stuff about flying him around in a jet, parties with other soul-saver bigwigs, putting on shows in back rooms. Here's where the story got sketchy on account of Red only let me in on so much. Said he couldn't never know for sure just who was who and who was listening in. He was going to keep quiet like some peoples told him, until they come through on their end of a deal.

Said he was here on business, said this was the perfect place to meet his man, the carnie: loads of peoples, noise, and colors, not a one thing to stick out from the rest. Told me I could hang with him until the man come, but after that I'd have to beat it like we didn't know each other, which I figured'd be easy since it was anyways mostly true.

"So who's the man?" I says. "He somebody from Boystown? You aim to go back there?"

"You crazy?" he says and his face gone screwy. "I'm trying to get away from them. Twisted motherfuckers made my life hell enough as it is."

And already by that time I knowed to keep my mouth shut, so I changed the subject to me. Told him how I knowed just exacty what he meant, just exactly, on account of I myself ain't had nowheres to go. How I seen what little home I got left just a few days before I come to the carnie—no go and get lost—and I's ready to head just about anywheres. When he didn't tell me to shut up, when I seen he's just looking away like he always done so's it might be he's listening, I gone on about my pa dying awhile back and what that done to what was left.

"He was sick on his bed for the longest time: alcohol, and ciga-rettes. Or so they says. Holed up top of the house in a back room, his bedroom but since he got sick it seemed more like a waiting room weren't nobody waiting in but him. He was on all kinds of pills, washed down with whiskey stored somewheres in there.

"Whichever, he was almost always asleep when I snuck in—got his head propped on a stack of pillows, body a sack of bones by then—and I'd know he was still alive from the way he's breathing: mouth wide open reaching up far as he could make it like to suck all the air in with whatever energy he got left. Sometimes I'd take some of them pills myself, slide under his bed. Hide for the rest of the day. In the beginning I laid on the wood floor, which didn't bother me none but later I brung pillows and a blanket and made my own bed to lie in. Figured I may as well set up camp.

"Sometimes he woke up after I been under for a while, and I'd be quiet, listen to the shake of the pill bottles, gulp of something to drink. I expected he'd get to bawling, like he just couldn't stand being in bed no more after so long without cigarettes and whatever else, no matter what Ma said about he liked it better that way, but he never so much as shed a croc tear that I could tell. Just the bottles rattling and maybe he'd holler for Ma but she generally didn't come until after dinnertime, when Pa was dead to the world. By that time he didn't wake up much. Just asleep and gasping like he done. Mostly I'd be under the bed trying to match my breathing to his, let myself near suffocate in that breadbox, thinking I could get to where he was so's I'd know how it felt.

"Course it was me found him dead, snuck into the room to find it was silence, no more breathing out of whack or breathing at all. I figured he just delivered his self to whatever dream he been having, right? Like they say peoples get to a point they like what's going on in their head better and want to go there so they just do; they just up and leave.

"Before I gone to tell my ma I searched the room until I found his flask: Looked in his drawers between clothes he ain't wore in years, under seat cushions and back of curtains, in the bathroom cabinet under the sink—all I found *there* was an invitation to him and my ma's wedding, like I'd want to go even if I could; it was pure white paper but for where the water pipes leaked lines on it. *Come join us for the wedding of So-and-So* and so on. Fell apart in my hands the second I picked it up.

"In the end I found the flask between the mattresses, half empty or half full. The whole time it been right under his nose and dangling over mine; now how come I wouldn't of figured that out? Should of knowed he wouldn't put it nowheres he'd have to walk for it. I took it, along with an empty pill bottle, and hid them in my room. Then I gone down to the basement where my ma was, told her Pa weren't breathing no more. She got her back to me, digging for something in the pantry, and I thought maybe I should just kick her in so's I could get rid of the worst too now the best was gone.

" 'In a minute,' she said without she even turned to look at me.

"Weren't until later I found out the real reason Pa died: He swallowed every pill out of them bottles on his bedside table. Ma never mentioned the one I got. Once in a while, until I lost it like everything else, I took the lid off and held it up to my nose, tried to smell what been in it before, like hearing the ocean in a shell. Just a hint left, but I got me a sense for it. Ain't made me feel better, or feel anything in particular, but I found myself doing it again all the same. By the time I finished the whiskey off I got a taste for that too. Still got the flask in my bag."

And I motioned to it at my hip.

Red made a sound like to laugh, though you wouldn't of knowed it by looking at him.

"Sounds like maybe *you* would of been better off at Boystown," he said.

Least I knowed he was listening.

"Maybe so. You ain't the only one's said it. But for the longest time the only place I wanted in was my pa's head. After he died my ma locked his room up, cause only she's got the key, and cause it took her so long to get her hands on it. That woman's all about keys. Once or twice she left it unlocked and I snuck in, looked through the drawers and the closets where all Pa's suit coats was hung, ones he wore to work before he's in bed so long. I took some of them—no more'n two or three—and put them in my own closet. Later Ma found out I got them, said she didn't like the idea I's sneaking around like a thief in my own daddy's room, specially since he was dead now and couldn't do nothing about it. I told her I didn't know what she was talking about: Even when he was alive, if that's what you want to call it, he couldn't of done nothing.

4

"But I ain't lived in that house for a long time now and don't expect I ever will again."

We was at the edge of the fairgrounds looking in, and I shut up cause I seen he weren't listening now, if he ever been. Instead he's watching the riders get ready for the rodeo—every one of them got a number taped to his back, all the papers flapping at once from the wind. I looked at Red and wondered about somebody like him— wondered was he like me, more ways than one, what would life be like the two of us moving through it together. Course later he'd take off for good, off to Colorado, where I's at now, shaking myself silly trying to kick this crud I been on. Red told me not to follow him but I ain't never been a good listener and anyways by that time I ain't got no choice. I knowed if a body's got a fate, I got one too. He's mine.

Two days already and don't nobody seems to know him. Wish I still had the black-and-white picture, one where he's leaning against the bleachers. Behind him you seen the riders, Ferris wheel, stuffed animals hanging by the neck, awning. He's at the carnie but not really, way he's away from everybody else like ain't a one of them he needs, and not even a look to what's around him—something bigger than him on his mind. Even in the picture he wouldn't look at me, got his eyes off to the sky. Sky takes up most of the picture, shoulders on up is shine white and the puff of his cigarette smoke and clouds. He's in the denim coat with the sheepskin collar, pack of Marlboros front pocketed, peeking from under the flap. Striped T-shirt, dusty-red hair. Eyes squinted and his mouth puckered up towards his nose like he's thinking hard.

That's how I describe him to anybody I think maybe's seen him around here in Colorado Springs, on account of it's how I remember him, even after I lost the picture like everything else.

First day here I ended up in what my ride called the Garden of the Gods. We been on just any old road, passing empty fields what just kept going on until they run into mountains and sky. Nothing but a trap in all directions. I ain't never met my ride, until a few hours back down the highway, but anyways I turned to him and talked like maybe we'd knowed each other longer, which is what I always done. Talked like he'd drove me all along and seen everything else I did, out the same windows, same eyes, and I said:

"I don't see why he'd want to get to a place like this so fast so bad.

Nothing here what won't wait for him, be exactly the same three weeks or six ahead."

Or something like that. And like he knowed what I's talking about my ride said, "There's plenty to see when you know where to look." A few miles up he turned into some of that emptiness like we's making a run for it, down a gravel road through red dust, around a bend, and into this garden.

So I take back what I said cause even though I didn't see Red there I seen now maybe why he come. All around the car was rocks piled mammoth high, fiery red as the guts of a volcano turned inside out, like pictures what flash by too fast in disaster movies and the news. Here it was; standstill. For all I know it *was* the middle of a volcano, and we'd drove right into it—like to get swallowed up. That same color lit the vinyl seats of the car on fire, and I squinted my eyes so's everything become just that and nothing else, got warm enough I felt maybe I's on fire too and so sleepy. Then too soon my ride said "Well let's go now you've seen it," and he drove me to a spot downtown where I lied peoples was sooner or later waiting for me.

This here's my third night without no shut-eye to speak of, and I's set to fall over. I left New York a week ago for Nebraska with no dope and nowheres to get more. Now I's empty-handed and ain't got connection one in Colorado Springs, and no cash even if I done. But I promised I wouldn't do the stuff no more anyways, so I been keeping a lid on things with the little joke bottles of liquor I lifted off the train. I got to make them last on account of I can't afford no more until I get set up, but try to tell me that once I's feeling good off one or two.

Even the YMCA ain't cheap enough I can square it here: muscleman at the front desk give me the merry ha-ha when I showed him what little money I got, just what's left of the dough from the carnie. I give him a look like if he weren't already dead inside that jug he might be soon, and since then it's been pass the time at whatever pinball machine I might run across, line my quarters on the deck of the game and take up as much time as I can pay for. Nights I crash in the fountainbed of Something-or-other Square, Courtyard Such-and-such, downtown; for now. Somebody's bound to come along.

Me and the Madam figured out going back to Nebraska was the thing to do. She said give it one more try and I done like she asked.

Ain't my fault it didn't work out. No way we could of knowed all that from New York City. So I took the train and give it a chance. Just weren't meant to be. And once I seen Nebraska ain't got nothing for me, and I ain't got nowheres else—nobody nowhere and so on—I seen I's free, go where I want. Don't know a soul in Colorado Springs, or anywheres else no more, and might be I'd of been tore up about it if things was different. But I can't say it makes no nevermind anymore.

ONE

I come to New York from Memphis.

Sort of.

To understand one you got to understand the other, if you can keep them straight. If you can keep them straight you's one step ahead of me. Like I say I's in Omaha, Nebraska before I's in Colorado Springs, and before that I's in New York City. In New York City, I's at the Madam's. It was Nebraska first, straight out of the womb, then Memphis later on, from Memphis to Buford, Arkansas but don't get me started on that cause I decided I best just forget Buford altogether if I can.

So: New York City, like I say. I go over it in my head again and again but it's a circle and soon as I get to a point I think I can stop I see I's still caught up in it, with as much of it ahead of me as behind. For now, just behind's Nebraska, and right behind that's the Madam putting me on the train headed there. Before that, back farther or maybe just ahead, when I first come to New York, is coming to her house fresh off the bus from that place in Arkansas don't exist no more.

When I first come in I got everything a body could want. Made me feel like that was life; you know, figure out it ain't working one place you go on to another next in line. Course that was back before I come to feel there's limits on these things. I been kicking around Forty-deuce the day my bus come in, happy to have my feet on the ground after being on the road so long, until I come across some guys hanging out front of Howard Johnson's just down from the big co'cola sign. They told me about working at the house, for the Madam, on account of we got to talking about how I's broke and got no place to go. They took me there and Bam straight off I's making the dough; got a room of my own and anything else I want or so I thought.

They could of at least half warned me.

There was all kinds of rules. No drugging in the Madam's house for one. But there's ways to get around that one: always was and will be. I learned that—how to hide it—from my pa. No drugs, and keep up appearances. Madam practically spit-combed her boys' hair, told us what to wear and what to say and when to shut up, which is the part I ain't never been good at.

Turned out she was right on a lot of things I didn't want to give her credit for. I can see that, now. She said I'd be big for a couple months but don't start to count on it. Said I'd do good to keep a thought to the future. The johns like a new face makes them think well maybe this here's a Hardy Boy, one of the Brady brothers. Just a kid next door. Act like you's in it but ain't, like somehow you stumbled into doing this for a living, which is anyhow mostly true but not like they got it, on account of I kind of been down that road before, in Memphis, road what led right to this house, even if I didn't know I's on it or what address I's looking for.

Madam said after a while they'd figure I's there to stay, that maybe once I was next door but now I's stuck *here*; for good. And she was right. After a while I's sitting on my ass in the living room—john after john—trying to remember all them things she told me to do would get get me sessions once I got to start working for them.

My only chance was to make myself good at what I done, get to be a pro as they says but I ain't never knowed just how to do that. I'd finally get a guy up in the room and wouldn't know what to say or not, fall all over myself to the point the Madam got phone calls about what the hell you letting that boy up in them rooms for and what kind of house was this anyway.

"What are you good at?" she asked me one time after yet another john wanted one thing and I give him everything but.

"Don't know," I says. "I can name wildflowers. And I know geography."

"I mean up in the *rooms*," she says. "We're talking about the rooms here. What can you do upstairs that gives you an advantage? You've got to think about these things."

And I racked my brains. But I couldn't never come up with noth-

10

ing. All I knowed was to try whatever she just told me downstairs—I tripped through it like I ain't never done it before, which the Madam said would of been okay if I didn't always look like I's set to vomit. The other guys was always talking about the money, making the cash, but I didn't see why nobody needed it. Who needs money when you got a warm place—the bed and eats and the whole shebang? Only thing I needed that the Madam weren't about to give me was my dope, the friend I made from the guys what first brung me to the house—better friend than Pa's liquor and pills ever been. When I needed that, I got it out on the street from a guy they knowed called Mannie—good old Mannie—who didn't care if I looked like I's about to chuck up, long as I put out.

"Just remember, you got the power," one of them other boys told me when I first come in. "They don't know why they're here; why *you're here*. They think it's just about sex."

But I didn't know what *he* was talking about neither. He was twenty-nine and been doing it since he's fifteen, so he got more time to figure it out than I done. I just wanted a place to stay and room to do my own thing, didn't care about money cause what did I need it for.

Thing is, even though I didn't need no money to live there, to live there I got to make some, which is another circle I couldn't make a straight line.

So after a while Madam said she couldn't do nothing with me no more; I's a lost cause. Said she weren't stupid, she knowed I's on drugs; said I got about two minutes left there. Course then I started trying harder, gone up into the rooms and squinted my eyes to stay awake and figure whatever it was needed doing to make this thing work, like it done back in Memphis in the bars. Said to myself *I got the power* over and over until the words run together. But the dope kind of set up camp in my head so's everything seemed like it was happening in another place, and I couldn't figure out the system.

One of my last days at the house—the last of the few minutes— time I's in the Grey Flannel room with yet another john wanted it without the condom, I done already give up. If I got all the power how come I got to keep telling myself's what I's thinking when I's thinking at all. In the back of my head, in the little pocket where things still made sense, place as impossible to get to as any other I's set on getting, I knowed I's on my way out, and weren't all the power in the world could change that. *I been through this before, so what did I care.* One john was like every other, and *still* I couldn't figure him out.

"Now you can make some money with this man," says Madam downstairs, after I left the guy in the Grey Flannel room—what's decked out like somebody's office, like any minute somebody could hold a meeting there all hush hush and ain't we all important— telling him to get comfortable like the day he's born.

"He's a regular. He'll try to get you to go without a condom. Don't tell him no, even if you don't intend to accommodate him. Remember what I told you? About suggesting something else before he even realizes he's not getting what he wanted? It's all about suggestion. Make another suggestion and show him what you're talking about to make it stick in his mind. He'll see you again if you do it right. Keep in mind he doesn't like you if you're a day over twelve, so don't talk much but keep a smile on. Think of high school prom, like it's next weekend. You're one of those shy boys: Everything's okay by you, sure, whatever."

"Are you listening?"

The john told me to stand a ways back so he could get a look, which was fine by me. I smiled doing it. Then he asked what was my favorite rock bands.

"Pretty much everything," I says, grinning cause what the hell made him think I got time to listen to the music.

Before long, it was just the floor I's looking at. He'd started undressing. If I watched him, all I could think was how white he was, how his dark socks left a purple ring around his legs when he took them off. If I looked at the floor I could think of something else, try to keep a grip on what I's supposed to do next and who he's supposed to be, manage half a smile.

He gone on talking phedinkus; about his wife, just a little, and a lot about his brother. How his father built up a business for him and his brother to divvy, but it was the john's idea his brother's getting greedy—said he lived with him all his life and knowed him like the back of his hand. He wanted somehow to get rid of his brother, kick him out of his half.

"Ever since we were little we were at each other's throats," the john said. "That house wasn't big enough for the two of us. He's always, *always* thought he could get his way."

12

But it was all says which to me—business and partners and shares. And I ain't never lived long enough with nobody to tell one thing or the other about *always*. I looked at his wingtips over by the white leather chair in the corner, stared hard like I's sober. Them I could figure—not a trace of dirt or wear, polished slick like he just bought them, like they was still a commercial what put the idea in his head to get them in the first place. Only thing give them away was their smell. From across the room it was office carpet, cold sweat socks, lady's perfume, the guts of a house on the edge of the suburbs.

"I like to have my balls licked. Can you do that for me?" as he set the lettuce on the bedside table, pulled the bedspread down, and jumped on the bed like he was still a football star.

Course I didn't want to; I tried to think was there anything Madam ever said about something like that, tried to think up a suggestion what could make something else seem just as good, but weren't nothing come to my head, and meanwhile he's staring hard at me like I weren't the grinning boy wonder he paid for no more. So I just smiled and said no.

"Only with peoples I know better."

"How do we get to know each other better?" he asked, like it was some game he could figure out.

Then he picked up a smut rag from the pine trunk, foot of the bed, started flipping through it. Every other page or so he stopped, made a sound like *hmm*, or *there we go*, or *now we's talking*, but it was only him talking, studying the magazine hard like to get ready to tell me who I was. I made my way to the bed and sat next to him, which point he tossed that one onto the floor and picked up some other from the trunk—this one all out; got the pictures of guys in action. Weren't no way I'd be able to come up with anything could beat that.

"Here's what I'm talking about," and he pointed to a full-page close-up of some guy licking some other's whatnot.

"See that?"

I leaned over just a little; just enough.

"How well do you think *they* know each other?" he asked, looked straight at me and pushed the magazine closer so's I felt like I's being surrounded.

How should I know? I wanted to say, or *Scoot over*. But all what come out was, "Search me."

"I know you better than you think," he says and nudged my arm with his elbow. "Hmm?"

Then like we's talking about something else he starts telling me how I probably got lots of boyfriends, I's a little princess; said I never been with a real man like this before, never had a real man I done nothing with, said I got to have some Italian in me—that he could tell I get lippy. If I ever got lippy with him he said he'd speak Italian like he knowed I understood; he'd beat my ass to a pulp then love me just as hard the next morning. Kept going on and on like most the rest of them, like we weren't where we was, which would of been fine if I could ever figure out just where it was they wanted to be instead. He didn't seem half as real to me as he thought he was.

"If you want me to I will," I said. "With protection."

And boy he shut that magazine quick, and pitched it past the foot of the bed, where it landed on the floor with a noise like somebody got slapped. But I paid him no mind. I reached over for the dental dams and lube out the bedside drawer. Before he could say bugger somebody or something up I's rolling a condom on him, thinking:

Must be I's still smiling. My mouth's got a butterfly cramp.

"When I see that other boy," john says, "what's his name, the one from France, the rugby player: *He* doesn't make me wear a condom."

I didn't know whose pack of lies he meant—no telling what the others said in the room—where they was from, how old, how turned on. And I couldn't let that get to me, couldn't let it break my concentration, so I just gone on with what I's doing. Getting my dope from Mannie on the outside was one thing: Got to do what you got to do. But this guy weren't doing me no favors. I weren't about to touch him without something standing in the way. Weren't much the Madam said I could remember but I remember she said weren't no reason not to use a rubber in the house. So, as long as I's there, I figured I got every right.

After I lubed my palm he took the condom off; pulled it at both ends so's it let sail across the room like a rubber band. He looked at me with a make me stare, folded his arms over his stomach.

"They aren't foolproof anyway. The number of times you use them a day, you might as well not."

Well my head gone empty, I just blanked. Couldn't remember nothing Madam or nobody else told me, not ever, just that I's in one

14

of them dreams, where you's on stage and ain't even knowed you's in a play until you blinked and seen you was there: Weren't nothing to do but go on with it. Just barrel through, and if you screwed the thing up so be it.

I told him he weren't half as big in some places as all around, like he thought. I ain't never had a boyfriend, I said, not really; just almost, right before I come to New York, in the real world I put out of my head to make room for cockamamie make-believe like this here. I ain't had a boyfriend cause I never found one, and just when I found one—just when I thought maybe I could get what he seemed to think should be so easy for me to find—it got took away. That was real, I said. That was real. So I didn't know what the hell he's talking about and he could eat shit, and not mine cause I weren't about to let him near me. If he didn't want a rubber he could call the rugby player and see was *he* game for playing without a net.

*   *   *

Before the place what don't exist no more it was Memphis, Tennessee. When I get to remembering without I can stop myself, it's all the flowers. That part of the circle's so many flowers. A body ain't seen Memphis until he seen spring, what's got the azaleas running up and down just about every street, and all in between them it's iris, bright yellow daffodils and forsythia, hydrangea. Columbine, what's got seeds so tiny you can't see them and the wind blows them all over to far-flung places—so far from where they started they might of come from the place I first learned all them flowers' names, and maybe like me they won't never go back. All them's something to lay eyes on.

But for the longest time Memphis was about wondering where was I going to grab a wink at night.

Finally I hooked up with a place for seventy-five dollars a month. It was downtown Memphis Main Street; way past the decent houses respectable folk lived in. This was deepest downtown, busted lip of the city, few blocks up from the Mississippi. Vacant lots and hollowed-out buildings left over from the cotton trade and immigrant days. Place called **MOJO'S**, or so the faded sign hung out front said. Maybe used to be a store or some kind of business. Now it was just a blank two-story, north end. Ground floor's one big room and a wall

15

of windows what faced the street. Second floor up creaky stairs was strictly flophouse; two empty hallways broke off into small rooms, every room got a fireplace didn't work and a window wouldn't open. Only way to lock the doors was from the outside—so's it felt like anybody could come along and trap you in. Plaster hung from the ceiling in big chunks over a floor what weren't but splinters.

I got family in Memphis, or so I thought: Nana on my pa's side and Aunt Edna on my ma's. Across the river into Arkansas, at *that* place, I got me another grandmama: If things didn't work out on the one bank of the Mississippi I could cross on over and try my luck with her's what I's thinking. Cause like I say, back then I thought that's how these things worked. Already I been living in Nana's house farther uptown. Ma sent me there from Omaha after Pa died, said I'd never go to college, get a job, do with my life like better peoples done. She been telling me that all along, so I didn't figure there was any use trying, on account of I got to take her word for it, she knowed me longer'n I knowed myself. She needed me out of her hair she said. *Well, good,* I figured. *I'll go to Memphis, where I got more family to choose from.*

I's in there pitching but turned out living with Nana weren't but a kettle of fish. Not two months moved in, come to find she wants me out. *I'm too old, I'm tired, I just can't do it,* she said, and all kind of baffle-gab without she never really explained herself. But maybe even if she tried to explain I wouldn't of understood, not from the looks of things anyhow, on account of she done a lot didn't make sense to me. Like sitting in some part of the house arguing with herself, or so I thought at first. After a while I come to think she been arguing with somebody else, like the grandpa I never met, like they got some unfinished business never got took care of before he died. She'd say her part, then she'd say his, so's both of them was putting their two cents' worth into the same slot and weren't neither getting closer to coming out right. The whole house was them arguments—voices raised and fists drawn.

I tried to keep to myself, thought maybe if I stayed out of the argument I wouldn't get dragged into it. Set up behind closed doors in my pa's old room, one he growed up in. Like to think it was just how he left it. Got its own bathroom and staircase; own separate digs in a way. I stayed up late nights tearing through drawers and cabinets, hungry for pictures or letters or just any old bits I figured maybe been his one time, anything he left behind, like the flask I brung with me from Ma's. Soon enough I felt more like him than me, so's things half made sense. Even looking out his window I seen the view he his self seen growing up. It was just like flying from Nebraska to Memphis in the plane Ma sent me off in to get rid of me quick as she could, give me my running shoes and told me to sprint. Way up there and looking down at everything it all seemed like just so many squares and rectangles, and things was just a matter of organizing; like if you stared long and hard enough you'd see how things is in rightful order and make sense of it all, not like on the ground where everything's just one big never-ending, what seems throwed together and shook up.

I set all them pictures and everything else up on shelves. Found old schoolbooks with my daddy's name wrote on the inside cover, scrawled like he just learned to spell it; set those out too, like they's a picture told what he looked like when he sat for it. Yes sir I got so cozy up there like to thought of it as my own home, only one I ever got, like Ma been wrong about me not being able to start over out there the way other peoples done.

Until the day Nana walks in like she just figured out she got a bone to pick with me, says:

"So did you find a place of your own yet?" in a voice so sweet you'd think she's singing me a love song.

It was the first I heard of it, and from there things got worse. Got to be she asked every day, Did I find it. I knowed I's on my way out, I ain't stupid; I been heading there in one way or another since I could remember—ain't never even got a chance to sit down. But I didn't know Memphis, and couldn't afford another plane to go up and make sense of it for me. And I didn't have nowheres else to go, so I held out long as I could. If she wanted me to leave she'd just have to carry me out herself.

But she started accusing me of lifting things, talked to me like I been in on the argument all along. She'd get to looking for something, couldn't find it anywheres, gone around the house searching, complaining under her breath. Longer she looked the angrier she got, and she'd talk to me like I's working as hard to hide things as she was to find them. More than once she asked me where'd her flashlight or receipt book or opal necklace get to. I never knowed what else to tell her but to try to think where she put it last, but seemed like anything I said made up her mind I's a thief storing loot.

Then calls from Ma: The phone rung echoes through the pitch-black halls of the house. She heard from Nana about things missing and made a case against me long-distance; told Nana watch out for me and my sticky fingers, told how I'd stole stuff from my own pa on his deathbed and weren't no telling where I'd stop if someone didn't stop me before I couldn't stop myself.

Mostly I kept on trying to keep to my own. Nana's house was big enough to get lost in anyhow, least for a while. I gone up the steep steps to the attic, where years of boxes was stacked along the wall, full of family things. Dug through them, found things like a navy medal of my grandaddy's, missing toy parts from games left pitched by aunt or uncle whatsisname; put all them things on the sill of a window looked down at the front yard. Figured: *Long as I keep it all up here I can make like its my own without it's stealing.* Stared at them and the green of the lawn behind them like they's one solid something I made myself.

But Nana always found me. Wondering where I got to sent her into fits, acted like I left the room before she's done talking to me. She'd call out all over the house until I answered—I could hear her underneath me somewheres, we was two ends of a tunnel calling through the dark for the other. Usually I's walking out the attic door when I answered. Out the attic door and right into her. Course she got on to me about being where I weren't supposed to be, looked at me with her eyes wide and the head backed away a little like she didn't trust me. It was extra proof of my criminal nature.

Finally I had to leave. She just asked one too many times when was I on my way, and weren't nowheres in that house I could go to get away from it, not without she thought I's somewheres stealing something else she lost her own damn self. After all that time living with her, she still ain't cleared out drawers for me to put my things in. I still got everything in my bag, like from the beginning she knowed I weren't there for long. If she seen I touched anything or put it where it weren't before, she got on to me about changing things around, said I's trying to confuse her. Got to be I's afraid I'd come home to the locks changed and that blamed on me too.

And that done it. Mr. Wingtips put in a call. If we was in a play, he wrote it, and he didn't take kindly to me changing the lines. How dare I this and that? What kind of place was this? Did we want the police called in on us? *Look*, Madam told him, *we can't make the boys do anything in the room. It's between you and them.* Then she offered him another session with somebody else on the house, and when she got off the phone she said I better start taking orders or my two minutes was up; said the only reason anybody ever picked me was I didn't look a day over fifteen, but then I gone and ruined it when I opened my mouth. I's either going to start doing what she said or I's out of there. From now on I'd have to sit in the phone room with her, between johns.

"If that's what it takes," she said.

For the rest of my time there I's on the couch across from her desk, and when I weren't plain nodding out I watched her crazy busy on the phones and at the monitors like popcorn on a skillet. All six phones ringing at once, and seemed like everybody asked the same questions: How many you got to choose from, what they look like, what's their names, how much, and sometimes did we get into this or that rough stuff, like we's as excited about it all as they was.

If anybody knowed their lines it was Madam. She said the same things to everybody.

"We have five handsome young men to choose from, we're located in the upper Fifties between First and Second Avenues in a lovely, well-appointed townhouse furnished in the Executive Style: Our prices are one-fifty for the half hour, two hundred for the hour," and blah blah blah.

I heard it so much it was sheep I counted in my sleep.

Then on about us guys, or peoples what sounded like us only better-looking. We was generally all-American frat types, and if that didn't work she just give us another name, said we was the exotic kind and jacked the price up. She tried to set up an appointment, saying we was so busy with school and frat stuff and exotic whatnot that we was hard to pin down, but most of the johns just said they'd call back when they was in the area, like we didn't know they worked right around the corner.

On a shelf over the phones was three black-and-white monitors,

One for manning the street outside the building, one for the quick hall between the two front security doors, and one for the living room; all of it scrunched fat by the cameras. To most anybody it wouldn't seem like the Madam's paying them no mind at all. But she could just as easily notice a chip of paint falling off the door or a finch landing across the street as a masked man with a gun. Between the phone calls and the johns at the door and the other guys what come in to pay up, she trained them eyes on me, got herself worked up telling me straighten out, until something come in or sounded off to interrupt her. But don't you know weren't none of it would get me off the hook.

"I've about had it," she said. "You know you're the laughingstock of this house, don't you?"

I's ready to laugh *with* her, but she weren't smiling. She lost plenty of money on me, she said, and pretty damn quick I'd have to do my job in the living room and behind closed doors with the johns or I's out of there and she really meant it this time.

"You're more like everyone else who comes in here than you think; looking to get something for free. All you want is money and taking care of but you have no intention of earning it. I've given you a room of your own to live in, food from my cupboards to eat as you please," and huff huff, puff puff. "But this is a hotel to you, isn't it? Just a hotel and we're all your room service. You think you own this house?"

Later, in the living room, my only chance to get away from her, I started thinking how nice living on my own'd be. That's why I come to New York in the first place, on account of living with somebody else never worked out. Some reason—beats me—I just fell into this job. If I ever wanted to be on my own I needed money: The other boys was right on that count. But I didn't know how to get the sessions. I knowed what the Madam told me: Look the johns in the eye and laugh when you hear them talking like it's the best joke ever. But I knowed at least some of what they said weren't supposed to be funny. I got tripped up trying to figure out where to put the laughs in. Maybe that's why I weren't no good at this.

I started thinking about other things and couldn't stop from drifting off, doped up as I been. Looked at the sunflowers set out on the coffee table and thought about down home Memphis, how the ones there grows six or seven feet. Then how it seemed like I ain't seen my

Nana in as many years. Remembered her house—dark monster of a thing—trying to get inside that last time I gone over. For all I knowed she could be dead, rotting somewheres inside, them doors locked on me forever.

I tried adding up how many sessions would it take for me to make it back to Memphis to try her again. But I lost count when I remembered the slim pickings I got for tricks there anyways, guys what just as soon dump me off at the train station with my things stuffed in a bandana and tied to a stick, don't care exactly what happens to me. Least at the house I got somebody looking out. No, it was crazy to think of going back to Memphis, since anyways I more or less just come from there. Wouldn't be in the Madam's or New York neither one if it wasn't for how bad things turned out in good old Tennessee and that other place. By now my Nana wouldn't even remember me.

While I been thinking all this, the john picked somebody and they got up to leave, and where I was come rushing back to me. Boy beside me snapped his fingers in front of my face, said, "You better come to. You know she's watching on the monitor."

Sure enough, the Madam's voice come in over the intercom; screamed "Get down here"—made all the guys in the living room jump.

"Good luck," somebody said like they only half meant it. Everybody got a turn with her sometime. If you didn't know how to sweet-talk her it weren't nobody's fault but your own.

She's on the phone when I come in and got another one resting on her shoulder; seen me before I's even full through the door. With her free hand she jerked a finger towards the couch and rolled her eyes the same direction like to say I better park it. And when she got done with them calls and told one of the other guys get down there and man the phones, he was there lickety. Now she rolled her chair to the couch, shoved her face into mine, looked mean at me a second, said:

"I mean, I'm just not wasting my time with this. I've got plenty of boys who need work. Plenty call here every day looking for it, and the ones who have it want more. You're sitting up there like you're in a different time zone."

She took a breath, sized me up. And I flinched, on account of she got this way of looking at you made you think she aimed to hit you even when she ain't lifted a finger.

"Now if you want to keep your arms and legs, and you want to go on living here . . . you better get a smile on and keep it on. As long as you live in my house under my roof you do exactly as I say. Want to try your luck on the outside? I know what you're thinking, right? Think you can go out there and make your own way, think you won't have me breathing down your back. Everything will come up roses? You be my guest. You'd last five minutes out there. You think it's so bad in here, it's worse than you can imagine for someone like you outside, somebody who can't play it straight for two seconds. But you don't see that, do you? Don't see it, and won't, until you see it for yourself, right? So you be my guest. You have about two minutes left here."

I knowed she meant it, least the part about my arms and legs, cause I heard the stories; about the chairs flying and her choking peoples up against the wall. "Tough love," one of the boys said. I knowed if you got something to say to her you waited until she left the room. So when she give me my get-go, I cursed her all the way up the stairs back into the living room, shut it off neat once I stepped through the door.

Then I started brainstorming about how I's going to make it on the outside, get out on my own—finally and really on my own—where I wouldn't need nobody and couldn't nobody tell me what to do.

* * *

Red hair, freckles. Blue eyes.

I kept looking away from him as we gone, watched peoples thinking maybe I could catch sight of whoever he was supposed to meet, or figure where the two of them was going. All I knowed was any second his man could show up and then where would I be. He got that look to him like waiting, mind on other things barely listening, barely there. Whereas the thought of being anywheres else scared the daylights out of me, and not just on account of I'd be that much closer to dope, which I weren't about to go back to, no matter how hard I got the shakes and shits. I's taking swigs from them joke bottles on the sly, whenever the cramps got to be too much, and just following him through the carnie once I done told him my life story—elbowed my way through the crowd to keep up, every step thinking, *What can I come up with to make him stick around?*

22

Walking down the midway, manic rows of stands on either side, followed by the calls of barkers trying to get us or anybody else to step right up to this or that booth, where the prize or promise offered was more likely'n not some overblown stuffed animal got felt polka dots for eyes, furry things hung captive from a rope at the neck, down from a roughed-up lip of awning, some got bright pink tongues what lolled out like they been choked. Below them and inside the dark of the booths was the targets; circles inside circles red and white, scuffed yellow ducks floating down a stream; a row of cardboard Dobermans what moved straight across a wall until they reached the end of the line, turned over on theirselves, and started back to the other side. More than once I stopped long enough to get taken in by the racket, only to find I'd near lost track of Red. Suddenly I'd snap out, remember he weren't the kind to stop and wait. I'd turn looking for him, seen first the mosh of bodies and carnie litter folding in on itself, afraid I lost him until at last—some kind of luck I got—I spotted him ahead getting swallowed up.

We ended up at the cramped group of tents, center of the fairgrounds. Wide-stripe canvas, red and yellow roped to the ground at the corners and sloped except for the centers where they pointed, reached for sky or roller coaster or Ferris wheel behind them. Round the bottom edges they was worn brown from dirt and kids sneaking underneath to get a free show. Outside each tent a sign advertised what you could see inside if you got the mind and money to. Red looked at a few of them sideways, I couldn't be sure which ones, until finally he stopped, his gaze come back to me, and he said:

"Don't see him anywhere. You know, if it was him couldn't find me he'd be awful mad—I'd never hear the end of it. Time's money, he'd say: That's the way they is. But here I am trying to find him, see him nowhere, 'specially not where he said to meet him, and what difference would it make how angry I am? I guess some people's time's more expensive."

"I know **just** what you mean," I said, getting closer to one of them signs: **SEE MADAM ROSA** in bright green letters, so bright I figured maybe they'd catch his eye and put it on me.

"And when he finds me—and it'll be him does the finding as far as he's concerned, no matter who sees who first—I'll have to hear for a while, or the whole time we's together, how impossible I am, for my

23

age or somebody like me, cause see: They got their own ideas about who you are, they got it all figured out, and they'd tell you all about it at the drop of a hat, whether you ask them to or not. He'll say I been looking all over for you, like I been hiding from him when really he just makes it onto the scene whenever he damn well pleases."

"You want to go inside?" I asked and pointed to the tent what promised Rosa.

Done already asked him a ways back did he want to ride the roller coaster, take my last five bucks and get on, mostly so's I could get him up there to myself. Told him they'd let us go through much's we wanted, long as there weren't a line and everybody else on wanted another go. But he said no, and when I asked again he snapped at me I's a pain in the ass on top of being the liar and thief my ma called me and "so's your old man." I jumped him and we was in a bitch-slapping fight before he knowed what hit him, got me a few swings in for my ma's good name, even though weren't but later I seen she wouldn't of done the same for me. When it was all over, which's to say I took one last swing and set sail over him on account of just then he bent over to pick up the pack of Marlboros what dropped out of his pocket, he offered me one of them cigarettes and said he didn't half mean it. Said I should keep my five bucks: I'd need it sooner'n I could get rid of it. Said he got so much stuff on his mind he didn't know just *what* he been thinking or saying. I's welcome to hang around he said, even though he spent the past couple hours telling me to get lost; long as I promised to make like I didn't know him once his man got there.

Now, he looked at the sign, at me, and at the tent next to the both of us like for the first time, and quick, said:

"Don't give up, do you? No. No time. What I really wants to see the Gator Boy. Got real alligator skin it says."

He reached into his pocket and pulled out a postcard he bought somewheres in the carnie, black-and-white snap of "Alligator Boy" what showed him standing front side of a tent in his skivvies. Stock straight up and pinched hard between the eyes like he's in the worst kind of pain, got skin so scaly looked like it was mud caked on good; dry and brittle and set to flake off. Just as quick as I seen it, Red shoved it back.

I moved away from where I been leaning on the sign, over the part what said **You must be this tall to enter**, got a picture next to it of a clown holding out his hand to show the size of born short and slapped down flat.

"Won't take but a few minutes," I says. "And you ain't got any one place you's supposed to meet him. Just the fair in general, right? And he's late anyways so let's go."

*　*　*

I figured I'd make one more stop at Nana's house, big stack of bricks looks like a castle unless somebody lets you in. Hitched a ride with the crazy man down the hall at Mojo's, set to get the last of my things I been getting bit by bit since I's kicked out. I rode passenger seat in his El Camino clunkety straight up Union Street until it turns into Walnut Grove in a better part of town.

Dan, crazy man—crazy driver—brung his parrot in the car, parrot perched on the neckrest of the seat between us. Whole drive Dan and the parrot singing to each other, Polly want a cracker sonatas, a capella whatnots, to the point I wanted to ask about the radio—like, Do it work?

Maybe Nana would invite me in—"sit down, you hungry?"—and like nothing ever happened she'd be in the kitchen whipping up whatnot. Or maybe she'd still think I's a burglar, come to steal just about anything from her just about for the sake of it; see me coming and run around inside shutting all the doors and windows heavy-bolt. Last time, she shut the door in my face. When I come by to ask her for the window unit air-conditioner she offered to borrow me one time—finally made it over to take her up on it so's I could maybe shove it in the window at Mojo's—it was like she never offered, like I just come to steal or beg for whatever she got, even stupid things neither one of us got use for. When I tried to point out I's only asking for what it been her idea to give me, she said:

"Now Jed. Doug . . . I mean . . ."

And to help her, mostly cause it was hot enough to burn a polar bear's butt on her doorstep, I told her my name.

"Earl," she says, and let out a huff like how dare I interrupt her. "Now I'm going to have to ask you: Have you found my opal ring and necklace?"

I stepped back a little—foot or two—just so's she could be sure I weren't aiming to pounce.

"No, I ain't, and I still don't know what neither one looks like."

I didn't have the first idea what she's talking about but it ain't made no difference to her. She gone right on like you'd maybe talk down to a dog what can't say nothing back, whether it done what you thought or not. And by that time I's the kind of dog makes it easier. Dog talked to that way again after again gets a look to his eyes like he knows what you's full of, no more doe eyes hid under lids loving you still no matter: He looks you straight up and in them eyes, in that look not letting you away, sees right through you to whatever wall you got on your side, says just get this over with and don't think I don't know.

"Well if you can't find them, maybe the police can help me."

So I took my leave, told her maybe she *should* call the cops. "If that'd make you feel better. But I's afraid I can't help. I *do* want to thank you for all you done, and I'll be seeing you."

Now here I was, Mr. Stupid trying it all over again, in an El Camino turning finally off Walnut Grove, wide four lanes bordered by forever green trees, into froufrou Chickasaw Meadows, past all the black maids waiting at the curb for the bus to take them back downtown. To get my mind on something else, I thought back to once a long time ago when Nana told me Memphis streets was laid over old Indian trails, covered up what them Indians done just like down by the Mississippi where the army turned an Indian worship mound into barracks during the Civil War, hollowed out the inside of a view of the river and hid in it where all you seen was dirt walls, tin canteens. "*Leave it to civilized folks to make a custom cell out of a view,*" I thought out loud. Dan nodded like he knowed what I's talking about. But maybe he did know, on account of the time he said the whole country's like that: the Indians got it first and then whitey took it away, kicked them off the land, or anyway give them a corner, said sit.

He parked the El Camino at the foot of Nana's driveway like I asked him to.

"I'd get out, you understand, but I got the bird here," which was fine. Still, I told him circle the neighborhood a couple times, without making it too obvious-like.

"If I's standing here like I never left this spot when you come back round, don't be fooled; don't mean time's playing tricks on you.

Means I ain't been any luckier this time than ever, been turned away again and I's ready to go."

He backed out the driveway barely looking over his shoulder; front of the car dipped hard at the curb so's I thought he'd lose his tail end right there in Nana's driveway, sure that'd do her for a heart attack. But save for the scrape of metal along concrete weren't no big sound but that Polly squawking, few feathers darting out the window.

I walked up the cobblestone sidewalk runs snaky through the grass in Nana's yard, come up to her door, big arch thing, solid wood set behind locked wrought iron and a pane of glass. Sucked in the smell of hot asphalt off her driveway, held it, then ding-dong.

No answer for what seemed so long that Dan's El Camino'd be rounding the corner any minute. Then the inner door swung open, and there's Nana big bifocaled like nobody's home, hiding most of herself behind it like maybe here in broad daylight she's dressed for bed. Took her a few minutes to gather who I was, didn't seem to recognize me and her fish eyes got all bent out of shape behind her glasses. I thought maybe she expected I'd talk to her through the glass and wrought iron of the security door, but I weren't about to. I just looked at her deadpan and harmless as I could think to, until her hand reached careful for the lock, clicked it to the side, and peeped the door open just a slim crack like I could slip through what I got to say by letter.

"Hello, Nana."

She searched herself for my name until I guess she could come up with anything at all.

"You know, Jed, your mama's been calling here every day worried sick about you. Where are you living now?"

Which was big phonus balonus. Like it made no nevermind she kicked me out, like anybody was calling anybody else about me except to make sure I been going just as rotten as they always said I would or was. I done told her a dozen times before but anyways I told her again where I's set up.

"Downtown, Nana: Got me somewheres downtown."

"Nice place? You have everything you need down there?"

"Yes. Reckon I's fine—just fine. It's a nice building downtown right off the river. I got me everything I need, a fireplace even. Don't work but it got marble all around it. And a mirror up above."

She smiled, and I knowed that smile. Same one she used when she really couldn't be bothered but didn't rightly know what else to say; way she used to look at me before I gone to live with her and I seen she weren't half the happy granny she seemed like.

"Well, that sure is nice, Douglas. It is."

"Everything's fine. I just stopped by for a how'do," I said, turning to go, on account of I could see whatever I come here for weren't going to work out; figured whatever she still got of mine she could have—just take it. We said our good-byes after she told me to call my ma and tell her how I's getting along.

"Your mama really does love you, now you know that," she said when I turned to leave. I looked back and weren't even sure she said it, couldn't even be sure she's ever there. Already she gone back inside and locked the iron door.

* * *

Don't take an idiot to figure what I done. Instead of waiting for her to give me the pink slip I left on my own.

One day when I asked her could I make a run to the store she sent me with a list of things the boys all wanted from the outside—mostly the usual, smokes and sodas; handed me a wad of twenties to take care of it. Before I left I gone up to my room, got together some of my things; not much but what I could take with me, put them in the scram-bag I brung when I first come to the house, stuffed the lot up under my shirt so's the Madam wouldn't see it on the monitor. Stopped, looked around. Told myself: *I won't never be back here again* and good riddance.

On the outside I called from a pay phone to say I weren't coming back. She yelled and stomped and banged things around on her end; told me I better not even *think* of it. Nothing to think about I said cause I done decided: *I can make it on my own.* Just remember, she told me, when you's broke and got nowheres to go, "you can't come here." Well that's just great, I told her, so good of her to tell me what I already decided myself. Didn't need her or nobody else to tell me I's leaving for good. I got plans, I's going to work for myself, be on my own—screw living somewheres I got to follow stupid rules made up by stupid peoples without I even got nothing to show for it. I's all done with that. She laughed like it was the whole house laughing, then she told me how if she ever got her hands on me she'd break every bone in my body.

Yeah, well I's free, I thought, and hung up the phone. Stood in the booth looking around at the peoples walking by.

Wide open out there. They's all free and me too.

*   *   *

Inside the tent was crowded, sweaty, dark, and snug; made me forget worrying about anything else but where we was. Even seemed like Red finally give up for a minute on finding his man. Weren't no more of the looking around focusing always somewheres way off in the distance. We was both of us eyes glued to the round stage, far end of the tent, then back to each other crazy excited to see what'd appear any second, this boy they screamed about all over the carnie, saying there weren't nothing like it you wouldn't believe, and not just the carnies saying it but peoples who gone into the tent and come out to tell it. Oh they could hardly believe their eyes; There they was, just sitting, waiting like to see any other old thing when here he come, whap-bam, a boy like you never seen in your life. Some was religious, fanatic about it, grabbed our arms and tried to draw us away into the story—into the tent to see it with them and come out to spread the tale for ourselves.

Like when we stopped so Red could get a soda-pop in a cup what said **Thank You** kindly cross the front. He already got his change, got the money fisted, and we was turning to look for his man again, when a hand grips my shoulder and jerks me to a halt. Well, course I thought it was Red put the arm on me, just maybe wanting me to slow down, give him a chance to pocket his change, but already when I's turning I remembered he weren't the kind needs nobody to wait. Sure enough I turn to find Red's still walking, off in the other direction, and this man's hand's on me, got his arm out like hold it right there, fingers digging into my collarbone enough to take out blood.

First I thought, *Well here's the man's supposed to meet Red, one he didn't really want to meet nohow; here he's mistook us one for the other, wouldn't you know: They think we's all the same.* But just a whit later this man's telling me all about how he thought he'd die of heart failure before he got to preach the Gator Boy, got me with the one hand and in the other a fist of them postcards what's like Red's, waving them like they's holy rosaries.

I told him let go or tried to over his voice, cause looking around I couldn't see Red no more, he was absolutely all gone. All I seen was backs and fronts of peoples fit close like a moving jigsaw puzzle. Then I pushed the panic button, thought, *Well this is it, they's all going to leave and even the tents'll get dragged away, just blank concrete and I'll never see him again.*

But I weren't eager for it to end that way. I grabbed that man with my *own* two arms, said into his eyes, "You need to let go, 'less you want me to take your hand with me: You might just die of heart failure *yet*," which point he even then held fast to me saying, "I kid you not, that boy is one of a most peculiar kind. You'll regret not seeing him."

Then thank God he let go.

Now here we was, stood together to see the Gator Boy, almost holding our breath we's so excited, and Red couldn't of disappeared if he wanted, what with the crowd even bigger inside than outside the tent, absolutely still going nowheres, not a muscle moved except for some of them fanning theirselves with them postcards.

A spot of light come up on the stage, leaving just seconds to wait until here come somebody. But he was tall, too tall to be Gator Boy; wore a dark suit and tie and a hat to match, no face what showed from under that except down at the mouth where he weren't but a stern set of lips. His hand took the microphone—skin clear and smooth like any other regular human's, said: "Ladies and gentleman, I would like to prepare you for what you are about to see."

I's breathing hard and heard Red's as furious next to me, let down but building up again already.

"He was born premature to young parents in Kentucky, left off in the swamp for good to be taken by time, or even eaten—yes eaten alive—by the alligators who roamed the area. But lo and behold a miracle will sometimes happen: He was set upon by a male group of the species, who might have eaten him—folks, they almost ate him—they had their large mouths open to swallow him whole but something happened. Miracle has struck many a time in this boy's life. These savage beasts decided to care for the boy, to take him in and raise him as one of their own. They took turns carrying him over the long journey from civilized society to their reptile lair, their jaws fixed gently, ever so gently open like a cradle. Took care of him and taught him their ways, folks, thusly he was more of their world than ours by the time he was a young man. And years later, after all the alligators were taken by time, when the boy left their home and the swamp to head back for the land of mankind—a stranger to our ways, an outcast wanderer in a strange wide open land—he was barely recognizable as a human no more. To make it among them, he'd got to get himself a thick skin, but to make it among us he like to need even thicker."

With this and a drum roll, the lights come up full; the man stepped away with the microphone, canned sound of chomping come on, and out of the dark, edge of the tent, a small figure made way towards the stage.

Me and Red couldn't help but yell on account of everybody else in the tent been—we's just a locomotive of hoots and whistles and clapping our hands. I thought, *Here's one of them times peoples says there's a miracle and they's right, no lie.* Weren't even the boy actually done nothing spectacular, no kind of trick or special feat of the eyes. Only stood there as is without he got to move at all except for just barely raising his shoulders breathing, but even that weren't nothing it was so steady you couldn't barely see it. I's glad to see him I guess just on account of he made it as far as he done, like the man said.

And once he was on stage and they got a good look at him the crowd got quiet, not the smallest word or sound, just dead quiet surprise, shock, and awe. Only noise at all come from outside the tent, just the general screaming and the tinkering music-box singsong from different parts of the fairgrounds. I's looking at Red next to me and the haze of frozen crowd behind him when the roar of the roller coaster fast on its way down cut through the top of the tent from somewheres outside, brung the scream of riders on us—one long, steady wail. And with the noise of that dying—that is, the cars slow-coasting in for a landing to drop off and pick up more—Red started like he been in a trance and come to his senses, and turned to me quick.

"Well, he's here now. I got to go."

* * *

So two steps forward and two steps back.

I's in the clover shacking up in this man's digs, *somewheres* in Colorado Springs: For all I know of this city, could be it's just about anywheres. But it ain't the lousy fountainbed; I know that much.

I was playing pinball at a hot dog joint, satisfied there weren't nobody else around to play; got my quarters lined up ready to get the most out of each and every one. Done played five games, getting better every time, played long enough to figure how to jerk the machine—just when and how much from what angle. Getting bored, even, at how easy it got.

This was in a cubbyhole away from the rest of the place, which give me more privacy and made it easier to concentrate. That way I didn't have to watch nobody eating and think how hungry I was. I could smell french fries and hamburger, relish and mustard and catsup melting on top, but long as I couldn't see it it was just an idea like most anything else. I just stared hard into the game and sucked on one of them fifths of firewater I got in my pocket, bought and paid for with the Madam's money on the train—that or stolen, I can't remember which. Then this man, this maybe in-his-thirties guy come into the doorway of the cubbyhole, stands there blocking the light, watches me play from the behind. Maybe he thought I couldn't see him, but even if I didn't miss the light he rubbed out I seen his reflection on the upright part of the pinball machine, between the picture of Pimp Flashjack skinny and fur-coated and the harem of bathing-suit beauties he got at his side.

First I thought he worked there, thought maybe he come to tell me get lost, so I ignored him—really got into the game nonstop like I got no mind to notice nothing else. But then he come over and stood at the side of the game drinking a beer, where I seen he weren't wearing no kind of uniform at all but a snug three-piecer, which's a whole nother story.

Didn't take me nothing to guess what was he looking at. Even when he lifted his beer to take a sip he kept his eyes steady on me there, looked through the bottle below his eyes which I guess cut the rest of me off except my hips, or made them small like things is through the rear-end of a bring 'em close glass. I figure the only reason he looked at my face once in a while was to make sure I didn't know where he was really looking, or didn't care too hard.

I put one more quarter in and played it, but his standing there got my focus worked down and I couldn't rightly pull out my bottle in front of him neither. Now that I's more keen on my hips moving than watching the ball, it was like that was the game—like putting the quarter in made me myself move this way or that. The ball was just something else gone on, decoration or somebody else playing. Turned out I scored lower with him breathing down my neck than on my first coin, so when **GAME OVER** rolled across the screen I turned to him and switched gears. He held out his beer and I took it from him—took a sip. Later on he bought me one for myself: "Drink it back here," he said. "We could both be in trouble if anyone out there sees you with it."

I almost told him I's old enough, so's he might relax, but I knowed right off that's the kind of thing would wreck his fun.

Like I say, drink's the only thing aside from enough cigarettes to smoke out a firesquad can make me forget being hungry, and make them shakes seem like they's sitting still. After getting through half a bottle of beer myself I's fine. He already finished his but kept standing next to the game with the empty rested on the deck, watching me nurse mine. Every time I lifted for a sip, them eyes gone down around my waist, and I watched him through the thick glass bottom of the bottle. When I swallowed the last of it I held the thing up to one eye, closed the other, and waved to the little man like he's standing outside a peephole. He laughed nervouslike, and I thought maybe he didn't take well to it, so I brung the bottle down and set it next to his like things was puppy love.

Ends up we's talking at a table inside the joint, and if the guy wanted more he never let on. Seemed he was more curious about what brung me here to Colorado, where I been before, and how everything else I talked about figured in. We talked about me the whole time, to the point felt like nothing much happened to the man before I come along. It was, "But you lived in *Memphis*" and "So what's this about Nebraska?" like if he was to figure it all out he might write his self the book on it. I's on my third hot dog—compliments his—and figured the more I talked the more grub I'd see.

"Well I started out in Nebraska with my folks, then got shipped off to my nana's, then by and by I's back in Nebraska, after a few stops between. And now I's here with you. *Hello.*"

He seemed confused, so I decided it weren't a good plan to tell him about New York and all the rest, on account of maybe he'd be less interested now it weren't a tight little cakewalk no more.

Then I made the mistake of asking him for a cigarette, motioned my fingers to my lips to make the sign for one after he looked at me funny when I first asked. When I realized I maybe shouldn't of said it there I was, stuck with my fingers midair. He shook the stunned mug off his face, drew up his eyes, said, "A rather deplorable habit for a boy like you," which left me wondering just what he could mean.

"Look at your fingers stained yellow, and you'll have your teeth ruined before your first kiss."

I decided I better act like I never said it, keep the conversation going so he might forget; figured he's the kind got off on helping so I brung up a problem needed solving.

"Maybe there's something you can do me for."

Which point the man scooted up his chair, set his elbows on the table, propped his chin on his fists so serious you'd think he was fixin to operate on the salt and pepper shakers. All of the sudden he's Florence Nightingale.

"I need to find somebody," I said. "Been looking for a while. He's maybe a little older than me—"

"In his twenties?" The man seemed to think.

"Older. Late twenties; maybe even thirties but I doubt it."

"But you don't look a day over *fifteen*. You *can't* tell me otherwise."

"Not much older but listen. This guy I need to find's got red hair, little taller than me, wears a red denim jacket, freckled as a turkey egg. Almost never smiles. Eyes seem dark but they's blue. And this you'd remember: he smokes."

Now the man leaned in even closer, whispered like he didn't want nobody else should hear and I didn't neither.

"And this boy, he's your . . . a brother? Relative, or . . ."

Even after he licked his lips I couldn't figure how he wanted me to answer. I tried to think of the best thing to say, and when I didn't say nothing right off it seemed that said plenty. He gone on without me.

"And do your parents know you're here, looking for this boy—this *friend* of yours?"

"They don't know where I's at, no, but my ma knowed I's leaving and that was okay by her. I got to find him so's I'll have a place to crash."

The man smiled, relaxed his arms enough to ease away from the table and lean back on his chair.

"I can certainly help you with that, and since that seems to be your main preoccupation with the boy, you can stop worrying about *him*."

And here it was; how peoples sometimes worked me around a certain ways, made me think to say one thing only to end up caught meaning something else. Then there weren't nothing to say at all—just me stuck sitting mouth open speechless, trying to think back over everything I could figure I said, until any word I might remember meant too many different things in all directions. The man acted all smug, like the salt and pepper shakers was all fixed up now.

But they looked the same to me.

Now that I's shut up, he wouldn't stop talking. In the car driving to his house it was almost the story of his life, which maybe would of held my attention, if I weren't busy thinking how good the cushy seat felt after all the standing and walking I done. Which got me looking out the window, watching all that space opened up what seemed forever until just a crease at the sky; thinking how so much headway was got for a car, held up to the distance I covered the past few days—really only right around the courtyard which I figured was where most everybody in Colorado Springs was at, shows you what I know. Then I got to thinking how long was it going to be I wouldn't be able to smoke, how this here was just too typical; once I find somebody can give me enough money I can afford cigs they says there ain't no smoking allowed. Cursing myself to no end, on account of I's heading right back into something I said I's done with.

The man's apartment's small enough we's always in the same room. Whenever I go out I feel him watching from the second-story window, holding fast to the glass maybe even after I leave the block. When I come back in he checks me over, smells my fingers, looks in my pockets for smokes. But it's a relief I got my own bathroom, without it's in a public space I got to finagle myself into, let me tell you—what with all's been going on with my body lately, stomach hassles and everything else. Feels like somebody's stomping on my gut and slamming my head into a wall for good measure. I been in the bathroom a lot, which don't make this guy happy when he's around. He ends up standing outside the door the whole time, asking What on earth are you doing in there? But I don't even know what's going on myself. All I know's everything was stopped up forever, and now—

ever since I left New York and the dope—all of the sudden I ain't been able to keep a lid on it.

You'd think an asshole could understand something like that.

Two days I been here, lying in a double bed just next to him at night: When he first goes to sleep he grabs me hard like I's a teddy bear what might wrestle its way out of his hold, then he's out light-like and pushes me to the other side of the mattress without he knows he done it. I got the chills and his breathing keeps me awake. Whenever I shift in bed, or anywheres else really, he starts. Asks me in the morning how come I pulled away in the middle of the night.

Only chance I got to myself's when he goes to work, which point I raid the wet bar for everything it's worth—keep myself booze blind enough I ain't feeling nothing. Sometimes he looks at the bottles like he knows I been in them, but if he knows he don't say nothing, maybe on account of he likes me sweet and dumb, the way the firewater makes me. I seen his kind before, but for now it's a place to stay, red carpet I can't hardly step off. Things outside seems like always; like they'll be there forever, plenty of time. Lately I ain't asked nobody about Red.

But a body's got to eat.

* * *

"No no. You can't leave yet. He's just now got on stage."

I spit it out quick cause already he was walking away from me—*excuse me, excuse me*—parting the crowd, got his hand stuck out front of him. I grabbed his arm without I could help it but only stopped him a little, barely enough for him to hear me out.

"Look: I thought you didn't want to meet this guy anyhow. That's what you been saying all along. Why not stick it out here, at least get our five bucks' worth?"

"Whose five bucks you mean? I'm the one got you in." And he motioned with his free hand up in the air like to tell somebody some-wheres he'd be right over.

"So now you paid that makes me part of the show I guess, and you can walk away from me just the same."

"Let off my arm," he said. "I got to go."

When I forced myself to turn him loose, I could only do it cause instantly—like a blow to the head—I seen I hated Red, from now on anyways. Hated him as much's I thought I liked him before. Maybe even hated him more than you would anybody else on account of I done wasted so much time and thought on him in the first place. Was hate set me free with him to where I felt I could say any old thing come in my head.

"You know, I liked spending time with you before," I says. "Figured maybe you wasn't like nothing else. But now I see you ain't much. Any half-wit living on the street could come up with something like you in his feeble half-wit head. I seen'm like you all over, fling some cash and walk away."

He moved faster than I did, shaking his head like trying to get me out of it, but I made sure my voice kept up. Most everybody under the tent was looking at us or for us, instead of at the Gator Boy—the one they's supposed to all be antsy to see.

"Oh, we's getting our five bucks' worth now," I yelled out in general like to slug everybody in the crowd at once. Red cut through to the left, got his eye on whoever he aimed to leave with. Made me crazy not knowing like he did who was he looking for and where was they waiting, otherwise I could of gone over and headed him off. As things was I tripped over the peoples got throwed in his wake.

"Fuckup, you are, yes sir that's what you is. Calling me a thief and what, a liar? Look at you. I think every person in here should know just what a liar you is yourself. Says all day how he's got to go with this guy but don't want to, nobody makes him do what he don't plan to already but look here he's off and just try to stop him."

Red stopped and turned, spoke over a few people's heads between us. "You don't even know me," he said. "You're making a scene. Shut up and get lost before I kick the shit out of you."

Then just as quick he turned and walked on.

"Couldn't kick enough to force as much shit out as you got bull-shit in your big head. Fine. Oh that's fine. You keep walking like you don't hear me."

He stopped again but when I caught up I seen it was only cause he come to the man been waiting for him. Some midget what got a briefcase and a look on his face like he seen a train crash right about where I's standing.

"What the hell you looking at?" I yelled at him. "You ain't paid five dollars to see *me*."

"Jared," the man called Red, "who is this boy?" Still looking gape-jawed my way.

"Maybe I's little, Shorty, but I got five fingers to make a fist so you shut up but good, and take your eyes off me if you like them there in your head."

The guy been holding a bottle of co'cola, and now he handed it to Red who drunk from it without he never once took his eyes off me. When he finished the bottle was empty, and he chucked it to the ground and took the man's arm to pull him out the tent.

"Don't follow us," he said. "I don't want to see you around again, hear? We had a deal. A deal's a deal. Now you make sure we don't run into each other again."

When they turned to leave his foot kicked the bottle so's it spinned, and now everybody looked at me like it was my turn to say something. But I just stood there quiet until the bottle sat still. Looked at it thinking, *empty, or full.*

* * *

With all the quiet sitting thick in Mr. Colorado Springs' apartment, weren't no way to keep things from running riot in my head after a while. And nothing to do but sit shack-wacky with it. Weren't like I could smoke, or drink, or nothing else when I wanted to, not as much as I wanted, and I needed as much as I wanted in the worst way. Food's one thing and don't I know it, but—once the stomach's full up a few days and hunger ain't such a bellyache—there's others. So there was them thoughts, and all the rest, and without I could do enough of nothing when I damn well wanted I's jones-ing this side of hell. Sleep, when I could get it, just seemed to make things worse.

Final straw's when I passed a mirror he got over the sink and caught sight through lips parted just so of the yellow what was left of my teeth. Brung out a smaller mirror, set it up in front of the window to check this out in a different light, take a look at my self like a doctor once told me. Sure enough, before I opened my mouth here I looked clean, regular Joe from right good family, tree-lined block and everything else. Open the mouth you seen I's rotting inside.

For a while I gone back and forth between open and closed, until I realized, what's the use, it's there whichever way. The thought hit me how much's happened, all the things I bit on since I can remember, if I remember, without I get too cozy like this here to spit this sour crud out. No, ain't none of it makes sense, ain't none of it I can put together the right way so's it stays long enough to get a good picture, but seems like as long's I keep my mouth closed everybody's fine letting me sit pretty while them memories of mine pop into thin air like firework brain cells. *Smile*, they says. *You look so* **good** *when you smile*. Sure enough, them memories look fine popping, but once they's gone, so long.

This was morning and the guy was still asleep on his bed, though he snapped up once or twice from what little noises I made, over there breathing easy chest slow up-down, eyes not a sketch busy. Didn't take me much longer to figure all I's doing around there was running into myself sitting still, that I should be out looking for Red, asking anybody I could corner, smoking and drinking both, and if I got to give up the bath and bed and food what come without them, weren't nothing my teeth'd miss.

He'd laid thirty dollars in a cookie jar, kitchen counter, made a big nickel-nursing production out of it with a "this is just in case" kind of talk, these *I's putting this trust in you with utter confidence, fingers crossed* eyes, staring me down hard like if they looked to the side for more than a second I'd be off packing silverware. That money stayed there long as I did, what with everything was taken care of. But now I's tearing out without I knowed where or for how long, it was just in case thinking when I lifted that lid. On my way past the wet bar I grabbed me a couple of bottles. I left him a fiver to show I's good for them.

I could swear as I pulled the door to I heard the springs of the bed squeak alert, but course I's walking fast down the hall carpet, tiptoe prancing high speed. Instead of walking across the street where I'd of been seen, I kept to the same side of his apartment building, up against awnings close to doors and windows. Out here, middle of suburbia, anywheres I might head was far from the courtyard, where I'd figured I need to be. But now it struck me—there's whole other worlds to Colorado Springs. What with the guy upstairs brung me out here where I never been, where plenty other peoples live. I figured I'd hang around out here for a while. Ain't like I got another choice. I'd just comb every inch of this city as it come to me.

First things first—I bought some smokes. Guy behind the counter give me the once-over, asked for ID until I showed him my twenty-five bucks. He give me a pack, but a talking to along with it; how he got a boy my age and what he'd do if he ever found out he's smoking coffin nails. Blah blah. I told him I ain't nobody's kid no more; anyways I ain't a kid, but smoking ain't the half of it. Then he started in about some guys he knowed what lost their noses from smokes, cancer this and that, and did I want I should end up like them. Was they kids when they lost the nose or what, I asked, and if they wasn't then what was he telling *me* for, and didn't *that* shut him up but good.

*   *   *

Least I still got the picture when he walked away. We's standing somewheres in the carnie, before we ever seen the Gator Boy, when poof there's this flash like to blind us both. Course right off we looked over to where it come from—like we's ready to beat whatever and whoever senseless—and seen it was the cameraman. I myself got a little nervous, on account of seeing him made me think of Buford and my grandma, and other things, and I weren't about to go there without a fight, but weren't nothing compared to Red, who started straight for the guy yelling he's going to rip his hands off so's he wouldn't never be able to sneak up on nobody and take his picture again.

"Look," I says, "it's okay. He's just taking pictures," and I pointed to the guy like maybe Red ain't seen him clear.

"Give me the film," he says, and the guy starts to back away.

"*Give* it to me."

Red got his hand held out at first but then he's packing it into a fist.

The man said he's selling them, the pictures, said it's a free country and he can take anybody's he wants, and whether they want to buy it or not's their own business too.

"Yeah well I decide who takes mine," says Red, and "what makes you think I shouldn't be charging *you?*"

I reminded him he's making a scene, and didn't he say he ain't wanted to, and that calmed him a little, but not enough.

"He's got my picture," he says, raising his voice. "And if I can't tell him not to take it I can't tell him who not to sell it to either. No telling who's going to get their hands on it."

There's no negative, the cameraman says, shaking his head. Just the picture, and if you buy it won't nobody else get it but you. And that got Red mad all over again, on account of he said the guy was trying to dick him around.

"I'll pay for the picture," I says. "Give it to me." And I took out my fiver to clinch it.

"No way," says Red. "Nobody's buying it but me, and I ain't buying it because he owes me for taking it."

But the guy wouldn't budge, no more'n Red, and finally Red didn't hold back no more and grabbed the guy by the shirt. Started shaking him up, so hard the camera was slapping between the two of them—sound of switches I don't know the name of breaking—and finally the guy puts his hands up says all right already, and quicker than you can holler howdy he's took the picture out of the camera from where it been hanging the whole time, ripped a piece of darker paper off it, and there's Red in black and white, looking as mean and somewheres else as ever.

The guy left cursing the day we was born, and I said well you ain't the first, buddy. Which point, for once since I knowed him, Red had a good laugh. He held the picture out, said, "You really want it?" And course I said hell yes I do. "Promise me it won't get into the wrong hands," he said, and I told him he couldn't know how serious I was when I told him wouldn't nobody ever see it but me. I said I wouldn't never leave it behind like some peoples do, wouldn't never let nobody get their hands on it and lock it up.

"Whatever," says Red, and rolls his eyes. "Just keep the damn thing to yourself."

Like I knowed what I's talking about or something I said he could be sure of that.

* * *

Today I seen a kid in one of these playgrounds out here in suburban wherever, kicking it up in the sandbox. Stood by the fence watching him push one of them big yellow trucks through the sand, bury a load of cars and dig them out again; watched so long I forgot about being hungry and no sleep since the two days ago I left the guy's apartment, my money run out on fags and whatever else, and all the booze gone too, and didn't even mind trying to shut-eye upright that way. Somehow the kid was putting me to sleep.

Then the gate opened with a quick metal clink, slammed against the fence, what slammed against me, and back to place. This woman stormed across the playground, head turned my way—hair's flapping behind her from her speed. She grabbed the kid up, yanked him off the ground's what, sand flying like a landmine gone off. Her eyes was still on me as she dumped the truck's load for good, started to leave the sandbox but the boy panics, screamed for them buried cars. Took her awhile to figure it out, on account of she's so busy looking at me, like I's the one started the boy crying, like any second I might just break through the fence and head over. But finally the kid got it across.

Digging for them cars she screamed all along at the kid to point out just exactly where they was, but course he couldn't find them now she made him disremember. He started crying.

Finally she set the kid and the truckload of cars one by the other on a bench, the kid's eyes wide, got his hand fast to the toys like he's worried they's going somewheres. This lady walked right over to where I's standing at the fence, stopped not two feet away on the other side, crossed her arms, said:

"Is there something I can help you with?"

Matter of fact, I says, "I lost a friend and now I's trying to find him," holding the fence each side of my face like to break out. "He's got red hair, red jacket with a sheepskin collar—"

"As you can see," says Lady Smarty-pants, "my son has brown hair. Dark brown. And his coat is *blue*. He's not even wearing it."

"Okay. Can I use your phone?"

Absolutely not, she says. "We have a neighborhood watch here, twenty-four hours. They'll be passing by any time. We've all seen you roaming around here the past few days. You can't do that."

"Look," I says, "it's just I's kind of half stuck out here—ain't nobody I could call to come get me anyways. If you could—"

"I can't help you," she said, and she brung her elbows closer into her ribs. Then she just stands there waiting like for me to leave first, but I stayed exactly where I's at and how while the kid's bawling in the background. Them low sobs and chokes what comes after being so excited then worked up and wore out.

"It gets so hard to breathe here," I says, idle-like, just to hear myself talk, just to make sure I still could. "Is that on account of it's so high

42

up? Do you ever have trouble taking in breath; ever feel like you's gasping, like maybe you'll pass out? Like if it gets fast enough you'll just suffocate yourself and pass right on out?"

Then I told her how I gone without cigarettes a spell, few days back, and did she think that was anything to do with it, without I added how I gone without dope too, and she stood there more straight-up than ever, like the sign to a drive-in movie what weren't showing no more, so hell-bent on protecting the kid she wouldn't go over and stop his crying.

"I think I should wait here for my friend. Peoples says if you's lost stay in one place so you's easier to find. Do that count if nobody's looking for you? Up until now I moved around a lot, actually looked everywheres so to speak, that I know of; think I need to take a bench here for a while, like the kid." And I nodded towards him, which got her all aflutter with nervous twitches again.

Finally she shook her head snap-fast, walked to the boy—"Let's go"—helped him with his truck even though her hand on it got him crying all over again. She looked at her hands, seen the sand and dirt on them, got angry I guess cause they's full and she couldn't clean them right off. Swung the gate open with her foot, toys in one hand, kid's hand in the other, marched off out of sight through trees and station wagons and rows of houses.

Really I aimed to leave then, but a rest on the bench sounded good when I said it so I sat myself and lit one last cigarette. Watched the smoke curl up above me, gray snake dancing under white clouds—far up a plane, slow-moving left a trail, thin streak of white like icing on a cake, wondering who's on the plane, and where they's going, lucky dogs. I could hear it, that propeller sound smudged by the distance, sound of somebody leaving somebody behind somewheres, sound of somebody getting away; least I thought I could. Hard to tell what with the thick blanket of suburban dinnertime buzz, kids called inside to sit at the table with the folks, cars coasting into the driveways, garage doors rattling up and how would I know how the rest of it goes.

That got me on how things is different from place to place, but still all the same. For all my trouble catching breath here in Colorado Springs—for all it seems like it ain't never been this bad—I remembered in Memphis there was so much pollen in the air, floated off all the flowers everywheres in spring. Breathing weren't no piece of cake there neither. Your sight got so full of that pollen you'd like to keel over from the haze, eyes tearing up something awful from the sting. And not just that but waking up early morning without you could breathe. So after all maybe it made sense.

I was just then thinking about breathing back in Nebraska, and might be I'd of got to New York but a siren cut through the hum of birds, and backyard dogs wailed from the sound. Then I seen this cop car slow rounding the bends of the road into the neighborhood, and to the side the boy's mother come out of the trees to watch, standing there, arms crossed, just like she done by the fence. Behind her I seen how *all* the peoples was coming out to their driveways to watch the show, got their hands up to their foreheads to shield for a better view, hugging the kids close like to ward off any and all trespassers. In my head, I seen a coyote at stand-off, got its teeth bared.

Cop car—sirens off now on account of it just been making a quick sound of warning I guess—coasts up next to the playground lot, lights still spinning red and blue. Officer steps out once he's parked it, adjusts his hip weight, ambles over like to get a cup of coffee, says:

"Son, do you live in this neighborhood?"

I shook my head nuh-uh, dropped my cigarette and crushed it out in the bark chips below the bench. Cop watches me like that woman done; real close. Only he's more relaxed, got his hand near his gun. Motions his head several directions to show I guess what's the boundaries of the neighborhood.

"Where do you come from? You want to tell me what your business is here?"

Something like that—like he seen it in a movie where they got the answer they's looking for.

Course I wanted to answer all kinds of things, in fact they was right on the tip of my tongue. Instead I says I's "just visiting. Friend of mine lives out this way," and I pointed a couple ways without I stopped at any which one. "I's just taking a walk, out for fresh air and exercise; you know, got so tired I thought: Stop and sit for a rest."

"Well, you'll have to be on your way then, move on. This area's for private sitting only. Otherwise I'll need to escort you down to the station for loitering."

He stood there waiting for me to get up, which I done; slow-like, though, on account of I had to give myself time to figure just where

I'd be on my way to. Suddenly, all the streets was cartwheels, and everything around me started turning out of control. Then my vision started fading, like somebody's hand on a dimmer switch. Going down I tried to talk myself out of it, but my voice seemed warped, far off, and I's probably in the middle of warning myself when things gone dark for good. I don't exactly remember.

* * *

Every night drinks and smokes and whatever else a body hands me, and one night it's fall over dead drunk. All the peoples around me trying to figure what's the matter, got their fingers in my face snapping, slapping, waving in front of my eyes I guess to see was I there or somewheres else.

These was the ones what drunk with me every night, downtown Memphis locals I bought a few, rounds on me after a trick turned wherever I could get one, only back then when I first started I didn't say tricks; it was just what the men called it—"making friends." So easy back then, mostly just getting smashed and talking without it was as hard as things turned out to be at the Madam's house. When I weren't making friends I's making drinking buddies, but the drinking buddies only knowed what to do with me when I's drinking. Now that I's something else they wasn't so sure.

So they carried me back to Mojo's, dug the key out of my pocket, stumbled up to my room and dumped me halfways on the mattress. There you go buddy, they says, but I don't think I heard it all.

I lay in the dark, things aspinning—all kinds of words on the wall, circling me—thinking well do I try to read what they's saying or leave be. And course I's all for leaving be on account of them or anything else only made my head worse.

Instead I blocked them out and tried to think about not thinking at all. Every time a thought come into my head, like Nana telling me I stole her opal ring and necklace what was first her mama's then hers, I squeezed everything hard until it gone away. It was a long time before I got to sleep, not until after turning circles and the other way and flips and whatnot, point I thought I might hurl; then crash.

Next day I's up in the bright and early heat what come through the window of the room. Gone over to try it open, get some air in; but don't you know that thing wouldn't so much as budge. I got on the mattress again, on my back and thinking sleep thoughts, didn't feel like nothing but being in a hot box, with the roof caving in, where nobody'd ever come along to find me. So I gone downstairs and out to the curb to sit and get some breath.

Crazy Dan strolls along with the cockadoodle on his shoulder, singing or whistling I don't know what, comes to me stops dead says *whoa!* Whoa what and would you mind shutting up, I says back, only he asks me ain't I looked in a mirror lately, or do I just don't care I's blue or purple or some other color a body ain't meant to be.

I gone back inside, looked in the crappy mirror over the fake fireplace in my room, wanted to laugh and would of if I didn't know how bad it'd hurt. Nobody ever told me what to do when you turn colors like that, so I got back on the bed to sit it out, figured if I ain't looking at it and couldn't see it it'd go away.

I closed my eyes to get some rest. But whenever I opened them again, seemed I'd bled *everything* blue, the walls and bed and even what sun still come through the window. I figured I better go down the hall to Crazy Dan's, get him to call my Aunt Edna and see what was up.

* * *

Redheaded.

Blue eyes, red hair. Freckles.

Thinking this in the ambulance, right up until it sped through a portico into the emergency ward garage. Sign says, THIS WAY, **THIS WAY**.

"But I want to . . ." *I feel better,* I's trying to say, but the paramedic was opening the doors, taking the front of my stretcher, and here was another paramedic meeting at the end to pull me out. My personal paramedics—One and Two—coasted me one on each end through the hospital's sliding doors, past a waiting room, down a hall, where they parked me and left I guess to go pick up somebody else.

Red hair, freckles. That red coat; looked like catsup stain on the cuff. And blue jeans. Got on blue-black Wranglers, boot cut, scuffed dark at the knees from dirt. When he smoked you could see the black under his fingernails, fingers theirselves yellow from nicotine; "a rather deplorable habit for a boy like you," I thought, and laughed in my head where it didn't hurt to.

And nobody's seen him. Colorado's where he come to: I know it cause he told me. Told me not to follow him here, and now I done it don't matter anyways. Must be he's hiding out somewheres in somebody's house, or out another part of town. Or maybe he's dead. Maybe it's just the second I turn around they disappear or die. Only thing kept him alive was the picture, and now I lost it, was me killed him. Maybe it's he come out here and something happened, and nobody noticed. He gone poof just like his picture.

But I can't think that way just yet, else this here's my last ditch.

Nurse at my side, takes my arm to check my pulse.

"You are not in such good shape," she says. "Have you been fainting much lately?"

"Been keeping it under control," I says.

Then she wrinkles up her nose like she opened a bottle of rubbing alcohol.

"Certainly not by eating anything to speak of. Obviously not at a loss for drink. I want you to understand that you're dangerously malnourished. Do you eat at all—ever? Is it because you have no money? You're in withdrawal, aren't you?"

I couldn't answer, my mouth was so dry. But what was she going to do if I said yes, give me a lifetime supply? Ain't nothing but trouble comes with charity; kind hearts and bayonets.

"We found a number in your wallet, a card with a gentleman's phone in case of emergency. The front desk has placed a call to him. He'll be here shortly. Until then, if I could ask you to remain comfortable here. We'll be taking several tests on you before your release."

Course all through I's opening my mouth like to say *No you can't do that* but she kept right on to the end like she rehearsed it somewheres beforehand, then she smiled quick, patted my arm, turned, and disappeared round a corner far end of the hall before you could say *Now of all the johns in the world why'd you have to go call that one.*

All sorts of peoples laying around like I was, on stretchers. Apart from stretchers there was three more chairs across from me, all of them full. Figured out these was the next three in line to get seen. Mostly they was still groggy from sleep out in the waiting room, but trying here to stay awake, eyelids flickering—thinking, I guess, *any minute*. Any minute and the pain'll go away. Weren't but one or two doctors what seen to the lot.

I myself weren't really in no pain, no more'n the past few days. I fainted but now I's awake, needed a cigarette and wanted to leave, only they'd took my coat and bag while I's out, my wallet too, which didn't have a lick of money or nothing else in it but the card the man stuck there when he give it to me—card what says in case of emergency call the owner of this here. Still, superstition got me thinking I'd be back later if I left that behind. It was just the thought of the man coming was enough to risk it and make a run for it. I thought maybe I'd know how to talk to him, but didn't have no energy to, even though it was more or less a script I learned by heart this point.

Course like Madam always said, some things work out best when you hold your tongue; don't even need to look them in the eyes, that way they can just pretend you ain't there, or there just the way they want. The bigger the mouth, the better it looks closed, she said. Maybe after all this time I could swing it without opening my big trap. He been trying to get me to shut up since the day he met me— smile, *smile. You look so good when you smile.* Weren't he thought I looked good as much's it kept my mouth too busy to talk.

But I'd took his money, without I asked. For once he'd expect me to do some talking. Weren't like I got nothing to show for it to explain it away. I thanked Jesus I left that fiver, though when I done it chances is I knowed I'd be back to him soon or soon enough, which case I'd need it.

Guy in one of them three chairs got bored I guess, walked around with little steps, not much place to go—they got him hooked up with clear plastic tubes to some blinking thingamajig on wheels, looked like a vacuum cleaner he couldn't shake. He seen I's looking at him, and come over, no nurse in sight to stop him. Got a mess of white hair smudged yellow some places and crusty thick, constant wheezes. Some breathing gadget what come out of the machine, held it up to his mouth like there's glue on it might make it stay.

"Got any cigarettes, Chief?" with a voice smelled like an open bottle of booze.

"In my coat," I said. "But they got it somewheres."

"You let one of them take your coat? Not good, Chief, not a smart thing. Now, listen, think of a way we can locate that coat," his mouth to the mask—took in air, then, "It's pure principle, gotta know where your things is and how they're doing and, if not, where they're headed. That there's, in a nutshell, the only way you got to feel power in your world."

He started looking around for a nurse, just scooted with that machine out into the center of the room, craning his neck both directions, then he come back over.

"Somebody'll have to move through sometime," I says, trying to make him feel better, like it was his things we's trying to track down.

"When. When is what to know. As long as they're gone we're stuck here alone, we're waiting for something only they can tell us. Now does that sound like power in your world to you?"

"But this ain't *my* world," I said, and shrugged.

He rushed at me full of nervous speed, near forgot the machine until he pulled the tubes far as they gone and decided he better stop there.

"What are you doing here if it's not your world? Your world is where you are. You have to keep your world together, you have to keep track of it. Where does it put you when everything yours is in the hands of somebody else? Means you're stuck, and without being altogether."

"I guess the coat's not as important as my bag. They got that too. Least I think so, else I dropped it somewheres."

He'd took the mask to his mouth but here he yanked it away fast like to near hit me with it.

"You better hope they got it, but still you need to get it back. It's *all* important, anything yours they got. Now you got to get them back. Where's that blonde, the blonde was in here before? She's the friend-liest of the lot: She'll find out for us."

But she didn't come, and after a while the man gone back on over to his chair, sat down, and parked the vacuum next to him. Stared at that machine long and hard enough to invent it all over again, then his eyes gone down and he fell asleep.

A long time later, once my own eyes was drifting off, the doors swung open, and the nurse come in followed by the man I owed money. He got my coat and bag slung over his arm, looked dirty now I ain't seen them for a while; got them away from his self, afraid I guess they'd rub off on him.

*　*　*

The nurse wanted my address and symptoms and some other information, wanted me to say all that through a slit in the glass, and when I weren't saying whatever loud enough she barked at me raise my voice.

"Five Main Street," I told her.

But she kept asking What—*What*—and leaned into the intercom she got on her side.

"Address I live at's number Something-or-other Main Street, north side of downtown, here in Memphis. What else?"

"Is this a house?" knowing full well weren't none of them down there.

"Do it matter?" I says. "Look, it's a storefront what used to be a liquor store. Or something. The symptoms is: I think I got a migraine."

"What?"

"I said I got migraines, and—"

"Have you ever had a migraine before?"

"I don't know: Don't think so."

"How do you know you're having one now?"

"Look," I says, "I don't know. That's why I come here. A little while back somebody told me I's blue, the color blue, or purple or something. I got a pain in my neck won't go away, like somebody's digging into my collarbone."

Then there's more sitting around in the waiting room, next to Aunt Edna flipping through *Reader's Digest, Better Homes and Gardens*, spent a long look on *Ladie's Home Journal* and *Redbook*. She never did ask me what was wrong exactly, how I got to feeling this way, which was fine by me except her being quiet made me wonder do she already know—about everything, like maybe she expected it from the second she first whiffed the room at Mojo's, like all this stuff's as prefigured as they all says.

Waiting room packed full, all of them doped up in the chairs on account of their every aching joint bored stiff. *Maybe the real draw of this place's you know help's on the way once you get here*, I thought to myself. *Help or relief either one. Right in the other room so's you can rest easy.*

But watching all them peoples comatose made me feel straitjacketed.

I turned, casual studied Edna's profile. Looked almost the same as in the picture I seen one of the few times I been in her ma's house, her face in between two others, my ma and sister Millie number three—all of them young girls, froze in charcoal like to never grow up and get color, trapped inside large, gold frames. This was my other grandma's—Ma's ma—Lady J they call her, one what lives in Buford, Arkansas. I promised I wouldn't talk about it, but I can't tell part of the story without the rest. I can't look ahead or behind without Buford gets in the way to trip me up.

I'll tell it like it happened, but I's stopping there, I ain't going back.

It was a long time since I seen that grandma. I thought probably she didn't remember me. Or maybe it just seemed like that cause I couldn't barely remember her myself. All I knowed was mostly what my ma and her sisters told me, and mostly that didn't make sense. I been trying to put it together since as long as I can remember, like everything else.

Like how Grandma had a husband, but before I got born he left her for a woman my ma said was young enough to be sister number four up there framed with the rest of them. He left her or she kicked him out. Or she kicked him out and it was somebody else cheated on somebody. When he married my grandma, he was making good money working at a hospital or in a doctor's office or I don't know, took pictures and a few other things on the side. Later on he designed a lake and a beach for part of Buford, built it around a big hill, and on top the hill he built a photo studio. They's doing so well he even got a plane at one point. Or a boat. A plane or a boat or a sports car.

Then he spent all the money. Had to sell the plane or boat or whatever it was to get some of it back. And he started to sleep with some of them women he took pictures of. One time I heard Ma say whenever she had friends over he got awful friendly with them, and sometimes they was friendly back. Millie said weren't none of that was true: He weren't never with nobody but grandma, and if he done anything wrong who wouldn't after so long with just her, on account of she wouldn't never settle for him being nothing less.

When the last of the three sisters moved out's when he left my grandma or she got rid of him. I guess it's good least they waited until then, and he did leave her the photo studio, or she kept it, added on to it enough to make a house. So that's anyhow something to make up for some of the rest, depending on who you's listening to. He left or she got rid of him. Edna says she got rid of him, kicked him out without she'd let him take nothing, not even his pictures, with him.

Ma never mentioned him much after a while. Nobody did, except sometimes to say the bad things he done, like to make sure to remember them parts. I had to ask until my jaw hurt what was he before he done all that stuff, but it was like since they ain't talked about it so long they couldn't remember. What I knowed about my grandma was just that, and the fact her own daddy died in a truck, him and his fifteen-year-old mistress. Carbon monoxide. Accident. Grandma never forgive him or nobody else for it.

I tried to see the gold frame around Edna's face now, her sitting next to me but like in the picture. Tried to decide how she changed by looking at her, if you could tell about all them points in time between the picture and now. Then my name's called, Edna looks up from *Redbook*: **FIVE WAYS TO STOP SAGGING**, bright yellow letters. I gone to another nurse took me through an electric door into a skinny hall of rooms cut off by curtains. Led me into one near the middle.

"Take your shirt off and have a seat on the cot," she said as already she's leaving the room. "Someone will be with you in a moment."

* * *

He laid my bag on the stretcher, handed me my coat and held up the pack of cigarettes he must of found in one of the pockets, nevermind I been jones-ing for one. After the nurse left us, me and him just stared each other down a few minutes, until he tossed them cigarettes next to me like he's spitting them out.

"They tell me you were found loitering around little children, scaring them half to death. You know, it's bad enough you're bent on making yourself a pariah; I guess you don't care you're making me one by association. Do you know—do you have any idea—how embarrassing this is for me? Look around you. Look at the class of people. Is this where you're happy to spend your life?"

"Can I have my wallet, please?" was all I'd say.

He handed it over—I mean to say he let me get my hands on it then held his own grip fast, so's if I wanted it I'd have to tug-of-war. But I let go.

"I don't see what you'd want with it. You spent all the money you took from me." Then he pitched the thing onto my coat, reached into my bag, pulled out Pa's flask and held it upside down to show it's empty, like to say don't think he don't know.

"Get your damn hands off that," I says, and swiped for it. But he let go that too, like he just wanted to see me get upset or something—let go and tossed the thing back in my bag. I started to cry without I could help it.

"You realize I have no responsibility for you. I was generous, enough to provide you with a place to stay, and with it a chance to settle down and start over. You obviously don't want any of that. I only came out of concern, though a part of me doesn't care what happens to you after what you've done to me."

"You don't know a thing about me," I said, turning over on the stretcher to face the wall next to it, my back to him so's he wouldn't see me crying and think it been for him.

"What can you think you mean," he said like anyhow he was talking to my face, like he didn't need my face to talk to me. "I know you better than you know yourself, because I can see where you're headed. It's not that hard to figure out the problems of someone your age. They're things not one of us hasn't gone through."

"What do you mean, 'one of us'? You don't even know how old I is."

He come closer to the stretcher, I guess on account of I raised my voice, and now he was folding my coat.

"Leave it alone," I says. "Last thing I need's somebody folding my threads."

"What you *need* is someone to wash them."

He ignored me, just gone right on and finished folding the damn thing, set it at the foot of the stretcher all tidy. I's done with the crying, or got it under control, but stayed turned just the same.

"Absolutely filthy. Probably germ-infested. Practically growing a *beard* for crying out loud. Why do you choose that over being clean and fed with a place to stay?"

"You don't even know how old I is."

"Smoking cigarettes and rolling around in dirt. Drinking. Drugs somewhere in there, or so the nurse seems to think, judging by the state of you. And to top things, following children."

"How you think you met me?" I asked and craned my head now to look at him. "I might as well be a child, young as you see me, and what's that make you? *My age.* And just so's you know, I ain't done a drug since you met me, and what's more you didn't seem so worried about me drinking when you bought me that beer, first day I met you. Why don't you just leave—just tear out?"

"And how do you expect to pay for the tests they're taking?" he says, like I got a mind to anyhow. "What will you pull out of your empty wallet to give them? You don't even have identification on your person."

"Don't matter. *You* seem to know who I is just by looking at me."

Made him mad I's still on that bit, and he didn't say nothing for a while longer, just stared into me. I could tell if he got his way he'd have me get lost so's he could straighten me up without no interruptions. But I weren't satisfied with leaving things how they was.

"If helping me's what you wanted you'd give me the help I ask for, so don't give me no line. I thank you for the place to stay and sorry I took off with your money but still you said it was in case of an emergency—didn't say who's to figure what one was. Think my life was nothing but me on my way to a place at your table? I didn't get no clean slate and neither did you."

"I was doing my best to help you. Are you saying you're just some child I picked up off the street, to have my way with at will?"

"Seems like part of that's true, anyhow."

He sucked his breath in slow and careful.

"You may be thirty years old, for all I know: You're right. But thirty or thirteen, you have no money to pay for this visit."

"So they can bill me, and so can you," I said.

"You have no home address that I'm aware of."

"Look. Charge it to the dust and let the rain settle it. I don't care neither way. I don't want them tests anyways—ain't even decided I'll take them. So why don't you leave like I said? I's an asshole, I pulled one over on you, just like you got it. I made you believe all kinds of things you wouldn't of regular, so now's your chance to get away."

"What about the money you owe me?"

"You yourself said I ain't got a pot to piss in or a window to throw it out; nothing in my wallet last time you checked."

He gripped the stretcher's bars and shoved them quick into the wall, so hard I thought I'd go right through. Then his hands stayed put, the digits white as powder, though he's beet red everywheres else. He was still trying to keep the look on his mug level, but he leaned in and spoke his hot breath on me and that kind of blew his cover.

"I gave you access to everything I own. I invited you into my home—my privacy—uncovered everything for you without any measure of protection for myself. When you were hungry I gave food, when you wanted anything, anything within means I gave you. You took advantage of all that, broke every show of respect on your way out with my money. And now you'd just leave it that way, without any kind of apology for the scene you're causing."

"And now you better get out of my face," I said, cause he was getting redder still, "or I'll hit you on top of it all. I told you I's sorry."

"Well it's not good enough."

I just shut up after that, and he left his hands on the bar like it was him holding the stretcher up, until the nurse come in.

Ready to go, she asks, put her hands on the stretcher, other end from his. All them hands made me feel shut in and locked up, ready to be pushed wherever, whichever way.

"I's just going to take my things and leave," I said, touching my coat and bag case anybody thought to grab them. Course she argued with me, said I got a mild case of what you call Altitude Sickness, on top of I's kicking and I should do this and that and whatnot else, get myself checked into some kind of treatment center with cash from who knows where. But I guess she realized she couldn't make me stay there. All they could nail me for was fainting.

"Well at least get yourself something to eat," she said, like it ain't never occurred to me.

After all this sound advice she asked would I wait right there so's she could bring back some papers for me to sign. When I said yes she left to get them.

The man took his hands off the stretcher, put them in his pockets, said:

"Are you sure you won't come with me so we can forget all of this?"

Which I couldn't figure one whit, seeing as how he just got done making everything a big deal.

"I can't," I said. And after I said nothing else for a while he turned and left without looking at me—kept his head down all the way out the swing doors where he come from.

Then I seen the man what been sitting across from me, the one what got the vaccuum hookup, seen he been looking at me the whole time.

"All right, Chief," he says. "Good deal. I see you got your things back."

* * *

It was maybe ten minutes later or so I made up my mind to go ahead and follow him, even if just to tell him when I caught up for good how much I hated him. In my mind it was suddenly I got to find him one last time to make sure he heard everything right, else maybe he'd of gone on forever thinking of me as his friend—still his friend, caught in time that way like a snapshot. Only way I could feel things was different for sure was make it so's he knowed.

I run through anybody in my way, kids and their folks just the same, stuck my arm straight out stiff moved it left or right as need be, struck whatever when there weren't no other way. Them peoples stumbled to the wayside, crumpled their legs or over each other, and once I got past them they was out of my mind. I just kept my eyes mostly ahead to watch out for a shock of red hair flashing in the sun or ringed in smoke. Thought I might even see his coat or whatall else, like if I could part enough of the crowd they'd flip off like dominoes, make a path right to him—everything else knocked down, even Shorty with the stupid three-piece and briefcase. Just Red standing there, all by his self.

Two carnie hands, got wise from the commotion, started tailing me, they was waddling after me in their baggy pants tripping over theirselves. But I's smart enough to throw peoples in my wake, and them clowns half falled over and again before they could catch their balance and keep it coming. Didn't put them out but give me a chance to stay ahead.

Finally near the edge of the carnival I seen him, no flash of nothing, just him and Mr. Collar-and-Tie, two little stick figures way up ahead, getting into some car surrounded all sides by a bunch of others. The man got Red by the elbow, helping him get in I guess. Opened the door, passenger side, his free hand on Red's back pushing him into the seat, shut the door firm both hands, then on his way around the car to the driver's side.

I yelled top of my lungs WAIT, and other stuff I forget. Knowed sure they couldn't hear me, knowed even if they could they wouldn't answer. So I jumped the flag rope to the parking lot and run fast as I could, my hip or arm or thigh slamming hard against this or that car trying to squeeze through too fast. Behind the scatterbrain of carnival music and chatter and the crank crank of the roller coaster making the long ride up, I could just barely hear the car's motor start, and still I's so far away.

I hopped the hood of a car, then run along like on a path, over one then the next. Up ahead their car shook like Shorty just put it into gear. Whole time I's yelling stop and cussing up a blue streak, top of my lungs—all panic, figured I done lost my chance. Them clowns falling behind, on account of they wouldn't jump over cars like I done. They kept to the ground, fought their way around bumpers and fenders, them wide-ass pants of theirs like to fall down to their ankles. Once in a while they yelled out something but I weren't listening so I don't know what.

By the time I caught the car—that is jumped onto the hood and sprawled myself across the windshield looking in—it was steady backing out its parking space, slow cause it was a tight fit, and when he seen me Shorty—who been looking over his shoulder to back the car out until I landed on it—slammed on the brakes and like a smart-ass laid his hand on the horn.

I slapped the glass a few times, maybe made a face like to show him what shape he'd been in if I could get at him. Which point he locked his door. Red and him was cuss-fighting a little, least Shorty was yelling at him, and Red raised his own voice over the horn to answer back. Once or twice Red looked at me through the darker part, top of the windshield, screwed up his eyes, said fuck you and go away. I's stuck just so on the car, since getting down meant them driving away. What could I do but bang my palms on the glass and shake my knees thunder-hard against the hood. And Shorty thought he's a laugh riot. He was half out the parking space already and figured he could floor it a hair to throw me. But I thought and held fast to the lip of the hood, bottom of the windshield, screamed louder once his hand was off the horn.

A flash in the corner of my vision: them clowns moving closer through the cars, damn near ten feet away. And now Shorty's jerking the car, foot dancing on the brake, which made my voice skip. Just when the clowns reached the fender I jumped down, started faking left and right so's all three of us, spread out and moving, blocked the car from getting anywheres. I's on the driver's side when Shorty rolled down his window a crack probably to yell at me, but I hollered right past him to Red.

"Wait," I says, while Shorty's trying to shoo my hands out the window so's he could close it. "I just want to talk to you for *one more minute*. Can you leave the goddamn car? Then I swear I'll go away." Without I got no idea what I's trying to say. But by then—since I been still—the carnies caught up with me. They swooped in one on either side, grabbed an arm each, told me I better get off the fairgrounds altogether. They forced my fingers out the window, which point Shorty rolled it shut and started moving the car like to drive away.

Then—funny thing—Red put a hand on Shorty's arm, said something to him got him to put the car in park, steps out his side, holds up his hands like to stop a brawl. Says to the carnies, "All right, guys," and they let go like he's a referee. He come over to my side of the car rubbing his forehead.

Shorty's watching keen, but it felt good there weren't nothing he could do. I seen my face reflected over his in the window and thought, *HA*. When Red reached me, I turned my back on Midget Man to give us some privacy, from him anyways since the clowns was of course still there waiting I guess to take me away to the funny farm.

Red reached into his coat pocket, pulled out his Marlboros, offered me one.

"I wouldn't share smokes with you for money," I says to him, and stared at the one he got held out for me like it could light on fire by itself and burn away useless down to the butt for all I cared.

"Suit yourself," he said. He stuck the cigarette in his own mouth and hung it off his lip while he searched his self for a light.

"Look, I don't know just what's up with you, but you're wrecking what I got going down here. These ain't the guys to mess with. You want my blood drawn so you can take it away with you or what's the deal?"

"The deal—" I said. "What's going on here is . . ."

"Go on." He found a lighter and brung it up to his mouth, lit the cigarette. "Go on, now. He's got the car idling, and I'm going to have some explaining to do when I get back in it."

"Well, what are you going to do?" I says. "I mean—where you headed after today?"

"You're drunk," he says, like he's just now noticing it, and shook his head. "Not it's none of your business but they's 'relocating' me to Colorado Springs. Setting me up out there in a brand-new house and everything else or so they keep saying." And he smirked. "Is that why you chased me down?"

"Why? Why out there? *Who's* relocating you for what?"

Shorty give a quick honk to the horn like all right already, and Red leaned past me to blow smoke at the window.

"Okay okay just a minute," he said in a careful voice I ain't never heard, then he come back to me, light from the fender shining on his hair and filling up his eyes.

"I got into something and these guys are getting me out."

"How come they can't get you out of it here?"

"I can't say nothing else. Look, I don't even know what to expect, know what I mean? Colorado Springs is just a name I pulled out of a hat. It looked better than some others, and it don't make a difference no more. I don't know a soul out there, no family, nothing. But if I stay here I'm good as dead. Didn't you know? I'm expendable."

"So . . . can't I go with you? I ain't got a house myself, like I say. Maybe you want somebody should come along, make the trip easier."

He shook his head firm but he weren't mad. "Course not. Look, I'll be fine. That what you's worried about?" and smirk, and giggle. "I don't know what's got you so bent out, what you's on and trying to kick. You *are* trying to kick, ain't you? I mean you been shaking like a wet dog all day. You hardly know me, you know? You hardly know anything about me."

"That's how come I'd ask," I said, giving the elbow to one of them carnies got too close.

"Look, you're a sweet kid—"

"I ain't a fucking kid. It's just . . . I's on my own, too. Home free.

Been that way for a long time—got nobody. I'm twenty-two, and there ain't nobody else but me. Oh Jesus where do I start—I mean it sure is hell when it's this way, and it's this way now. You never let me finish my story, else you'd know I ain't never felt right and it only gets worse, so bad since I come back here to Nebraska from everywheres in the world kicked me out, seems like, and can't even step foot inside my ma's house, coming to feel it's now or never, go-no-go on lots of things. All's I's asking ain't nothing to you, just you let me come with you to Colorado Springs, nothing else. Seems like it's the only place left I ain't tried. And believe me when I say I can make like I ain't even there, so's you can feel you's all alone. If that's what you want. I done it before."

Red turned to the carnies and told them get lost. "Can't you see we're talking here?"

Them clowns said I's trouble and it was me needed getting lost, they was there to make sure, but Red said they couldn't touch me, me being his brother and all, and this was just a hard time for me, I's snapping like anybody else could at any spur of the moment, so why didn't they just dog-tail it back to a pie-in-the-face routine. They said I's in trouble for the damage I done to the cars alone, not to mention the peoples and blah blah all else, which point Red dug a wad of dough from his pocket and handed some of it over to them.

"Okay? Just take it. Take it and no questions asked, long as you get out of here."

And they left counting it.

I made sure my back covered most of the window and hid my face cause now I done lost it, now them other two was gone. Red, cigarette held in his lips, reached over, used his thumb to wipe under my eyes one after the other. Let his thumb stay there, then moved down my cheek, to my nose, on to my mouth, said:

"Kick this shit—it owns you. It'll own you if you don't get a grip on it."

"I *done* kicked it," I said. "I ain't going back."

"What's it been—a couple of days? A week? You ain't kicked it just yet, and you ain't going to by following me. You know, twenty-two's nothing like it feels like. You've got all the time in the world, you'll see. Come with me, I guarantee you nothing, nothing would change much. How else you think I know to tell you this stuff unless I been through it already? You think it's so bad not having anybody to look out for you? What about you can't do anything without somebody somewhere seeing it and getting you into trouble for it? One day you'll get where you want and won't any of this hurt so much no more. Maybe. But not if you ain't looking for it, not if you give up and you ain't ready to jump on it. Now you just go home and work things out. I mean it."

He give me the rest of the money what was in his hand and closed my fingers over it, laughed when I tried to give it back, said, "I'm like a grandmother, trying to take care of everybody; now you run on home."

"But I *done* all that," I said. "I ain't got a home. I told you. Stop saying that already."

But he was backing away, and when I started after him he put his hand up.

Course I heard it all before, but what else was there to do, so I held off, even when more crying come over me and blurred sight of him turning, going around the car to the other side. I thought I seen him wave, so I waved back. I waved all the time it took him to get back inside the car, and I didn't touch that car at all—made no move to stop it. I just kept waving until it was out of the parking lot, then out of sight where sure they couldn't see me neither, stood there waving and shaking, smell of his smokes mixed in with my tears and spit and sweat.

And that's the last time I seen him.

TWO

Later that summer Hurricane Andrew ripped cross-country through Florida, landed on the *New York Post* and *Daily News* under headlines like, *Andrew's Aftermath* and *Andrew Goes for Broke*. Day in and out it hit the papers until maybe by force their front pages tore straight off and laid waste to the curbs and gutters of the city.

August was the hottest month yet, and I spent it in the company of one Herbert P. Myers, man who favored dark suits with stripes run up and down them. I hooked up with him after I been on my own for a while and things wasn't working out, after I seen I couldn't make heads or tails of peoples on the outside; like Madam said but I weren't ready to give her that. Figured if I didn't want to end up with Mannie owning me like them others I seen out on the streets of the Square, I needed a steady, some place I knowed I could stay no matter what, without I got to think about it all day or sleep wherever if I ain't come up with nothing. If I aimed to make it on my own I needed to get myself set up with somebody.

Myers was near bald, told me he was in the habit of wearing hats but just lately it was too hot, he'd have to go without. Without meant the top of his head got red and shiny from sweat and later sunburn. Sometimes when he talked to me I watched up there, focused in on one or two beads to see how long before they'd roll down the bulb of his head onto the hair just above his ears, which point he'd reach up a hand to smooth them over like pomade. Most times this hair round the nape of his neck took slick and looked like the bristle-whiskers, steel-gray and wiry, of a walrus I seen at the Omaha Zoo; big old fellar sat mostly up on a rock fountain middle of his pen. In my head I got to calling Myers Walrus.

Walrus worked on Wall Street nine to five, five of seven days a week.

"It's all numbers and slips of paper," he said, "figures, tall buildings. Everyone stressed-out silly. You're lucky if your office has a window, much less one that looks out past a brick wall."

That's how he described Wall Street, but really I couldn't say, cause I never seen it for myself. Before Walrus I only seen Omaha, Memphis, the Madam's, the insides of hotel rooms. More or less. So what'd I know? I only seen Wall Street from pictures, I guess—just skinny buildings scrunched up together, window on top of window all the way up same size.

I thought about Myers waddling up to a revolving door where other walruses slid into the hyped-up lobby of a building, all eyes straight ahead, not so much as a friendly shake of whisker to any passerby. I figured this much cause whenever he come home he talked about his day like that, and he weren't none too patient with me as he scrambled out of his clothes like they's on fire, couldn't barely bother to look my way.

"It's all fluorescent lighting inside," he belly-ached. "Along the ceiling in rows all the way down; a sick green color to everything from them and the glow of each man's computer on his desk. We are all in rows there, right up against each other but you'd never know, never a word except about business. That's not really talking. When I leave my things at the end of the day to come out into the light, it's like getting out of a dark prison. But you don't want to hear about all of this."

Once all the talk about work was done, Walrus mostly kept quiet with his hands to his self. In his cramped apartment, high up off Times Square, we sat one on each side of the couch watching movies; all day and nothing but on weekends. Disaster flicks like the one where peoples dressed in furry clothes gets caught under a giant avalanche. Everything fine—drinking and laughs in the ski lodge—until suddenly through the window the mountain breaks in half, comes crashing down to bury peoples without it so much as give them a chance to set their drinks aside, sirens coming from all over, the lights dancing funny on the snow.

His favorite was the earthquake movie come on one Saturday, five o'clock.

"Just when everyone's getting out," he squealed like the revenge of the living dead.

The part he laughed hardest at's when downtown splintered into cracks gone all crazy directions. The skyscrapers toppling; tenth floor become the third become the first. Boy he laughed and laughed. "Just when they'd be getting out," he said again, watching all the suits run out the crushed entrances, some of them jumping out the windows, their coats left behind—course, those was the ones didn't make it. They landed on the ground like weren't nothing but gravity and concrete.

"Those places are death traps," Walrus said, and he shook his head firm like it just gone to show.

He never really did reach across the couch to touch me, only sometimes a pat on the head or leg, which was fine by me. Still, he wanted me there at all times, even when he his self weren't. He made no small talk about how he give me everything I could need, and how, it being so hot, there weren't no reason for me to get out.

"I don't like not knowing where you are," he'd say. "I like to know you're right here."

And he'd pat the couch between us.

When he left for work, I waited five minutes or so to make sure he wouldn't turn around and come back, cause early on sometimes he done. "Oh, I forgot something," he'd say, rustling some papers before he gone again, only after he give me a sharp once-over like even though he could see me right there I might actually be gone. Then I took the phone off the hook just in case.

For the rest of the day I turned whatever tricks I could find. Sure, Walrus give me things, but not "everything I could want or need," like he put it; more like what he thought I wanted and needed, and what did he know. I didn't know neither, really, but that was for me to decide. He made it sound like he'd never get lost of me, but I couldn't never be sure just from what he told me when I pressed him. Ain't like I's exactly used to peoples keeping their word. If there's one thing I learned by then it's a body's got to make sure to put away for the future, and even though I ain't never got that far I knowed from the start I got to get out and try. Never aimed to get locked up somewheres like at the Madam's all over again; I just wanted a place to come and go from, place I'd know was always there. So: Walrus gone to work, and so'd I. Made my own rules, not like in the house. Even if it just been to show I could; even if just to practice for when I'd start setting money aside. If things gone wrong doing it, weren't nobody to kick me out of nowheres.

I mostly made it back before five, which point I put the phone back on the hook and went into the bedroom to lie down and make like I's asleep. Like clockwork in he'd come, make some noises in the front room, walk into the bedroom where he'd stand over the bed and pat me quick on the back of the head, scruff up my hair. Undress saying how hot it was, then lay his self down next to me with enough room between us to raise a family, start rubbing my arm. Cluck cluck at me for tying up the phone all day.

"You're not making any long-distance calls, are you?"

Like I got friends all over in high places—a direct line to the Oval Office.

But that was all just talk and he didn't so much like talking. I knowed what he wanted, cause we been through it so much before; so I gone down below the belt and done for him what I been doing most all day on good days.

And after a while he'd say: "I'm ready to get off. Are you?"

It weren't no different than with nobody else that day who paid one way or another, cause see, like I say: He didn't touch me. None to speak of.

Still, sometimes I'd be bold, say:

"Well I myself might need a little something," though I'd of decked him if he tried, and anyway the dope I's on weren't exactly a firestarter. It was just the principle.

"What do you want me to do?" he'd grumble.

So I'd just say nevermind to him, and *sure enough* to myself.

Underneath his bed he kept a big cardboard box full of dirty magazines, and he'd dig one out, bring it up, turn on his side so's his back was to me, start playing with his self. I could hear the pages flipping, like he wouldn't be ready until he seen a little of every one. When he got done, he'd turn back my way, start to come, look at me out the corners of his eyes like to say, "Thought you said you was ready."

Then like he couldn't be bothered, out his mouth like he held it in all day or week come language what could fry bacon, the likes I only heard from cops. "Fuck damn, Godammit, I mean FUCK," and in-between these blasts of breath like the steam shooting out a time whistle, end of a workday shift.

* * *

Doctor told me, said. "Take better care of yourself."

But what he never said's how. I thought I *been* taking care of myself, what I's doing. But he said Son look at yourself, now you need to take a long, hard look. Guess that's something I ain't never done up to then, running all over the way I been; never once really stared myself down, said, *Self what is you and don't you lie.* It's just nobody else ever seemed to care neither way, and it didn't make no difference to me what I thought of myself: Thinking never got me by. Thinking was think harder; think again.

This doctor told me, but you see how it gone in one ear and out the other, cause how should I know. He said I maybe got a thing called spinal meningitis.

"Fine by me," I says. "Give me the pills." Them I could make use of one way or another.

"No, no," and he shook a rubber-gloved finger at me. "I don't know for sure that you have it."

"Guess," I said; and, "Can't you just give me them pills case I do or don't?"

"This is fatal," he says. "I have to do a spinal tap to make sure."

I knowed that meant a needle, got some idea what he aimed to do. So again I asked him, why not just pretend like I got this thing, go ahead give me the pills. I's willing to take my medicine. And if it turned out I ain't got it, why, I'd bring them back. Swear on the Bible.

No no, again; He said he'd be right in with the needle—"just relax"—then turned, flipped the curtains aside, and there I was, with myself, shirt beside me on the cot, cold chill goose bumps from the hospital air. Thinking; *How fast can I get that shirt on and self out of here: how to find my way out the maze of curtains and cots, through the waiting room, back to the street, screw Aunt Edna wherever she may be in there.*

But it was them pills in my mind more than any needle. Sure, I's scared: It's just I told myself for a sharp pinch I'd get a big bottle of pretty swallow things, restin' powder to help me get over it. So I sat there, listened to moans and grunts through the curtains, until here come the doctor again, black case in his hand like an assassin keeps his gun in. He set it on the rollaway table next to my cot, flipped one lock then the other, and up come the lid on the longest needle I ever seen. I thought while I watched him piecing parts together, *Sure here*

I's watching my very own assassination. That needle'll go through my back and out my stomach, and what good'll all them pills do me falling right through that hole.

"I need you to lay on your side, back to me, and curl up in a fetal position, like the day you were born," Doc maybe wisecracked, got that needle held upright next to his show-nothing face.

But I's stalling: I got my hands held tight to the edges of the cot, not about to lie down.

"What's that thing feel like going in?"

He brung the needle down a whit, smiled like he's patient, said. "You'll feel a sharp pang, then not much else."

"Actually, I feel much better," I said; smiling like I's patient too. "Fact, I don't think I's ever sick to start with, just needed a look, like you say. So I'll take my leave and set to it. Just tell me exactly where to look and I'll be on my way."

But no go: It's a lost cause trying to hoodwink a real doctor. Few more questions later, he told me I should just grow up and take it like a man, did I want my mama should be ashamed of me and boy was that a laugh, so I laid down curled up like he said and held my breath like to burst, sure the needle'd pop me the second it hit my skin.

"Whatever you do, don't move once I've inserted the needle," I heard him say from behind me, "or I'll have to realign it and start over."

Course I's never one to follow rules. I jumped. It was too much, the way he gone and made it sound, and waiting for it without being able to see it coming. Seemed like I always done just what peoples said I would even as they told me not to. I jolted like live wire in water when the point of it got to my back. *Burst,* I thought—just that; then, *go back, try again, never should of, mama's boy, all growed up now, never again, how much time, wherever to, who in the world who.* And so on. It's just he touched some spot I guess ain't never been touched and needed to, or got touched once and shouldn't of, and triggered something set everything to clicking.

I heard him sigh like to say, Well now you done it, and I held my breath again waiting to see would it start all over. But turns out it was after all in there straight, no thanks to me, so I laid still, thought pills pills and rattle-happy while that thing was in me, felt his free hand on my skin, pressing steady-sure.

Here I was, supposed to look at myself, but how to do what when

I's free to be poked and prodded and carted here to there by whoever got a whim. How to look at me like to see clear what's mine to begin with when seemed like anybody else could give me a better picture than I ever could, long look or no. Thought maybe if I knowed myself better I wouldn't get shuttled off on a plane from one family member to the other, poked around, kicked out.

Laid there quiet after it was all done, waiting for him to come back, give me word. I thought I could feel the hole where he pulled the needle out, felt it grow bigger until it seemed to swallow up the whole room—the bedpans, cabinets full of rubber gloves and gauze, even that cot I's on. When he come in to tell me I didn't have it after all—whatever it was—just some silly stomach virus, the room was gone for me. It was him standing there telling me middle of nowheres I'd have to change the way I's living but for now he'd give me some pills, some something-or-others to make me feel better, make it all go away, or come back full circle.

*　*　*

One day, I almost didn't make it back before Walrus got home from work. I seen it was three-thirty—that I ain't got much time—but here I was, ain't made much cash to speak of, and some john's across the bar holding his beer mug up like to say "You game?" Right away I figured I could get an hour or a half out of the guy: I'd just tell him an hour was the longest I could go, then I'd have the thirty to make it back to Walrus.

I walked casual down the bar, said well hello, "My name's" blah blah: "Buy me a drink?" Which point of course he done.

He said: "You know, I was just thinking about a boy like you."

"I'm sure I don't know," I said, like I seen somebody fancy do in one of Walrus's movies, "but what are you thinking about now?"

He smiled big, then lifted his mug and filled the smile with beer, swallowed it until the smile was just a grin, said: "I'm wondering how old the boy I have is."

It was a question but I didn't answer it. Instead I said, "Well we can talk all that over come the next beer," and he motioned to the bartender with his little finger.

Already I seen how the john was like more than a few other guys I knowed before. I felt comfortable, like as long as I stayed sober until after it was over I could figure out how things'd go, and if I's wrong so what; so I'd get my dope and make it back on time. By now I's what you call a professional; not but a drink or two while I's on the job. Still I acted like I's supposed to—giddy drunk like for the first time and stupid so's he'd think whatever happened was how he wanted it. I just watched him cool, sized him up, and got the conversation going.

"How old you *think* I am?" I asked.

"I could be wrong," the john said, "but I don't think so. I think you're not a day over eighteen. I doubt you're old enough for that beer without some amount of trouble along with it."

"And where you think I's from?"

"I'd say . . . a small town somewhere, though I don't know what brings you to New York City. Maybe you ran away from home because you like older men like me, and there weren't enough of them in that small town that didn't know your father well enough to tell him what's on your mind. Your mother died when you were little. It's just you and a father and maybe a brother. If you have a brother you like him more than you should. Maybe that's another reason you're here."

He was in his own world of thought and didn't hurt things none to let him go on. One thing I knowed by now was sit down and shut up, on account of the more they's talking the more you can watch what they's thinking. Weren't always easy to do, but it got easier the more I done it. If you kept quiet you got a better idea what they wanted you should be, and wouldn't mess up the pretty picture they's drawing. So I just sat and listened, kept an eye to my watch, kept my mouth shut when I ain't supposed to got nothing to say, and only said anything what made him think it been his own idea.

"You might be in school but I doubt it. You probably live with friends your age in the city, or just outside it, two stops into Brooklyn maybe, artsy fartsy neighborhood. Wherever it is, you don't like it there. You want to be older than you are; or at least be able to do the things older men do. You like to be with older men: you like listening to them and spending time with them, laying next to them."

Course he was mostly all wrong. He could of gone on in circles, onward beer after beer, and still: All wrong. Like for instance, right then he was sure I's listening without a thought to nothing else, but I got my mind on Walrus and the time and money and getting doped up and drunker still the minute I got rid of him, and on Omaha thinking about the grave where Pa been buried, thinking how much to dig him up and what would I find; maybe just that suit they buried him in, that navy thing looked in better shape than him when the lid got shut down and locked. White shirt crisp and bright. He been hollowed out, weren't nothing in him, and at the time I wondered how did all his skin hold up and would a pin collapse him. Dig him up and sure there'd be nothing left, just that suit and maybe I could put it on, maybe it'd fit me just right except the sleeves too long, past my hands. And his smell, that cologne they got out of his medicine cabinet and sprayed all over his suit and him. I'd wear that smell and wouldn't have to worry about most things no more. I'd be inside his head and smell, his skin so to speak, and walking through life'd be walking through his. That'd be easy cause I already seen how most of it gone.

"Just like your father." Like Ma said once. "Mr. Used-to-be; never amount to nothing."

The john asked me soon enough did I want to leave this stuffy bar and light out for his place. Said he got a nice apartment over on Park Avenue, a right smart place he'd like to show me. Said we could watch some TV and have plenty more beers, get to know each other without all these other peoples around; meaning, I guess, the two or three of them what was sitting in the bar. I looked hard at him without he'd know it and thought about all he done said; tried to figure just what kind of person he'd turn into once we was in his apartment.

Outside, he held up his pinky until a yellow cab parted from the rest and coasted up to us like it got his name on it. Opened the door, held his hand out like to say "You first." I got in and slid across the seat, and now here he was next to me, the door shut on his side. He leaned up to the Plexiglas between the driver and us, and through the opening whispered where we's headed, like he thought maybe he could keep it from me. Then he sat back, closer this time but like he weren't used to being that close to nobody; like he could with me cause weren't nobody I could tell about it and even if I done weren't nobody would listen. Put his hand on my leg, looked into my eyes, said: "We'll be there shortly."

"I only got an hour to spend," I figured it was safe to say.

70

His look gone like a stupid baby doll's—fake sad face and a pout painted on. "So we'll have to spend it wisely," he said.

His apartment, up three flights by elevator and down a marble and carpet hall, was all knickknacks and a TV. Right away he turned on the TV and disappeared around a corner. I's looking at some of them do-funnies on the shelf of a wood and glass bookcase I's standing at when he come back with a beer. "Let's sit here on the couch," he said, and already he's there, holding the beer in one hand, rubbing the cushion with the other.

"Right here," he said. "Come on, now."

But I's too busy studying them knickknacks. Objects of art's what they called them on the shopping channel some of the boys at the house used to watch, waiting in the living room between sessions. Little pretty things to look at, made out of glass and clay and wood.

The shelf was crowded with boy figurines: a boy with a fishing pole caught walking in grass; boy kneeling by a dog, got his hand out to pet it full of trust like the one ain't never been bit by the other; there was boys sitting and standing and jumping and running, all frozen doing it forever, painted different colors but looked like the same boy over and over. Some got on overalls with a red bandana peeking out the back pocket, some in Sunday best, but like I said: All of it trapped behind glass, set perfect on that shelf, like if you breathed hard they'd break.

"Come on, now," the john said again. So after a few seconds more, I gone over to the couch and sat beside him. He picked up a remote control, pushed one button, then another, and the picture come on. Adjusted the color. "Too much red tone," he mumbled like things wouldn't be right in the world cause of it, and I watched a dot move inside a line from **RED** on one end of the screen towards **GREEN** on the other, until I guess he found what he liked.

It was some video what showed a man in a office, straightening up the things on a desk. Woman's voice called in on a monitor to tell him the Lowry boy's outside, should she send him in, would the man see him?

"Send him right in," the man said as he pressed a button on the monitor. He pulled a small mirror from his desk, checked his hair and adjusted his tie, then you could see the boy come in through the door.

Boy said: "I'm reporting to you as you asked me to, Sir."

71

Which point the man smiled and shrugged his shoulders.

"Please; call me Rod."

It was something about the boy dropped by to give some report to the man, but once the boy brought the report out and laid it down, he stuck around. The man come out from behind his desk, drawed the blinds so's the room gone dim under the office lights, then he come over close to the boy.

Here the john pressed mute on the remote control, but there weren't much to miss anyways. Only the man's mouth moving for a little while longer before the boy nodded like he agreed with something got said. Boy started to take off his clothes—some kind of uniform, Boy Scouts or military maybe, tan shirt and dark brown pants. Unbuttoned the shirt slow like to make sure he done it right, pulled down his pants not a whit faster, left his underwear on.

The man was close enough to touch him, and soon enough he done; put his hand on the boy's shoulder and rubbed it smooth, got a look on his face like he's talking to the paperboy about what his plans for the future is. He pointed to his desk, started towards it, got the boy walking in front of him. Out the desk drawer the man pulled a bundle of rope and got to untangling it. Boy got up on the desk on all fours, perched his self right in the center after he pushed the report off the edge.

The john laid out on the couch behind me and pulled at my shoulder for me to join him. "I like to lay together like spoons," he said, which was more or less okay by me, since that way I could turn my back to him and make whatever kind of face I wanted.

Now the man tied the boy; each limb pulled over a corner and rigged to a leg of the desk. Neither one of their mouths was moving no more. The man gone all stern, like if the boy delivered papers he weren't doing his job right: He worked hard to finish tying him up. And the boy just seemed kind of blank, like it was all happening to somebody else, just looked down at the wood of the desk or at the wall across the room. Once in a while he looked off quick to the side like somebody else was there watching, like the man tying him up weren't the only one got a say in telling him what to do.

I myself got my eyes stuck on the both of them, trying to figure out just what exactly's going on. But just as the man finished tying the boy and was leaning towards him like to make friends, the scene changed.

It was some other boy—this one in his skivvies but got the same blank look on his face like waiting for somebody to put something on it. He'd barely lift his brows then put them back flat again; again it was some man in a suit. These two looked like the same peoples, I guess. Different clothes but the same. But this man made the boy kneel on the floor, all fours, didn't tie him up but looked like he would if he could get his hands on some rope; so on and on same to the end.

Mr. John this point reached his hand around front, slipped it into my pants, rubbed up and down my leg.

"Can we turn it off?" I said.

"What—you don't like it?" His hand stopped moving, waiting for my answer. I looked back and seen he got the remote control perched midair.

"You know them or something?" I asked, nodding at the TV.

"Not personally. I know some of their names. Some of them. There's a few I've taken an interest in. I've made a point to learn their names. What does it matter?"

"Their real names?" I asked. "Do you know their real names?"

The john took his hand off my side, sunk away toward the back of the couch, stopped looking at me. He was talking to me but he looked at the video.

"You can't really be that stupid," he said, and he gone on slow like to spell things out for me. "I know the names they use on the videos. I have friends I tell the names of the ones I like, I have my favorites. My friends know what I like, and when they come across it, they send it in to me. Sometimes I go to the video store."

"Do you ever wonder what their real names is?" I asked.

"What does it matter? It's not real. Do you actually think it's real? Give me a break. Don't try to come off so naive, so fucking gullible. You're on the streets, for fuck's sake. I mean, you've probably *been* in one of these things."

Course that was the typical rub, how they wanted to think you's so "naive" when you was taking the money but then when you told them you didn't know the first thing about something they's talking about they said you's a liar, hiding something—go figure. I looked at the TV, studied the boy's face, the way he was there, and weren't; how he's in some room, maybe a set, part of a studio. There was a window: light come through it, from outside or maybe from a stage lamp.

Then looked at his skin—his body; got a dark tan like he been out in the sun a lot, and at his waist a tan line, thin white flesh from some skimpy bathing suit I couldn't picture him wearing in public. The man was behind him, rubbing his white ass. I knowed it weren't real, but so what. So what was? It's just it come to me watching it how much everything was like it been in the house. Just when I thought things couldn't be more different outside than in, I seen they's exactly the same, and I wondered was I the only one what figured it out. I knowed I's supposed to keep quiet, but if things was still the same in the house they was still the same out here; I didn't want to.

"What's your favorite part?" I asked, not bothering to look at the john since anyways he weren't looking at me.

He jerked upright and pushed his self to a side of the couch.

"I don't have to answer these questions," he said.

"Sorry I said nothing. I just wondered, but it don't matter."

"That's right," he said. "It doesn't matter at all. I don't even know you. I don't care what you think: You think I care what you like?"

I thought for a minute, while he watched the video like that's where I's talking to him from. "Okay. So what do *you* like?" I asked. On account of I thought I knowed already, and now I seen I's wrong.

"What are you talking about?" he said, turning for just a second to stare darts at me, drizzle stray spit on my cheek.

It was just then I didn't care one whit about him; just then I realized he might be like every john in New York or anywheres else but all the same I didn't know him from nobody. Then I thought about the money, getting this over with, and making it back to Walrus on time, with a few minutes to go score from Mannie in between, now my work was done. Course back of my head I started to think how I didn't know Walrus at all, neither, and how he didn't know me. Like when I got home, after taking the dope, he'd be none the wiser, just pat me and say, "That's my boy: I like you dreamy," on account of I didn't practically do nothing but zone out once I's under. But I had to stop myself from thinking that way: Only thing it could lead to was me not knowing anybody anywheres and nobody knowing me.

The john got me all confused somehow. I felt stupid for wondering or asking or saying *anything*. That made me hate him, want to hit him, stomp on him or something.

"I mean: What do you want to do?"

"I was doing exactly that," he said. "What makes you think I ever do what I don't want? I was doing it just now."

"That's all you want to do?" I asked. I put my hand on his arm to tranquilize him but it made him jump.

"I want to watch this video. I want you to sit down, shut the fuck up, and watch it with me, and we'll see what happens."

After that, I's even more mixed up. We gone back to watching the video, laid out like spoons, me with my back to the john. He started rubbing me again, all nicey-nice, like nothing ever happened, no words exchanged of any kind. I let him feel inside my pants all he wanted, until he said:

"Turn over: I want to see you shoot."

And I done like he said—turned on my back, played with myself while he tried to make up his mind was it me or the video he wanted to watch. He studied me like I's something he almost recognized, like he might know my name or it'd come to him the harder he looked. I couldn't look at the video and jerk off at the same time, so I looked up at the ceiling and pictured Fletcher, sweet Buford Fletcher, kissing my neck, asking me do I like it, smiling at me and laughing like we was good friends and this was just so stupid we couldn't get over it, until I come. Or made like I done, on account of like usual I didn't feel much of nothing and weren't like nobody cared, long as I faked it.

Which point the john pressed a button on the remote control, and the video gone into fast forward, the boy on the screen moving high-speed and out of control.

"Oops," he giggled without he cracked a smile. "Wrong button."

Then he got up and said just a minute, left the room.

A thought come into my head, and I rushed into my pants and over to the shelf of whatchamacallits. Looked quick over the figurines. My eye come to one I couldn't get away from—a redheaded boy with a dog, hair streaked straw-colored like he been out playing in the sun.

When I heard the john coming back, I slid open the glass, grabbed the boy, and shoved him into my pocket.

* * *

Take a look at yourself the doctor said. See what you find. Something like that. By the time I made it out of the hospital it was only partly I remembered what he said. More than anything I remembered the needle in my back; remembered laying there like a dead thing can't feel nothing but what should feel like pain. Getting out of the hospital, reeling out; remember that. Aunt Edna rushing after me: "Well let me see what they told you."

"Look at myself," I answered, "and this," which point I handed her the piece of paper said I got the right to some pills.

"So if you don't mind let's go get some," I said, and we done. Aunt Edna chatted up the clerk over the counter, kept him from getting me them pills sooner, and meanwhile me tapping my fingers noisy on the Formica like to say *ain't you forgetting*. But she got to go on about how she must keep him in business, what with three sons of her own always needing something in a bottle and now this here, her nephew.

"You're supposed to take them with a glass of water," she told me out in the car as I popped two of them pills into my mouth.

But I "Got spit," I said, "and a good imagination," on account of I done waited long enough.

Then she took me to her house and made a pallet on the floor for me to lay on, shut the shades and closed the door on the noise her kids was making in the other room. I could feel it already—feel nothing, that is—which is what I guess the pills was for, or anyhow it was fine by me either way. Remember that, too; drifting off to sleep like I's a leaf on the river, thinking every time I opened my eyes a slit, *This here's a coffin, this room—dark and quiet and sleep.*

Then on back to Mojo's the very next day, minute I come to.

"I need to get back," I told Edna, and she drove me and them pills downtown.

She said it was too hot for me to ever get better, too stuffy in that place I lived, what with no open windows and plenty of sunlight, middle of a drought.

"You shouldn't go back there," she said. Course she didn't think I should of gone in the first place. But my mind was too hazy to think out any other options. I kind of listed my choices inside my head, like go to my ma's in Nebraska—like she'd have me—or stay with Edna and her three kids—another mouth to feed. I made the list but all the parts kept slipping down before I could finish with it, I couldn't tell one or the other from which.

She left me on the corner and drove off, too scared to come in I guess, or she didn't want to get out from her cool car into the heat. Inside's where I thought to check out Dan and could be drive me over to Nana's. Yeah, that's it; Thought about it half the day, sitting in there staring at the window like I could open it if I wanted to, before I finally gone up and asked him for the ride. Popping the pills before he come around with the El Camino—one, two. Put them under my tongue to see if I could melt the plastic coating before I just decided, *Oh swallow them, for crying out loud.*

Feeling better, I remember, feeling I weren't feeling a thing at all, didn't matter what happened next, I could do any damn thing I wanted. That was how I felt anyways; cause like I said, might be I could do lots but getting into Nana's house later weren't so easy. No, she turned me away, or disappeared from the doorway, or she weren't never there. Could be she weren't never there. Dan drove me back to Mojo's, every once in a while give a pet to his bird on the feathers just above its beak. I watched myself in the rearview mirror, tried to really look; listened to how on the radio they was saying it's the hottest ever in Memphis, ever in recorded history. And I thought, *If you couldn't feel it you'd never know by the look of things.* But maybe you could tell at the river, cause like they said on the radio, Old Miss was so low the ships couldn't get through, all travel standstill.

Back at Mojo's, I's set to leave for somewhere, anywheres I could think up, and knowed I better think it up quick on account of I ain't paid my rent. After a few minutes, I got to thinking I could go to Buford, Arkansas, to see my other grandmama. Course I could. She was sitting up on top of that hill, empty house all to herself. Plenty of rooms towards the back what she never got to. I could stay in one of them, out of her way. My ma told me how her property's going all to hell—overgrown grass, everything rusted out, the gravel near gone from the drive, carried off by cars and trucks coming through and time, I guess. Sure, I could go live with her and keep up her land, get it looking back the way it used to. I could help her out around the house, maybe screw in light-bulbs or reach things she couldn't, make myself handy just somehow. I wouldn't never get sick or miserable, cause I'd have me a place to stay and room to unwind. In Buford things'd be all around better.

Once I decided that's where I's headed, I spent my time figuring how would I get there, how to make the three-hour drive: across the Hernando-Desoto Bridge, through West Memphis, Jonesboro, Hoxie,

Cherokee. And Buford, long last. Thought, *Bus ride*, but weren't no fare I could pay for; *Somebody to drive me*, but I didn't know nobody got a car would make it that far or care to.

Course with not much choice I ended up at the river, staring across to the West Memphis bank with all kinds of crazy thoughts in my head. I asked everybody I could think to: "You got a rowboat" or "Say, how long you reckon it takes to swim across the Mississippi?" And when nobody could answer I walked the few blocks over from Mojo's back to the cobblestones against the bank, held my thumb up front of my face, tried to somehow measure the distance and time by sight.

I seen it a dozen times before but never thought about going on the *Mississippi Queen*, riverboat red, white and fancy you could pay to take you up a stretch and back down the river. Until one day there I was sitting on the cobblestones, watching the boats go back and forth, and the peoples lined up along the pier to board, little kids all excited practically peeing in their pants to get on. That's when I thought about tricking and paying to ride the *Queen* myself; about jumping off midstream and swimming the rest of the distance to the West Memphis shore.

Once it got in my head weren't nothing else I could think about. Down Beale Street and into Schwab's dimestore, dusted up and racked hidden in a corner, I found a ten-cent postcard of the *Mississippi Queen* out middle in the river, red waterwheel turning out skinny falls from its spokes. Stole that and carried it around in my back pocket to the point it got chewed up, faded, and beat at the edges like a memory—like already I swum through the river and took it with me. Whenever I needed, I pulled that picture out and squinted my eyes at it until it like to fuzz near into three dimensions, so's before too long it seemed just as real as anything else.

More summer heat, then Aunt Edna showed at my curb again, white-gold sunlight caught up in her car and blinding, her sitting cool as cucumbers inside with the AC. "I think you better talk to your mama," she come all that way to say. Got this look on her face like I better listen up or something no good was set to go, like things could get worse. Might be I'd of got as worried about it as she was, but since them pills she got me'd left the bottle for good I been tipping drinks instead. I weren't feeling so bad that I could tell.

"Well, I can't," I told her, "on account of I can't pay for the long-distance."

But Edna said that weren't no trouble at all; why, I could come on over to her house out East Memphis, phone from there, she herself would pay for the call. She was willing to so's I might see how important it was to finally talk to my ma who after all been trying weeks to track me down or so peoples said. I couldn't figure that one—she been the one kicked me out but it was I's the one's running away like.

I weren't keen on going to Edna's again, its being a weekend and all and her husband Ike sure to be there. He bothered me, that one—made me feel I's supposed to say something, whereas turned out whatever I said was the wrong thing, like I been tricked. Bothered me the way he stood around got his hands in his pockets, all stern and dull quiet, and somewheres in their living room that big oil painting of a mountain range, lopsided thing trapped by four sides. He done it way back when, when he's in college. Him and Edna the both of them stood around and always soon enough they'd say a bit about how he really was some kind of a painter once, a real *arteest*—said fancy—and then something about how whatever job he's working now's just a temporary thing, "Understand." Made me feel silly, like we's all kids playacting at being grown up.

Still I finally said I'd come over to make the call and I can't say how come. It just struck me, I guess, that Edna wouldn't never let me be less I did. She got so excited she stopped at a pay phone on the way to call Ike. I watched her from the front seat, bouncing just so in the phone booth behind the smudged-up glass. Or maybe it was me excited, somewheres deep down, cause my ma wanted to talk to me after all. Even if it was just to yell at me.

When Edna got back in the car, she said:

"Ike's going to call your mama. She'll get hold of us at the house after we've had our dinner."

It was sitting stiff in the dining room I made the mistake of asking Ike where he growed up. I's just trying to steer the talk away from oil paints and the "burdens of home-owning." But don't you know he gone down the whole long list, without he never once took his eyes off me. Told me every job he ever held, every person he done wrong, the houses and apartments and the streets they's on. Voice droned on to the point I's inside my head begging for that phone to ring. And when he was done—or at least there weren't no more left to tell—he looked at me like to say: "I was lost and all over just like you."

And what, I thought, *someday I'll find my way to where* **you** *is; wife, three kids, house out in the middle of nowheres sitting on all kinds of wishes?*

When the phone finally rung I's swallowing back the yawns—chin on my fist. Edna popped up from her seat at the table, whizzed around the corner almost singing. "Oh, this'll be your mama," like just the call made things storybook again. Ike and me sat quiet at the table, just the two of us alone in the dining room, the kids off screaming somewheres else in the house. Weren't nothing left to say: I's afraid to add anything, else he might of gone off again. Done already gone through his whole life, from the second the doc cut the cord and spanked the rear on up. Weren't much more he could say without I got him kick-started.

I better get right back to my nana's house, my ma said. What'd I think I's doing; who'd I think I was? First my pa dying, and now me adding all this trouble to the misery stew.

"I's just trying to be myself," I told her, knowing full well it weren't enough.

"I want you to march right back over to your nana's and beg her to let you in again."

I tried to explain it was Nana kicked me out, how if not for Nana I'd probably right then be with her in that dark house. This was just the way things worked out. But Ma wouldn't have none of it.

"You do as I say or you're no longer my son; hear?"

And that was a laugh—just hysterical. I's supposed to go knock on Nana's door, which she got lock and stocked against me, say, "It's only me; can I come in?" Which seemed like a trick question, cause answering one way wouldn't make no sense, and answering the other'd make a mother done sent me away say it was just now I weren't her kin.

"Answer me," she said, and she sounded like a stranger.

It was coming on God knows how long since Pa died on his bed, and in that time Ma's voice'd took to sounding flat and cold and just as dead as him. Way she talked to me, I's some part of life she got to deal with like it or no, and mostly she'd just as soon not. But anyways here I's cropping up all over, making her do *something* I guess.

"I can't go back there," I said. "Nana told me leave. I don't know she's all together just now. She disremembers things, seems generally out of touch. But I don't think she forgot how she asked me to leave. I'm sure she remembers that."

"Now you listen to me," Ma said. "Are you listening? I won't have no son of mine running around Memphis like there's no care in the world. It's time you stop causing so much embarrassment for your family. I don't know what exactly you got inside your head, what you'd be thinking to act this way. But it's time for all of it to stop. You realize how much trouble you've caused? The money and everything else? You think we can all take care of you and wait for you to grow up for the rest of your life? Getting Edna to drive you all over the place, in and out of the hospital for God knows what got God knows how. And who's paying those hospital bills? Who's paying for Edna's gasoline? Where are you living—down with thieves and liars you could teach a thing or two? It's disgraceful. I'm telling you: go straight back to your nana's. I already talked to her, so you can stop with making her out to be the villain. She's worried sick, crying to me on the phone."

That's funny, I thought. *She says the same about you.*

"Doesn't know where you've got to, how you're living, God knows there's drugs involved. And I know all about the jewelry. She seems to think so high of you, nevermind what you say of her; she's sure you took it by accident. God knows it's sold now and gone for good. But if you expect to stay a son of mine, you are to go there—now. Empty-handed if you got to, and crawling on your knees. Tell her you'll work off the jewelry and everything else."

So I hung up the phone. Cause I thought: *What else? That's what she thinks of me and couldn't get no better, and it's mostly too confusing to figure it all out without her help. There then, let's make it easier. That's the end of it. I won't never cost you another plane ride again.*

Then I walked back into the dining room, where Edna and Ike was sitting. Just as Edna started to ask me how things gone, the phone rung again. She looked at me without neither one of us made a move, like things wasn't supposed to happen twice like this, it was all supposed to be done with the first time around. Then I just walked out the front door and stood by the car waiting for her to finish on the phone and come out with the keys, take me back downtown.

Walrus and me fought near the whole night over it, what to do with the thing.

I wanted to put it on one of his shelves, next to the window where outside you could see all the buildings of the Square, where straight across was the big neon soda sign lit bright red and some white what said **ENJOY**.

Or on the table next to his bed, where I could see it when I woke up, or before I hit the sack—maybe in my sleep.

Walrus didn't want it nowheres in his apartment, said:

"It doesn't go with the theme of my furnishings."

More than anything, he wanted to know where I suddenly got it, sure I stole it or—worse—found it in the trash.

"At least if you stole it," he said, "you can't entirely be blamed for the poor taste someone else decorated his home with. But if you picked it up after someone else had the common decency to throw it away, there's only you to blame."

Piss off, I told him. "I ain't taking up room here with nothing but my own self, so don't expect I got to agree with you on me not being able to put just one more thing out to show I's staying here."

"If it were anything else, I might consider it, but this junk is too much. Part of you staying with me, though we've never so much discussed it, is to teach you by example my good taste in things. You'd hardly be learning anything by having *that* here. You'd learn nothing about balance and theme and—"

"Yeah, yeah," I said, "balance and blah blah. Just so happens it's only this one thing I want to keep here."

This point Walrus come up close, took the figurine out of my hand before I could grab it tighter, held it to his eye, studied it, then brought it down fast with his arm like to drop it, said:

"It's not even nearly the real thing. If it were even close, even somewhat similar to the original, I might consider keeping it here, as some kind of mercy acquisition, but it's so far away from even being a coy reproduction. They sell these in fine stores, you know; the *real* thing. If you'd been in one you'd know, which tells me exactly where I must next take you."

I took it back from him, held it close. Weren't no way I aimed to let him get his hands on it again. I even stepped back deeper into the room thinking he might charge at me to wrestle it out of my hold.

"I don't know what you's talking about," I said. "And neither do you. None of it makes a whit of sense. Nobody but you'd get up close enough to judge it."

"It's simply knowing that it would be here," he gone on. "It has no value whatsoever, and if no one else but me discerned it, it would still be far and away enough to make me restless as long as it's here. I work hard. Very, very hard. Perhaps you haven't noticed. Look around you. All this—the look and feel and mood of this apartment—has been a great investment for me. I've had to sit through nine to fives since before you were born, since before that cheap clay trinket was slapped together and sold to the closest fool, all so I could find this place and make it different. Livable, and not *only* livable but so much more comfortable that I can forget where business hours consign me. So, if it seems desperately important to me, perhaps you can see why."

I looked around his apartment, at all the glass tops on concrete blocks, wood floors. "Streamlined" and whoop-di-doo. Other words: Bare. Funny—that's how I always pictured where he worked while I's out turning tricks.

"Don't see no difference," I said, which made things worse. He gone on about how I should just listen to his advice. Stop trying to be so independent, seeing as how it weren't getting me nowheres anyways but to bad taste. Many things I don't know, he told me, cause I's brung up the way I been. I didn't really see how he could say neither way how I's brung up or where. Never so much as asked me.

"Listen," I said, "You act like me being here's such a favor from you, like without you maybe I wouldn't breathe. I got a feeling I do something for you just as much as you do for me."

Which point he stopped all his huffing and puffing, said:

"And what would that be?"

"Well, you talk about taste and whatnot. What if I wasn't around to tell—to talk to? What if I wasn't around even when you didn't want to talk, just wanted to sit there quiet like you mostly do. Who'd you have to watch TV with you, who'd lay with you? And when you think about it that way—like I do at least something for you—makes

83

sense I'd want just maybe one thing to set out, one goddamned diddly-squat, so's I'd have something of my own to look at. Now I ain't got no easy life myself. I bet you'd never know that, cause you never ask what I do when you ain't around, and that's fine. But I's telling you: I bet I got it just as hard as you do, and seeing as how you say you understand hard knocks, you can see why I want a place away from a place myself. I can't live out of a bag the rest of my life. After all this I don't care much *where* exactly I put it, but you say I live here, and cause I live here, what little's mine do too. I don't care it's trash. Ever think it means something just cause it do? Don't matter it don't mean nothing to you. It don't have to. Sick of peoples like you telling me don't sit here don't touch that and I can't breathe funny but you don't want me out of your sight. Want me here but you don't. Well make up your mind."

My head felt hot like maybe I myself's making decisions, before I knowed what they was like I said something would turn everything around so's I'd end up losing again. All over a "stupid trinket," like Walrus said.

Worse, Walrus left the apartment altogether, without a word to me, not even an "I want you out of here when I get back" kind of thing like he usually done just out the door and icy quiet, like somehow he took the place with him.

*　*　*

He was surrounded on all sides by his handlers from the carnie when I seen him, and I's dead drunk. From where I stood he looked just like he done on stage, except now he weren't so high up and all above like nobody could ever think to get near him.

I been hanging out by the parking lot before I decided I'd come on back in: been buying myself drinks, or getting other peoples to, on account of I ain't got but the five bucks and the money Red give me to last who knows how long, and I's dying from shakes and pain like you wouldn't believe, all my insides wrecked. I'd got in my mind I'd go back, find a ride somewheres, but when the guy what was buying me the drafts decided I weren't about to give him nothing but my empty cup for more, he ditched me, after saying I's the worst piece of so-and-so he ever seen. And cause by that time I's too drunk to make another friend, I watched the area close by the booth what served the beers, waited for peoples to decide they didn't want no more of theirs, which point they'd leave it next to the overstuffed trash can on the ground and I'd swipe the bees away, make it mine. Got me quite a few cups that way, and some almost perfectly good cigarettes too.

Then there he come.

If you'd seen him out the corner of your eye you'd of thought he's anybody else in the carnival, wandering around to maybe buy cotton candy, see the rodeo, step on board one of the rides. But being he was one of the main attractions there, being his name was spoke on every part of the grounds, weren't nobody could look at him but straight on. Here was the boy they claimed weren't nothing like you ever seen or ever would, amazing feat of nature what for a price you could see behind lock and key; out in the open, free for anybody with the eyes to stare.

Most everybody kept their distance from him, crowded up in a bulk at the sides of the bright yellow tents, pointing and their eyes wide open. They was all of them whispering, but all at once so's it was loud enough he could hear. The women covered their eyes with their hands, peeped out from between fingers, squint-eyed; huddled their kids close into their dresses, scolded them when they tried to break away to see what was everybody talking about. The menfolk was braver I guess, or just so stupid they figured they ain't got nothing to lose: Stared right at the boy. They wasn't about to pass up the bargain.

As for him, he passed through them with his head high, like he ain't heard or seen nothing but his own two cents' worth.

That's the amazing feat, I thought. *That's what's like nothing you ever seen.*

His handlers, dressed in their clown garb with the serious-smile mouths and eyes still painted on, hurried him along like it was true he's made of eggshells and might break if anybody in the crowd breathed or stared too hard. They's so worried about him they didn't seem to take notice he his self weren't bothered one whit. Mostly he looked ahead to where the carnies was taking him like that was the only place in the circus or the world, though a few times his eyes couldn't help going out to somebody in the crowd, and he smiled like the queen walking through the projects to prove she's one of the regular peoples, only I don't guess her clowns is so funny looking.

Couldn't much tell where they's off to. Them handlers was

machinery oiled good—walked like getting from point A to B was a matter of winding themselves up and following a straight track, like they weren't put on this earth for nothing but to take care of and watch over him. Once I made up my mind to follow them no matter where they's off to, I started heading through the crowd too.

Yes sir, it was a golden opportunity; to see the one everybody was after, find out how come he got everybody looking out for him—following him around, trotting him up and off stage—when others could do jumping jacks from one end of the carnie to the other and wouldn't catch nothing but a draft. Back of his postcard said he lived with the alligators for so long he forgot how to be around other peoples. I wanted to know what showed him how.

Or I's just drunk.

But peoples didn't want to let me by. They shoved back against me: I nearly lost my footing a couple times, worried I'd fall into the mass of them and get trampled, carried off nowheres with the carnival. First I tried *Excuse please*, and beg your pardons, but pretty soon I figured out there weren't no chance of that working—being polite and all—no more now than never. So I started shoving; held my arm out straight and cut back and forth through them. When they started pushing back, I cut through harder, took out everything on everybody at once. Finally I got to where they was, just heading off the side of the midway, and found myself looking between the shoulders of the two handlers following him up in the rear.

I bobbed up and down on my toes talking loud as I could to make it over the whisper-voice of the crowd and the cranks and whatnot sounds of the carnie, just generally trying to get his attention, didn't know quite what to say, really—just whatever come to my mind. It weren't but the back of his noggin I seen, the hair like anybody else's, between them clowns on either side. He was shorter than they was but his head peaked out like it grown from where their shoulders met.

"I just want to talk to you," I called out.

But he kept walking. I couldn't even be sure he heard me; no turn of the head, weren't the slightest turn of his head to show some ear. The crowd was coming between me and the clowns and I's in so much panic, so near to losing him before the chance to see up close and talk, I reached past a couple of kids come in front of me, the both of them wearing T-shirts said "my folks gone somewheres or other and all I got's this lousy shirt" or somesuch claptrap; grabbed one of them clown's suspenders, got a good hold and pulled hard as I could. He come flying back towards me, knocked over them kids without a one of them knowed what hit. All of them stumbled on their heels back to me until they fell at my feet in a bundle. The other clowns stopped—turned, looked up, sideways, and down—before they realized their man's floored. And just then, turning his self, Alligator Boy seen me. I stepped over the clown and walked right up to him through the space left open.

He looked at me quiet and cool-eyed, said:

"Did you do that?"

My mouth was open but it took me a minute to speak, on account of his face weren't what I expected. From a distance and up on stage it looked one way—a little wrinkled, mostly dark was all, like covered in mud, and I'd thought for sure that's what it been. But up close here I seen all the razor-thin lines of red, like somebody pulled his skin off and here's all his veins and gristle staring me in the face.

Somebody's took his skin and won't give it back. That's how come he's got to follow these clowns around. They's the only ones knows where it's at.

I watched his eyes blink, how when his lids shut looked like weren't nothing to his face but a tangle of raw insides.

"Who did that to you?" I whispered.

"That's what I asked you," he said. "I thought it must be you tripped him, you're the closest one."

He nodded to the clown been floored.

"Oh, that. What's the difference? Now's your chance to get away."

But he looked at me confused-like. Two of them clowns was on their knees pulling the other apart from the kids. The last clown come over by the Alligator Boy and me, maybe noticed the boy was in a state and got into my face a little, said:

"Get a move on, punk."

"You're the one from inside the tent," Gator Boy says, his eyes wider and all the veins pushed up past them, strained to near popping. "The one that fought with that other guy."

"Listen," I told the clown, "just stay away from me. I ain't got business with you. I want to talk to the boy here. How's about you make tracks to a pie-in-the-face routine somewheres?"

The clown grabbed my shirt and come up close like I's the pie we's talking about, scrunched his painted smile until it was half grin, half smirk.

"Leave him alone," Gator Boy said, and he put his scaly hand on the clown's shoulder. The clown's face relaxed, mouth back to full-out smile, though his eyes still stared mean, and he backed off a little, then finally let go my shirt.

* * *

Woke up facedown on a scratchy-ass rug, staring at a half-empty rum and co'cola a few inches from my head. Before I looked much past that I heard a dog or two whining, locked out behind some door begging to get in. Then footsteps, the clunk of cowboy boots, drawers shutting. Them feet got closer until they stepped onto the rug behind me and tapped me hard in the ribs.

"Okay. Up now. I have to go to work."

I turned slow so's not to feel the pain in my head any worse, seen it's the man I gone home with the night before, one said he'd get me to Buford in exchange for . . . well, this. He's standing over me all gussied up in a suit, threw me, on account of it was so similar to the one I remembered him in I got the feeling last night or whenever never stopped, like I just closed my eyes for a few seconds.

Maybe I's in Buford, I thought. *Maybe this here's Grandma's house. He dropped me off and stayed over and now he's leaving to drive back.*

"Where we at?" I asked and shut my eyes.

"I told you already," he said. "We're at my house. No talking, let's go. Up and at 'em so we can get you home. I'm expected somewhere."

I pulled myself up the best I could, rubbed my forehead, said:

"You might as well take me to the bus station: I don't plan to go home. Maybe I didn't tell you last night but I's on my way to Buford, Arkansas, and ain't nothing I need but the bag I got on my person." Then I got frantic for a second, looking around to make sure I seen it somewheres.

He huffed and left the rug, walked a few feet over to a glossy chest of drawers, reached inside a container and pulled out a pair of cufflinks. They was the ass-ends of two horses, and when he clipped them to his sleeves it looked like they's headed north.

"I don't know what time the bus leaves," I told him. "But you can drop me off anyhow: I'll find out and wait for the next one to show.

Only thing is I don't got the money to cover the ticket. So if you was to float me it—"

"I don't like to be manipulated," he said, which took some nerve, seeing as how I must of already come through on my end of the deal. But with all kind of snitting around he told me to go ahead and call the station then, find out what time exactly was the bus coming. I done, and the operator said two in the P.M., which point I hung up the man's shiny gold phone and passed the message on to him.

"I can't take you just now," he said, adjusting a tie with stables and saddles printed across it. "I'm expected somewhere very soon. Straighten yourself up: I'll give you something to wear. You'll come with me and wait until I'm done with my business."

I took a shower in one made of glass bricks, after the man give me towels and a rag and said don't touch nothing else until I's washed off and shaved and even then keep my hands to myself. While the water run I seen his outline walk through the bathroom to the sink. Turned the faucet on and my shower gone hot, so I screamed, told him turn it off. But he gone on with what he's doing—busy busy—Mr. I Got Things To Do. Tapping his toothbrush and razor on the edge of the sink exactly three times each like any more or less'd ruin everything, flurried his hands around his face I guess to comb and pat and poke it perfect. Then without a word and just as quick as quiet he left.

When I come out he got clothes laid on his bed for me—a yellow, button-down shirt, brown pants, a tie with lassoes looping round. If you held the tie the right angle them ropes looked like nooses waiting for a neck; dripping wet and shivering, face bleeding from the shave, I stood there turning it every which way. And like he seen me standing there wasting his time the man called out from the other room for me to hurry it up.

It was a while since I'd stuffed a shirt and tie. Not since Pa's buryin', when Ma told me stand up straight, "get some starch in you," so many times I thought I'd got a steel rod up my backside. Didn't know how to put it all on and wear it then, and didn't know no better now. When it come to the knot, I didn't know just what I's doing. I got the tie slung over my collar and tried a few things with it but finally it was just a tangle around my face and I had to call at the doorway for the man to come help me. He rushed in carrying some papers, set those on the bed and swatted my hands away from my neck, said:

"Come on. Let's have a look at it."

Even he flubbed it at first, slipped the wrong end into the wrong hole, mixed up by my handiwork, but it weren't long before it was like he was tying it around his own neck. Slapped me in the face with the big end flipping it over for the final tuck. "You've got it all wet," he said: told me I got blood on it. When he was done he stepped back a few feet and squinted his eyes at my chest like it was just the clothes standing there passing muster.

Then he snapped his fingers, clapped his hands, said, "Come. Let's go."

In his car driving through a neighborhood what was mostly shrubbery, sharp-cut like crystal, I asked him could he tell me where it was we's going.

"I'm expected at Graceland, not that it's any of your business. I'm meeting with a team of refurbishers the estate has enlisted to restore certain key areas of the so-called mansion. I'm overseeing the affair."

Naturally, he says.

"While I'm preoccupied, you may keep yourself entertained however you like. If you wish, you may tour the grounds: I can arrange it. Or you may simply peruse the gift shops across the street. In case none of that appeals to you, I invite you to wait at the car until I return, though if you try to hotwire it or tamper with it in any other way I'll punish you to the fullest extent of the law. And swear I've never seen you before. Just so you know."

"Don't forget what time my bus comes," I said, but no sooner was it out my mouth than he's telling me how unheard-of it was for a person like me—"hardly famous for reliability," as he put it—to keep time for one like him.

"I'll meet you exactly four hours from now. That leaves plenty of time to get you to your little bus ride. You simply need to make up your mind where you wish to wait."

We drove down Elvis Presley Boulevard, toward Mississippi, past some of the older signs in Memphis—signs with neon stars, busted out from old age, and arrows pointing nowheres in particular since the shops they used to advertise was long gone, took over by others got nothing to do with the originals the signs was made for. Down that far on the boulevard it's all them and telephone wires crisscrossing, off wood poles shaped like crosses up high against the clouds, everything sun-faded, crumbling streets, heavy traffic. The rest fenced in and grown over with ivy and vine like once peoples aimed to make everything fancy but somehow give up and gated it.

Course I's mostly thinking about how this was miles farther from Buford, the way we's headed, so I didn't listen much to the man talking. Saying things like how glad he was this part of town was more Mississippi than Memphis, on account of its giving us a bad name. Elvis was born in Tupelo, Mississippi, he told me, not Memphis—that's how come he lived way out there where he done. He was like all them what was anyhow no different than most peoples in the U.S. of A; tacky and black velvet posters framed in gold. Wait all their lives to get themselves a nice house, and once they got the money what do they do but slap tacky dofunnies on the one they already got. Peoples like them shouldn't be allowed to own houses, he said, and he gone on for a few more minutes. But my mind was busy, and I didn't much feel like talking or listening neither one.

We parked across the street in a lot specially made for visitors to Graceland. Mostly it was full of mobile homes and family vans, tagged with license plates from all over. From there we gone to a tour bus under a pavilion on the same side of the street, boarded it with the rest of the sightseers, and headed across Elvis Presley Boulevard, after I told him I's going to wait for him around the house.

The yard was blocked off by a long wall of jagged stones, and over them was the scribble of thousands of visitors what come since Elvis died I guess. Writing so thick and overlapping it mostly looked like tangled-up barbed wire, and not a whit easier to make heads or tail of. "Long Live the King" and so on. I thought about just how many peoples must of come and wrote on the wall when what they really wanted was to get inside the house and for good; thought it was as hard to imagine as counting stars when you know there's more than you can see, or trying to figure how time goes on and on in heaven like nowheres else.

Through the gate the bus drove up a driveway what winded back and forth through the yard like to make it seem longer than it was, until it pulled up to rest alongside the house, which weren't as big as you'd figure. Got itself standing back so far from the curb and high up a hill you'd of thought it was big as Jesus on the cross, until up close you seen it's just a two-car garage type thing. Then we filed out of the bus, and while most of the peoples took turns snapping pictures of each other standing in front of the entrance, the man I come with took me by the arm off to the side.

"You'll be done with the tour before I'm back," he said as the peoples around us posed, hammed it up like maybe it was them who moved in after Elvis kicked off. I weren't paying much attention to the man on account of all the smiling—all teeth and gums and laughing guilty like they's in a graveyard. "So ride the bus back across the street. You won't want to wait here the whole time. I'll meet you outside the ticket office in four hours," and he walked up the stone steps to the front door, showed a card to a lady what stood there in a uniform, and disappeared into the house.

* * *

I sat on the couch most all of the night waiting for him. For a while I tried to get my mind off him being gone by watching the TV, but there weren't nothing much on. Just some peoples selling things, silly grins on their faces like "buy this and oh what a wonder your life will be." And the news: talk about peoples found dead all over the city, some girl sent to jail on account of she killed a little boy she been baby-sitting, cut up parts of peoples found in bags, then a quickie about how some fifth-graders was planting trees inside a neighborhood everybody's scared to go into. Junk like that, and old sitcoms with canned laughter.

No, I turned the TV off after one last search through every channel back and forth a few times so fast it was just a blur of laughs and crying. It gone off with a blink.

I got the figurine next to me on the couch, boy staring off, on his side, so it was like he's looking at the blank wall across the apartment. Seeing him stuck like that made me feel funny, so I picked him up and tried setting him different places to see where he looked the best, pretended I owned the place and couldn't nobody tell me not to.

Walrus been right, I guess: the thing didn't match most any of his stuff. Up against his things it was out of place. The boy seemed like he was out in the middle of nowheres, staring.

Finally I put him on the windowsill next to the bed and stood a few feet away to take in the whole. From there he was standing right in the middle of the bright red neon **ENJOY** sign. It blinked off and on all around him so's one second he was dark outline, the next lit up different shades of red, his face pink like he been left out in the cold. I left him there with all the other signs and lights and buildings of Forty-deuce around him.

Walrus stumbled through the door close to three in the morning after fiddling with the lock a few minutes like he got the wrong key.

"Where have you been, mister?" he said, his words slurred together and his eyes squinted up, which meant he was drunk like the night I met him in the bar.

"I been sitting on this couch, watching TV," I answered, not much looking at him. "What do you think?"

"I looked all over for you," he said.

"You got me confused with somebody else."

"Didn't you hear me trying to get in?"

He flipped on some lights.

"Turn them off. I want to go to bed."

"I think you're getting too comfortable around here," he said. "Do you think maybe you forgot already whose place this is?"

I got off the couch and walked into the bedroom, laid on the bed without I pulled down the covers.

"I don't want to talk about that right now. I's tired. I want to sleep."

But suddenly here Walrus was, all shits and giggles—wanted to talk. I tried to put my head into the pillow to muffle out the sound, but he tugged at my leg, then my arm. When nothing else worked he poked me in the ribs until I rolled quick over on my side and slammed my hand down on the bed.

"That is a very expensive bedspread," he said. "You be careful."

I rolled my eyes. "Ain't nothing in a slap'll hurt it."

"It happens to be chenille," he said, "which makes it expensive enough. I was given it by my grandmother: Which makes it . . . double."

"Maybe you'd like I should sleep on the floor," I said. "Or did somebody give that to you too?" I got off the bed and stood in front of the window. "Don't you think I know what things cost? You think I never seen a bedspread like that, think I ain't got a grandma of my own? I weren't born out in the wild like you think, raised by wolves didn't know their ass from their fangs."

He sat on the bed, after he made sure the tail of his suitcoat was out from underneath him. Like a sick drunk off the street he tried propping his leg on his knee and missed.

"Where do you think I've been?" he asked.

"I ain't playing your guessing game. I can smell where you been on your breath."

"I was in the bars," he said, with a stupid smile on his face like that was funny.

I didn't want to look at him so I faced the window and looked out on the street at the cars and peoples and trash dragging along, all of it under that red neon sign, got a big soda bottle and a straw, mechanical cap what popped open and out drained all the drink, then filled up again, then out and again.

"Do you know how many boys your age there are in those bars?"

"I ain't a boy," I mumbled. "I's twenty-two." But it seemed like only my reflection in the window heard me.

"There are hundreds, I think. Hundreds. Frankly, so many better looking than you. At least, not so sullen. They stand around with lazy slumps, and hungry, waiting for at least a drink, hoping for more. When you talk to them they're so happy to see you. They laugh at anything you say, if you're old enough . . . and dressed the right way. Anything you say interests them. They hang on your every word. If you're bored, they're bored. If you're sad, so are they. They're only happy when you are, and they're more than happy to arrange it. Hundreds like that. Probably nowhere to live, not a friend in the world, and not too bright which is what I'd suspect makes them so gracious."

"Got that all figured out from looking at them, do you," I said.

"I'm a lot older than you. The longer you're around, the more you see."

"Get off it," I said. "Don't mean nothing if you don't see clear."

"Several of these boys looked no more than fourteen or fifteen. Their faces are young, but do you know—their eyes are old. You barely know how to talk to someone like that. They have the experience of an adult and the understanding of a child."

"Did they understand your money?" I asked, but I didn't expect an answer and didn't give no time for one. "Look: I's tired. I got things to do in the morning."

"You were wrong when you said I don't know what you do. I can picture you during the day," he said, "while I'm at work and you sneak out. I see you walking the streets, with nothing much to do. Maybe you go to places where people your age congregate, a coffee-house or a diner. You go to be around them but you have nothing in common so you simply sit and stare wistfully out the window, all day, just like you're doing now. Feeling sorry for yourself and wanting everyone else to. Wondering what you're going to do with your life, whether you'll ever amount to much; wondering when that one big thing will happen that changes everything, you're grown up and no one can say different, and then you can relax."

"Think what you want," I said. "I's going to sleep."

Walrus sprawled out on the bed, an arm or a foot to each corner, left that grin on his face like to say "ha-ha," then hummed to his self until he said:

"Guess how many of them wanted to come home with me."

"Am I supposed to tell by looking at you? I told you; I ain't playing your stupid guessing games."

"A few of them practically threw themselves at me for the chance at somewhere to stay the night," and he laughed remembering it. I just turned him off, stared out the window at everything ant-size down on the street, thinking: Which is worse. There, or here? Seen the bottle and thought *empty, full*.

Walrus gone on, looking at me like he expected me to say something.

"They told me my suit looks nice, and I have a nice smile. One of them even said he likes a balding man. 'There's something very appealing about a bald man,' he said."

Yeah, I thought, *makes what they got up their sleeve slide over your head easier*. Then I remembered first meeting Walrus, how he was just like now on the bed that first night in the bar—breath smelled like booze, and he didn't know enough to keep his mouth shut. I remembered smiling at him and thinking about other things, like how many men was there in the place, and was it smart to be seen so long with him. Remembered looking up to his bald head, the red bulbs from up above lighting him up like some sore thing, thinking, *He ain't got a clue.*

Maybe I thought that was safe.

"What would you have done had I brought one of those boys here, for the night?"

I paid no attention to him.

"You start to think this is yours, don't you? That you own this place. You forget who pays the rent, who stamps and sends off the bills. Do you think those boys, any of them, would take all that for granted? I wonder. I wondered about that all the way home. They looked so gracious, so grateful, really like they'd do anything for a warm place to stay."

While he talked I opened the window slow-like, so's maybe he wouldn't see what I's doing. Watched the bottom pane go up, how it cut off my reflection on its way, like wiping myself off the glass.

"Most of them had nothing. Just the clothes they were wearing, I'm sure, and that's what they would have asked to bring here to my house—that baggage and that's all."

It was humid air outside, thick enough to choke on. Soon as the window got full up, the heat rushed in like Hurricane Andrew his self come from Florida, took over the cool of Walrus's air conditioner. Up come the sounds from the street—honking horns, car alarms, people's voices yelling at each other or nobody in particular—racing on his backside.

Walrus didn't notice. He was still looking up at the ceiling, I guess, going on about the boys he seen in the bars, singing their virtues like to say they's miles ahead of me, better in every way.

I lifted the figurine from the windowsill, brought it close to get a good look. For the first time I noticed what it was, really—what was going on. Boy got his hands behind his back, hiding a bundle of apples, looked down to the dog at his feet. Puppy dog anxious, eager for the apples, maybe, or whatever it was he thought the boy got. And on the base of the statue a label I ain't never seen, peeling at the corners, brown from old age, said: **NOT FOR YOU**.

Before thinking what I's doing, I tossed the boy out the window, then leaned over and watched him fall straight down with the speed of a bullet, until the darkness and distance swallowed him up I can't say how many stories down.

*   *   *

Just inside the door it was blue velvet, white lacquer, big crystal chandeliers. We was all crowded around the lady as she told us they had to take every piece of them chandeliers apart to get them through the door, then put them back together once they's inside. She told everybody how Elvis liked to entertain regular, have peoples over for dinner all the time or to watch one of his movies I guess, liked to show off his house from the get-go. She said we could get up close to the velvet ropes what barred the dining room, long as we moved around after we seen it so's everybody else who paid could get a good look.

Everything was set up like Elvis just run out to the store for a carton of milk or a pack of smokes. And the way the lady talked about him, he *was*, still living there, and we could have a look all around, long's we's out of the way whenever he come back.

Next she crowded us into the entryway, underneath another chandelier next to a staircase, looked up the stairs and said weren't nobody allowed to go up there on account of that's where Elvis's bedroom was. Elvis's family was everything to him, she said, like he told her his self; they's everything and he wanted every one of them in the house with him, so they all lived there together. Said his ma's dying got Elvis all shook up more than he his self ever could—some peoples still felt the ghost of her in the house years after she's dead, which probably got something to do with she been buried out in the backyard. Weren't nothing upstairs now but the ghosts and Elvis's aunt or somebody outlived him. Guide lady said she herself ain't seen it either, so no use asking her what it was like.

All I thought about the rest of the tour was Where the Hell'd my ride get to? Weren't nothing to refurbish, from the looks of things. After all it was like the lady-guide said: "Just as he left it." I wanted to get on over to Buford, didn't care about seeing this place; wished the man would hurry up and finish whatever he was there to do so's I could make it to the bus station—sit *there* and wait the four hours.

But she took us on: to the Jungle Room, all done up in monkey fur and green shag, said Elvis's daughter loved to sleep in that chair right there; to the yellow TV room with all the TV screens and stereo, said boy didn't they all sit around *that* room and have a good laugh; the pool room; the office out back with every kind of picture and painting of the King, and all the time it was don't touch and the velvet ropes, and the lady behind me saying we's seeing more of it all than Elvis ever done locked in the bathroom drugged up with his face in his lap and his back end on the toilet.

"Treat it with the same respect you show your own home," the guide lady kept saying.

So maybe this here's how it is everywheres, I thought. *Only one person to each house can touch, and that's the person what sets the rules. Everybody else stands in line and waits his turn.* Except in Buford at Grandma's, which is why I's going there.

She took us from the office, where we seen a videotape of Elvis sitting at his desk talking, and said she's going to leave us now. Pointed across the lawn to a bright metal shack past a stable and some horses, said we could walk down there to see some of Elvis's prized possessions, she'd be over to meet us at the door. While the others was filing past me, I cornered her before she could get back inside the place to answer a phone been ringing off the hook for the last few minutes like weren't nobody home.

"May I help you?" she asked, looking like she'd just as soon rather not.

"I come here with somebody," I told her, "and now they's gone. I's supposed to meet them later but I need to meet them now. I wonder could you tell me where they got to."

"How many people are you looking for?" she asked.

"It's just the one; a man. He's older than me, got . . ."

It come to me I couldn't think what he looked like.

"Are you sure he's not up ahead with the others?"

"He weren't never with them others," I said, "so I don't expect he'd be now. He's got on a suit and tie, and before the tour even started he dropped me off, said he got business to do and he'd be right back; well, four hours or maybe just three now, I ain't kept track—but I don't think I can wait that long."

The smile she got on since the start of the tour gone off her face. Scrunched up her forehead and looked at me like I's the sun in her eyes.

"I think he might be upstairs," I said, and I pointed to an upstairs window where the curtains was drawn.

"No one's allowed upstairs," she said, nervous laugh. "I'm afraid that's impossible. Don't you think he's across the street at one of the gift shops?"

"Listen," I said, "I happen to know he ain't across the street. He got off the bus over here, with me. I seen him go in. He's inside, rearranging."

She stepped back a ways from me, took the walkie-talkie off her hip-holster, held it ready.

"What is this gentleman's name?"

"I don't know. He's just . . . a man. An older man. Got on a suit and tie, and he's inside the house. Ain't there somebody in there can tell you where he is? What you peoples got these walkie-talkies for? He's supposed to take me to Buford, Arkansas. Told me to see this house, but I seen all I want to, no offense. I got one of my own to get to."

"I don't understand," she said. "You came with this man but you don't know his name?"

So I explained myself slow like I's giving her sign language for "Me or You's an Idiot and I'll Give You Two Guesses Who."

"He never told me. He don't know my name neither. Ain't you never met nobody and didn't get his name? Look, there must be somebody's allowed to go upstairs, cause that's where he probably is. Whoever's allowed up there's the one he's with. Call that one."

She put the walkie-talkie back in the holster and snapped it shut, like she made up her mind about something, said:

"No one is allowed upstairs. Elvis's aunt resides on the second floor. It's her home, her private residence. Now, I'm sure if you return to the driveway and wait on one of the benches outside the door, you'll find your friend in no time. If you'll excuse me, I'm expected inside for the next group."

That's when the smile come back on her face, and I figured that meant she weren't going to help me no more.

*   *   *

"I'm not sure what you want me to tell you," says Alligator Boy, and that was a laugh.

"*You*," I says. "You know everything. And I didn't get that from myself. I seen it on the posters around the midway, and everybody saying it too, says you know just about everything anybody could want to, so now I got you all to myself don't go stingy on me."

I expected maybe he'd smile, on account of I'd tried to sound so casual, like it weren't life and death, but knowing everything like he done he caught on how crazy I was to find Red; weren't a twitch of his leathery skin.

"Listen," he says, "I don't know what you think—"

99

"Whoa there; not another word. Hear me out."

I brung my hands to the table, locked digits and cracked my knuckles before I gone on.

"There's a guy. You probably know his name without I got to tell you Red. He come to the carnival, I come to the carnival, so on and so on then wham: We meet up. He don't want nothing to do with me but you and me both know he just ain't savvy, what he don't know's it's supposed to happen this way. You yourself know better than me and probably from the start whereas what I know took me a while to figure out. This here: **We's supposed to meet up and wait for what you call "Further Instruction."** I didn't see that until just now, until I seen you, why we's brung together; still I knowed there was something there and I's trying to listen. But see he kept talking, fucker wouldn't barely even look at me, and trying to leave, and me trying to keep him stay, him leaving, me trying, then we fought. *Then:* Shorty—the guy he says he's meeting—turns up, of all the fine times for him to show his face, so Red's all of the sudden *I got to go for good.* Well, I followed him, I—"

And here godammit I got choked up, the eyes on their way to the waterworks. I had to stop the story to get past it, thought maybe, *Well shut up and it's going to blow over.* But it kept on until I got both my fists banging on the table, putting on the weeps so hard I couldn't see straight, and felt the Alligator Boy's hand on my arm. That's what got me stopped: It weren't nothing like what I expected. Not near as rough or scaly or I don't know what—all them things they all said he's supposed to be.

"I got so many questions to ask you. So many," I said. "Like for instance how did you know to stay with the alligators. How'd you know not to go back to the peoples you lived with before? And did you ever miss them? Even after all they done, beat on you and cursed the day you's born and everything else like it says in the story of your life, back of the card?"

I reached behind me to pull his picture out of my pants but found I's staring at Red's, got the wrong one, said hold on and brung out the scaly shot of the Alligator Boy in nothing but his drawers, socks, and shoes. I turned it over and read from the back.

"Says you was beaten and abandoned by them young newlyweds had you, maybe cause they didn't know no better, and they left you off to die I guess but still did you miss them? Would you of gone back if they said come on? And how'd you know when the gators come along they's the right ones, the ones you's meant to go with, or didn't you? Did you have a choice?"

I seen he got a weird look on his face couldn't none of his scales hide, so I cleared my eyes and thought of letting off. But there was too much to know and God only knows how much time so I said:

"Who are you?"

He swallowed hard before he'd tell. Try as I might I couldn't get my eyes clear enough to make him come up sharp like to listen that much closer to what he might say.

"The Alligator Boy," he stutters.

"No, really," I says. "I know but I mean *who*? Don't you got a real name?"

"Promise you won't tell?"

He leaned in close, and I promised.

"My name's Eddie, and . . . I wasn't *always* an Alligator Boy."

Which kind of threw me, you know? So I didn't know what to say, like I's in the wrong tent or something.

"Yeah—so? What are you talking about? I know that. Don't you think I know that? It's what I been saying sitting here: You wasn't always but then when they come to take you you knowed to go, and *then* you become."

I cleared my eyes enough I could see him, finally, like coming out a bad windstorm, past the dirt on my hands and the sandpaper of his skin, seen he's dead serious. But I stared at him hard like to make him stay who I thought he was and hoped he'd keep his mouth shut.

"My name used to be Eddie," he said, "Eddie before I joined the circus. I'm a circus boy born and raised mostly, don't remember much before that except my parents meant well but had nothing to give, so I went to the circus when it came to *me*. For a while I did just the regular, had a buried alive shtick I did every night, had a private stash of milk balls to get by on when they closed me in. But that's nothing but small time, no kind of pay in it unless you got yourself an oddity. I wanted more than anything, more than anything you can think of, to really belong here, to bring in my weight. Not just a boy but a man kind of, you know? So nobody'd think I had it easy, like I was plucked out and made special just because I had a new face. So I saw me a doctor some of them knows in one of the stopovers, small town other side of nowhere, doc gave me a pill first, supposed to make me never grow an inch again: 'Retard the bones,' he said. World's Smallest Boy: That's the banner I saw in my head.

"But I took the pills with me on the road and nothing. I had to wait until the next time we passed him on the road again, and when I tell him it ain't no good what he gave me last time around, he handed over a tonic said well this is surefire. Rub it all over yourself and you'll see. See what, I didn't ask. Didn't need to I didn't think.

"Every day and night and practically all in between, I rub that tonic on; don't seem to me like a thing's happening at all, rub harder and harder trying to get it into my skin whatever it is. But I don't even know what to look for.

"Well. One night I go down into the casket, close the lid, hear the oohs and ahs and lower me down, lower until clunk, then the pitter pat of the dirt lands on top of me. I eat my milk balls, slow thinking what would I give besides my very soul to be a freak and make some money and a name for myself.

"Then there's this spark inside the thing, from the wiring they got rigged, and the place catches on fire in there and I got nowhere to go, I'm banging on it, you know, but nobody hears. And that tonic I got all over me takes the fire and spreads it across my body faster than you can think, and might of killed me if it wasn't for the routine was over or the fire started a few minutes earlier.

"I was laid up for weeks, wrapped in bandages. And the pain. I *mean*. And then the day come they was going to take them off, and everybody's in my hospital room. I didn't know what to expect, you know? The doctor said it didn't look good at all. But none of us was ready for what happened, cause we none of us never seen somebody after they caught on fire, for real. After they unwrapped them bandages, even the carnies, who seen it all, were eyes wide, so I know something's up. What? *What?* You know: 'What's wrong,' I ask everybody. Your skin, they tell me: Your skin. And I'm all excited thinking this is it, instant big time: I got it made for life. So they bring a mirror to me, and here's what I seen. Stranger looking me in the face, ever since. I got what I want. You know. I did. Can't say I didn't. Maybe not the way I wanted but the man upstairs takes care of all that."

I's so all-fired-up angry at him I couldn't barely speak. Just stared hard and mean at him, at his stupid no-good mug no better than a mask, his stupid little woe-is-me line.

"So . . . you . . . don't know nothing," I says. "Not a thing. Do you?"

"What should I know?"

"All about *Red*. What I's getting to. I need to know where to find him. He said he was off to Colorado Springs, but just *where's* the question. I thought sure you know it all. Everything. Just like the ballyhoo says. But you ain't even *real*; you got fake skin. Just lotion and fireworks. It just goes to show."

No different than the boys at the Madam's, I thought. *Go by different names, everybody's a different story depending on who's asking.* Big old phoney.

"*You* paid to see it," the boy says. "It don't rub off. It's just I didn't get it the way you thought."

Yeah, it was true. "True," I told him, but I didn't believe it.

After that we sat there staring at each other, Alligator Boy or whoever he was looking like he wished he wouldn't of told me, until one of the clowns stuck his head in the tent, let back in the sounds of the carnie outside, and some of the bright lights too. He give me the look but spoke to the boy.

"We got to get things wrapped up. Enough now with this goon."

Looked at me like all the other clowns told him about me, then without he give me a second to defend myself he was gone.

"What was it like in there, in that box?" I asked. "Before the fire. Could you breathe?"

"Did you go see Rosa?" the Alligator Boy or Eddie or whateversisname says to me, like we ain't talked about nothing, just shot the crap.

"I don't believe you," I spit at him, mad he's trying to change the subject. "You's a false advertiser's what. Just exactly what do I do now? You can't even tell me *that*. All you can tell me's a story, your story you says but that's a bunch of bull and you too. Don't know no more about nothing than a frog know about bedsheets. Everybody paying you money, you getting rich and for what? Just so's you can turn around when somebody's in need and say, 'Well now, I don't rightly know.' "

"I never said I could tell the future," he got the nerve to say, like I been the one to build him up.

On and on he says, "Go see Rosa," she's the reader. I already know how to read I told him, good as anybody. "Fortunes," he says. "She'll point you the right way." Frenology and stuff it's called. "You never heard of it? It's not anybody can do it."

"That's what they said about *you*," I told him. "And *anybody* can light themselves on fire." But I let him point me out, on account of I figured if she was as much of a hoax as he been I could finish with her what I started with him. I watched as he got up from the table, walked by me with that fancy smooth walk of his which now I knowed weren't nothing, got a real guy underneath. *Ha, I thought, I won't never be like you. Won't see **me** swallowing nobody else's medicine again.* He split the tent flaps, stuck his hand out, and pointed to a sign said **SEE MADAM ROSA** outside a tent where me and Red was earlier. Don't you know I's all mixed up, on account of I never thought about it the whole time we been standing there, how right next to us all along's a reader of brains.

*   *   *

One step forward, two steps back. And blah blah.

Same old same old, out again. When Walrus weren't looking I's out of there quicker than you can say *let me in*. Waited until he gone to sleep one night then decided what I already been deciding for weeks. Weren't no place for me there. Weren't room. Same old thing like Nana, who wouldn't clean out the drawers enough to make a space for me the whole time I's at her house, kept saying she'd get to it. Same old thing and I don't get it so I got to get out.

Stood in that apartment with the walls lit up red from Forty-deuce outside, blink on and off, empty or full, thinking what is it about this place with the either or's, don't feel like there's no space between them. Heard Walrus snoring in the other room, slow and steady, like it was a totally different place for him, sleep sound cause he knowed he'd wake up and it'd still be his. Stood there thinking now I got to go to Mannie, not just for my dope but for good, now I got to face up to the fact I can't make it on my own, not like I wanted. I ain't the kind of person, like the Madam and my ma, my grandma and all the rest said, kind what can make it out there. Well that's fine but I got to go somewheres, and Mannie's a start.

He been telling me all along I'd got to come stay with him longer—*take your shoes off and stay awhile*, he said—instead of just slipping in and out like I done, come in get my dope and leave, go back to Madam or Walrus or wherever else. "You'll be back," he was always saying, and didn't I know it, only I didn't think it'd be for good. Promised he'd go easy on me, said I wouldn't have to see nobody I didn't want, and up to now I ain't had to see but him, done the deed with him to score; he kissed me on the cheek and handed it over like he's giving me my lunch money, told me not to shoot it, just keep sniffing, so's I wouldn't mess up that pretty skin of his, then sent me back on my way. I didn't know what to expect now I'd be with him for good. But how hard could it be?

Snoring in the other room and I wanted so bad to go crawl into bed with him, nudge up and nighty-night. But I ain't as sound a sleeper as Walrus; I been trying that all along. Wanted to be but ain't. And he knowed it too, much as me; been saying more lately about them others, the boys at the bars and how he's going to have to go get one, bring back something what ain't as much trouble, wants sleep so bad ain't no problem getting to sleep once it's offered. Not like me, who's nodding off all the time but ain't never actually crashed. I jumped, inside I jumped, every time he talked about them boys, cause I knowed the more he talked the closer it was they got there, and I's out. But weren't nothing I could do about it, no more'n at the Madam's house. I got sent here, to New York City, on account of that, on account of there's so much I can't do nothing about, no matter how hard I try.

You done that on purpose, s'what Ma always said. *Just to get me riled.* And Nana saying I took things I ain't, just like Ma, to the point I thought maybe I got them and just didn't know it. If everybody's saying it, everybody what should know, it must be true. My ma's the one give birth to me. She watched me since before I could watch myself. And even way back then I's talking too much, or so my grandma told me the last time I seen her, said Boy you ain't never shut up. Well I tried; ain't done nothing but try to keep my mouth closed since I come to New York. Seen finally that been my problem all along—a big mouth—and I tried hard as I could to keep it closed but what do you expect?

"You got the power," the boy at Madam's said. Maybe so, but I been looking and it sure ain't turned up yet. Maybe the power here was I could leave on my own before anybody kicked me out, which case I got all the power in the world.

When I's sure he was as dead to the world as it sounded like, when the walls was so steady red and dark and red again and Walrus was as sure in his snoring, I gone into the bedroom and started digging around the top of his chest of drawers. Found dry cleaner slips; bar flyers what said *whoo-ee looky here at this piece of flesh come to our place and it's yours*; loose coins I figured I got coming to me so, quiet as I could, I slipped them in my pocket; little plastic rings what held together his socks so's they wouldn't get lost in the drawer; bottle of cologne reminded me of the night I first met him; and bingo—the wallet.

It was full of business cards I couldn't care less about, got family pictures too, somebody's baby and mama and papa and blah blah blah, little rosy cheeks all of them, slapped in front of fake posters and somebody off the corner saying oh *smile*. Smile for the camera; Happy happy. I took a few of them out of the plastic and folded them in four pieces just cause, four exact pieces just the same as I watched Walrus fold his precious underwear all them times. "Everything has its place," he'd say. "An ordered life is an adjusted one." I ain't never knowed what he meant and didn't care, just thanked him kindly under my breath now for being organized enough he left his wallet in the same place all the time, and full up of dough. For weeks Walrus been saying I's taking from him and just to prove him wrong I held off, but now I's leaving I didn't care *what* he thought of me. I stuffed that in my pocket too.

Looked at him on the bed, thought, *I won't never see you again. Hear? Never. No more going back to places. No more running back like I ain't got nowheres else to go. Might be. Might be I got nowheres, but that includes you. Take a good long look.*

Then I found my bag—trusty bag: got the few shirts and socks, pair of underwear or two folded exactly four times, took from Walrus's drawer, some chips from the kitchen, bottle of booze, the envelope I got out of Nana's mailbox one of the last time's I gone out to stare at her house before I left for Buford, rock from Grandma's yard, my pa's flask.

Grabbed all that and said good-bye, to the walls and the furniture, sound of Walrus snoring. Sounded so far away but good-bye to that, yes sir.

* * *

"Hello—Madam?"

And when no sound come out from between the flaps of her tent I called one more time before I gone in.

It was awful small in there, though it probably don't take a body much room to tell the future. Just a few feet round of tent and a table in the middle what got a crystal ball set out. First I didn't even make a move, like I weren't curious about the ball, on account of who knows if a fortune teller's got to be there to see what it is she sees. But it was too much to keep away from, what with the way it stood out smack dab in the middle of the room, almost glowed. Even from where I was I seen things moving inside.

I gone up close, stopped at the edge of the table then leaned in slow until me and the ball was near face to face. Seen the tent upside down—me staring into it, the opening of the flaps behind me, but that weren't good enough. So I closed my eyes and opened them again, stared as hard as I could, squinted like you see them do when they's making spells, grit my teeth for good measure—but nothing. *Hocus pocus toil and trouble give me a good look at Red,* and an abra-cadabra or two but nothing. Maybe you got to be sober. When there weren't nothing but just the steady glow I decided Mr. Fancy Pants Gator Boy done took me for a fool and ripped me off both, just to get me out of his hair quick cause he knowed I's about to rough him up worse than he ever thought a scaly-skinned body could be.

Thought, *So that's what you get when you's in trouble. Go to the last person you can think of, what ain't even what you'd call a person like everybody else, or is but says he ain't, cry to him and spill out the whole story how you ain't got nobody to help you in the world—and what? He's so set to get rid of you he spits out the quickest decoy come to mind. Maybe this here's a—what they say—frenologist's tent: Maybe, but she done checked out with the rest of the carnies, off somewheres packing up.*

Big old gnarly face shows up in the ball, near scares the bejesus out of me. Boils or whatnots on the face, bumps all over and dark hair, a scarf with designs gone every which way in every color you can come up with. At the sides of the face dark hair come out of the scarf, squeezed itself into ratty curls. And the eyes, well: Underneath brows thick as ditch grass was two dark spots staring hard at me like to strangle me with both hands tied behind the back. It was too late to make like I weren't looking in the ball—which I guess to a fortune-teller's like trespassing or reading her mail—so I froze the way I was, thinking what can she do to me from inside that thing. Course I knowed that if she could scrunch herself inside that there weren't no telling just what she could do with a little more size to her, but just then I seen the entry to the tent behind her head and how she come in behind me, same way I done, turned to see her standing there.

She got on a bathrobe like Walrus's bedspread, and I told her so.

"Is that what you're here to tell me?" she says, and so stiff you'd think it come out the mouth of a carcass. "Go on home, boy. Show's over."

And that I had to laugh at—"go on home"—on account of what could she tell me I didn't already know if she looked into my future and seen one of them.

"For your information I got sent here by Gator Boy. He told me you could answer my questions if anybody could."

She nodded real slow, said, "I know your questions before you ask them."

That was a relief, on account of now I figured I didn't have to talk no more. I stood quiet waiting for her to read my mind, make sense of it and give me the answers, wipe it all out; and waited some more, until her eyes rolled back into her head and she said *Well boy, do you have questions or do you need a few days to think about it*, which got me confused.

I didn't want it that way; standing up. I wanted to sit right down on either side of that crystal ball and really dig into the question of Red, get comfortable and get on with it, not standing one of us on either side of the tent's guts stiff as boards. She weren't even concentrating on me—just got her eyes set back for a snooze. I looked down at her feet and seen she got on fuzzy slippers, pink flip-flops got chi-chi pom-poms and all pointy at the toes like she's standing on the heads of two elves, ugly things; thought *What the hell kind of fortune teller's this?*

"You're expecting suit and tie?" she said. Then she took a seat and I knowed we's down to business.

Turns out she been the one what looked after Gator Boy, ever since he come on with the sideshow, one that sat it out in the hospital room with him after he gone flammable. She told me was a lot of peoples would take the boy for all he got or could bring in without nobody to watch over him, and when she seen that she pulled him under her wing, even though really he's grown up now and could take care of his self mostly.

"Yeah yeah, you can't hold a candle to him," I said, "but look: I met this guy. Red. You know him?"

She was nodding and got the eyes rolled back in the head so I gone on.

"He left awhile back, told me don't follow him, but I ain't got nowheres else. Do you believe in things like two peoples got something in common and they don't know what? I do," I said like I didn't need her to tell me *that*. "Either you pass it up or stick with it, and I don't aim to let it go. I let it go before and ain't about to again: That ain't a problem. What I got to know's how do I go about this here?"

Her eyes come back down just a bit—they was through slit lids and shaking—and she lit into a bunch of stuff I didn't exactly catch on to.

"Red because red hair. Redheaded. Blue eyes, red hair, freckles. The boy looks not but a day over fifteen until he opens his mouth. He's a lot older than anybody he deals with knows. That's why they like him. Do you know about the others?"

I jumped at the news.

"More? There's more like him?"

Full eyes for a second and she said, "*Nothing* like him, that's why they kept him," then through slits again. "They have him in it, so deep he thinks he can never get out. If he goes away from it but not far enough they'll find him, and once they see he intends to leave they'll hold him tighter still."

"I don't know none of these peoples," I said, thinking about Shorty and getting sick to my stomach. "I appreciate your poems or whatchamacallit but can you stick to—"

"*Shh*. Quiet, now. No family. That's why he went to them, why they wanted him. He's all alone. They made promises, all kinds of things they told him he could have if he got in deeper. His own mind told him he'd get even more. It's been years and they're still holding out. There's others like him involved, as trapped as he is. Some are hooked; those are the ones who think nothing of staying, forever if a day. First he stayed for them. He thought he could help them out of it, but now he sees they're stuck, all of them. He might have been their friend once, but no more."

Her eyes got so small I thought she gone wherever Red done, and for good, but then come the part what's been with me ever since.

"He's left to mountains, rocks, broken dishes, a small room he can barely afford."

"I know," I blurted out. "He was trying to get away from *me*. Ditched me in the parking lot and—"

"It has nothing to do with you. Nothing. He's in trouble. He's trying to get away. If you follow him you'll make things worse."

She turned her head down like to cast the thoughts out, told me she weren't going to think about it another minute. She got things to do with the rest of the carnies. I got what I come for she said, but I didn't. I didn't get nothing, just broken dishes, telling me I shouldn't follow him which weren't nothing I ain't already heard. Bunch of cockamamie about somebody or other holding Red hostage. I knowed that was bull: Anybody seen Red for a minute would of knowed weren't nobody could tell him what's what. Still she was serious enough, she shut down shop, eyes come back to her face: She weren't about to tell me nothing more. Got this look come over her like she seen something she didn't want to but she weren't giving an inch.

*   *   *

"Welcome home!!" Mannie yelled, when he seen me coming.

He'd heard from some of the others who seen me out on the streets the past few days I's on my way, heard I'd left Walrus's and knowed I needed somewheres to stay. He got his arms spread wide and a big beaming smile on his face like come to mama. *Whatever,* I thought. *Just give me my dope and send me up to my room.*

But he held out first, took me to the place off 42nd I always done him to score, up on the second floor in a room what weren't nothing more'n a bed and a broken light, window staring out at a brick wall, told me sit down on the bed now we got to get a few things clear.

"I just want you to know," he said, after he checked my arms for tracks, "things gonna be different. It ain't like you just visiting now, not like you can waltz over and visit like we your poor relations and hightail it back over to your penthouse. You one of us and you got to pull your weight."

And I's nodding like yeah yeah get on with it, practically got my hand held out for the dope, feeling like I got three different kinds of the flu—and counting, if I didn't get some soon—but he took his own hand and put it on my head so firm to stop it I knowed he meant what he said. Looked me straight in the eyes.

"I heard from a few of the others you been out here trying to do it on your own. That right? Since you left your daddy? Because you know it ain't allowed. If you out here doing it you ain't doing it but for me. And you got to understand that, that *I'm* the man. Nobody else. Because if you only been out here a couple days and already you breaking my rules what'm I supposed to think? So this here's it:

"You go with who I say. I bring him in, you make him happy, whatever it takes, and bring the take on back to me. No exceptions. Because I took care of you 'til now. Ain't I?"

And he nodded my head with his hand.

"But I can't take care of you if you break my rules. Can't take care of you and can't look out for you, can't say *what's* gonna happen. Okay? You make them happy and I make you happy. And don't ever ask me a question I already give you the answer for—just speak when you spoken to. And I'll take care of you good."

Then he handed me the dope, turned the grip he got on my head into a pat, "that's my boy," ruffled my hair and pinched my cheek, and told me to come downstairs with the rest of them the minute I's done.

I ain't never met men like Mannie's, like the johns what come to him looking for boys like me, and I thought I seen them all. But I knowed what I's supposed to do with them. These didn't even so much's look at you. Talked to Mannie, then Mannie brung them over, didn't bother giving them your name, on account of I guess if they got a question they'd of gone to him. We gone into one of the two rooms off 42nd Mannie always got ready for us, waited down on the corner with the guy if they's full, but they weren't never full for long. Gone up to the room and done whatever the guy wanted, on account of if you didn't you got a whack from Mannie, and didn't get your dope when you's done. The one thing I could count on if I done what I's told was Mannie'd fork it over, just enough so's I'd be burning a low blue flame—keep me quiet but on my toes, as Mannie put it—until late at night when we's all done he'd give me extra to sniff straight up so's I could really go under and take off floating, where I wanted, give me so much more'n I ever had before I couldn't complain.

And I thought about nothing, not a thing—just one steady blur of nothing much. Just flickers of things, and so slow seemed like they couldn't hurt a flea on their way in or out. Little flicker of Memphis, Nana's face the last time I seen her, the things she said but what did I care now; little flicker of Nebraska, Pa on the bed, mouth barely open breathing, but I didn't care no more what he'd felt like, on account of I didn't feel much of nothing and didn't want to; the Mississippi, then the Spring River in Buford, both of them lapping against the bank, water carrying things away, farther and farther away. I seen the boy there, Fletcher, one I's sweet on Fletcher, that face and the red hair what's made me think of him ever since, my mind kept going right back to him like I's tied there with string. None of it fit together any better than it ever done, all of it just as jumbled as always. But floating, just free-floating, and didn't make no difference to me no more anyways.

Months of Mannie tucking me into bed at night, in one of the two rooms we been using all days—so tired at the end of the day and so out of it already I's half gone by the time he took me up there. Slept two of us boys together on a bed, said sweet dreams and sleep tight, little peck on the cheek but I ain't ever hardly felt it. And I'd just black out like the sweet hereafter until suddenly he's back and tapping against the mattress to say "rise and shine for me." Most times we's so out of it, so deep under whatever it was that a tap weren't enough, and he had to nudge us, hard again and again until we got up. When nothing else worked, like towards the end with me, he'd tell us we weren't getting nothing, not a speck, until we got our asses up and out, and if we's going to sleep it weren't going to be in there cause he needed the bed.

Every minute of the day was took care of with Mannie, not a second to spare for yourself, and that was okay cause most times I wouldn't of knowed what to do with myself if I got one. But during them times he only half got us doped up the thoughts come back in more than ever, and it was them times I wondered about Walrus. Cause it was true I said I wouldn't never go back, but it was just as true I said I wouldn't never be with Mannie. And if I's the kind of person gone back on my word—kind of person keeps trying old places looking for new things—well, I might as well choose better over worse.

And one day I woke up in the room without nobody was tapping the bed. Not a tap but pounding on the door—owner of the hotel telling me *out,* get out of there. I got my bag of things and gone downstairs rubbing my eyes, seen it was the middle of the day. And no Mannie, nowheres. And nobody else. Asked around and nobody could tell me what happened, he just vanished, and here it's not just the middle of the day but the middle of the day without no dope, and next thing I know I's sick as a dog all over the place without I even got a chance to make it to the crapper. Before the end of the day I's in so much pain, got such screaming meemies I couldn't stand up right, and I ended up around the corner from Walrus's place watching for him to come home on the tail end of the nine to five.

He took me straight upstairs, stared me down in my corner of the elevator from his own.

"You look weird," he said with his nose pinched up. "Skinny. You don't have AIDS do you?"

I held my stomach from the pain and shook my head.

"Because I can't let you into the apartment if you do. I mean things have changed since you left—ran out or absconded with my money or whatever you've been calling it. I know what *I've* been calling it. Things are different. I don't bring boys into the house anymore. I will this once of course, because . . . for old times' sake. But generally things are at a point in my life where I need to think of myself."

And the same damn blah blah as ever only now it was like I ain't never heard it before. All the way up to his floor, telling me I ain't got no power over him no more, he don't give it to me, to peoples like me, he keeps it for his self and to his self, except this once.

Brung me upstairs and asked again do I got AIDS, like if I done he'd get it too just from looking at me, said he couldn't be too careful, but then he wants to do it without a condom, and I say whatever, just let's get it over with, since after all I been with Mannie so long, done whatever the guys wanted, and what they wanted's without a rubber, and if Walrus didn't get nothing I wouldn't get money for my dope. So I said let's go, but first he wanted to tell me one more time things was different with him. He hoped I ain't come up there thinking I could steal from him like I done last time; this was just the once and I'd have to leave.

* * *

113

Sat there waiting on his car I don't know how long, drunk and feeling good, beating the sun just barely by the shade of an overhead tree, sweating bullets anyways. Figured, *Well I'll wait here and* **sometime** *he's got to leave,* knowing he couldn't very well go without his wheels. Still ain't got any idea what time it was but cared a little less since I scored me a few drinks back at the food places next to the gift shops, from some Japanese folks I made friendly with, got wasted drinking out of cups what got the King's face winking up at me every time I took a swig, done my best nothing but a hound dog impression to pay my keep.

Thought about Buford every second of the way, going to see my grandma, how me and her was going to be the two to deal with, the terrible two, what with all what done us wrong and walked away. First thing I aimed to do was sit down with her and tell her everything, right from the beginning, get her story straight. We'd go down to her dock, sit by the lake, with the crickets and the whippoorwills going at it, and I'd tell her what her daughter done. How Ma treated her own husband, even after he got trapped in bed, practically wrote him off for dead. How I hid under him to get away from her and on account of that's the only way me and him could be together was without her knowed it, otherwise she'd of got her nose all in it like I better get away from him so's he could get on and sprout wings. Then after he did die—me going down to tell her there in the basement, saying *Ma, he's gone; he really is gone.* And she ain't said nothing but well she'd get to it.

How she tried to get rid of me. I's too young to stay locked up in a room. I run out from under her hold, else she might of put me in Pa's place. But she had to figure something out to do with me, some way to settle the score. Talked about how she's going to pack me up and turn me over to Boystown—crazy place out the corner of Omaha, with all them houses set up supposed to look like ones with real families inside, only I knowed better; and the statue in the middle of it all; dark metal man holding a little boy, frozen solid. Weren't no way she'd get me there to rot away.

How she gone over and over it again in her head trying to figure what could she do with me to make sure I wouldn't have no life left in me, stuffed me in a plane and flew me over and that's how I ended up here, sitting on the dock, all kind of things behind me I couldn't look at. Sure Grandma could understand a thing like that.

I ain't got no watch, but last time I looked in the Sock Hop Cafe over the tip of my drink the Elvis clock said one hour and a half until my bus left downtown Memphis for Arkansas. From the way time was dragging on, I been waiting on the tail of the man's car for close to that, and still no sign of him. Just the rows of cars gone on forever down the lot, and the sun bearing down on every last one. I could see my bag inside, on the backseat, started worrying I might never get my hands on it again. And just when I got to thinking about breaking in through the guy's window, I look back up and there he come—Mr. Stuffed Shirt—not a sign of sweat nowheres on his suit or self, says lazy enough:

"I thought we agreed to meet outside the ticket office. You've probably dug your own grave as far as making your bus on time. I spent several minutes back there looking for you."

I couldn't picture him spending much time at all looking for nobody but his self, but I let it fly.

"Look," I says, "Here I is and ready to go. We still got time."

"*Who* has time?"

"I didn't exactly enjoy sitting around in the heat in what ain't even my own clothes," I said. "You could drop me out the car without stopping if it's so out your way."

Then he giggled, little persnickety thing, said well he just happened to be in a good mood, on account of he made so much money back at Elvis's place. Even when we's in the car he didn't stop talking about it, he gone on about how stupid somebody like Elvis is, and how anybody with good taste could of pulled one over on him. Hell, even peoples without it, on account of look at his manager Colonel Tom Parker, what used to be the head of a circus geek show—took him for everything he's worth. I got my bag off the backseat and held it close in my lap, felt through it to make sure Pa's flask was still there, thought how wrong Ma was when she said a body shouldn't bother giving me nothing on account of I couldn't hold on to it.

"That's how these people are, these dirt-poor mossbacks, get-rich-quicks. They get a few dollars in their hands and all of the sudden they can have the finer things in life, only the closest they've ever been to the finer things is the high end of a Wal-Mart. They have to call somebody like me in, somebody who knows paper plates from Wedgwood, and of course it's rather easy, and almost necessary for all your trouble, once your foot's in the door, to jack up the price on the finer things. They don't know the difference. All they care about is making the Taj Mahal out of a breadbox."

And on we drove, veer here and there down the interstate what twirls in and out and over itself before getting you wherever quick. More cars, more shiny paint jobs, whiz past and fall behind, to the point I figured between the parking lot and the highway I sure must of seen all the cars a body could see. Before too long we passed a green sign overhead said downtown so and so many miles away, and my whole insides set on edge. Then the road split in two and one part took exit from the rest—that's the one we took what ended us up downtown, and a few blocks over, past busted up buildings not far from where Mojo's was, the Greyhound station showed up, two dogs running fast off either side of the sign like they couldn't get the hell out of Dodge fast enough.

Figures I got to go all the way out to Graceland to get a ticket for a bus right down the street from my digs, I thought. Then I thought about everything I's leaving behind—well, anyways, Mojo's—Crazy Dan and the parrot and what all. But let somebody else make sense of that. Knowed I wouldn't miss none of it, specially not Mojo's, where like I say I owed all kinds of rent, where nothing but good old boys come looking for me. But I almost felt bad about it—about ditching all the things in the room upstairs. Nothing, nobody, should get left cold like that.

I figured the man was sure to throw me out the speeding car like I told him to, but at the last minute he turned polite, come to a full stop right outside the building, said, "Enjoy your trip."

"What about your clothes?" I asked him, tugging on the tie. But he told me keep them, so's to make a good impression on my grandma. Then he stuffed a wad of bills in my pocket and took off smirking.

* * *

All I know's I woke up facedown in my own vomit to pitch-black and one hell of a pain in the ass, somebody going at it back there, grumbling. Took me a few minutes to figure it was Walrus tearing at me in

116

my sleep, got me pinned on my front side, so heavy on me I couldn't hardly breathe, smell of booze come over my shoulder like he been out while I's sleeping and come back.

"Well get off me," I says, "Now you had yours."

But he kept at it like I weren't there, until I could wrestle out from under him and throw the lamp from the bedside table over his head. I maybe killed him for all I knowed, and not much caring I wiped myself up and started to gather up my things and some of his. I got my shirt and the pants I come in with, my bag, whatever else I seen I wanted and thought I could carry—the money out of Walrus's wallet I come for in the first place. And when I's done, and weren't no sign of Walrus coming to, I gone over to the couch and had myself a sit, on account of standing took too much effort.

Got to think gone through my mind. *Got to get this together*. Weren't no good in the dark, so I hauled up and turned the overhead on, lit up everything at once, even Walrus over in the corner slung out across the bed. When I seen his apartment like that, laid bare, for the first time in the months I been living out on the streets, I realized *Well now you's somewhere cozy, like where you been thinking to get back in*. All them nights with Mannie thinking I got nowheres else to go, so much I put everything else out of my mind, just floating. No thought of going back to Nebraska to try my ma and the house with Pa's spook locked in it, none about going back to Memphis, where Nana like to own the city for all I could make it on my own there. No, all I got left, only home to go to was this little trap in the sky, where instead of clouds and a load off it was concrete and glass.

So now I took a good look at it—now I clawed my way up here again, practically scaled the side of the building to do it when you think about it and I could be thrown out faster than I come up, any second Walrus thought to come to. I gone close along the walls, stared at pictures he got hung there since I been away. They was every last one pictures of him: Walrus at three or four, few years later, all the way up to the zits, when he got the hair puffed up front looked like a duck had his self a seat there. And nobody else in the frame, not once, just little Walrus before he even was one, shot from higher up than his self, neck craned to look at the camera.

I gone full around the room that way, my nose up against the walls, until I made it to the window next to Walrus, seen myself face forward as I passed the pane, then come to the bed. Mr. Walrus ain't got on no pants, no undershorts—just the dark socks, suitcoat, tie. He was arms spread, face to the side, pieces of the lamp tossed around him, and from the skin of his bald head out come an ooze of red. Must be he tossed a bit cause the blood'd got on some of his grandma's bedspread, took to the ridges so's it was up and over, under and again. *If I knowed anything about what things's worth I'd be tore up about that,* I thought. Whenever he took a big breath the streams of blood run faster.

Up that close, with his eyes shut firm and none of his usual sass, he scared the daylights out of me; I didn't know just how to take him now he weren't telling me what I was or turning his face quick away when I looked at him. I backed slow away from the bed, and kept going, until I got far enough back to where I thought I could handle him. Stood there shaking and thought a minute.

Thought about Mannie and how's I supposed to get my dope now, boy did I need it and quick. Wondered why somebody couldn't hit *me* over the head with a lamp—I's the one wants out. How I ain't never done nothing right; never. Never wanted nothing but in one place and out another, and couldn't do neither. In my head I seen Nana arguing with herself the way she done, like thoughts constantly in her head and now didn't I know why. So sick of talking to myself but what to do, what to do, now I run out of places. Knowed there's more out there, knowed there's got to be, out of all them there's got to be one what lets me in, but I got the wearies so fucking bad it's like they's the never-get-overs.

Can't do it on my own. I seen—finally—I couldn't do all this, my life or whatever you call it. Thought how I started out like I thought Pa done, followed in his footsteps trying to see where it might get me to; maybe all along I's just looking for a bed to lie in like he got, bed I could lie on in peace where weren't nobody'd bother me. But a steady bed's the one thing I ain't been able to get myself. Boy how I done it all else; first the pills and the whiskey, and when that weren't enough I got the dope—"Mother," like Mannie called it: "Come to Mama." Thought, *well finally,* Finally. Thought I'd always have a home there. Stupid me. Just as hard to get the dope's anything else, and just as likely to go without, like now.

This must be what they mean when they says you got to think

about these things—think about your future. Mine was I knowed I got no aim to go back to Forty-deuce, except to score and pass on through. Took me a while, with Walrus laying there on the bed, to realize I got at least one place left—only small price to pay was could I swallow my pride. After I figured I ain't never had much of that to start with, my mind was set. For old times' sake, and to take something besides his money away with me, I gone over to the bed, put my head up to Walrus's belly, closed my eyes and listened to his breathing.

* * *

So I's standing outside the door, knock-knock and all that, only at first there's nobody answers. I step back, check the address again, but I know this place, lived there long enough to remember where it's at. Knock again: No answer. I'd look in the windows, try to see past the curtains, only I know somebody's got to be in there, and anyways the windows is boarded up from the inside so's nobody can see through neither way. Ain't none of this is real.

Finally the door buzzes. I push it and get through to the foyer, where I know I's being watched. Where is that little thing, little camera hole? Oh yeah—here we is, right over the door, points right down at me: Hello there.

"What do you want?" over the intercom, and I recognize the voice straight off.

"In," I says.

For the longest time, ain't nothing else comes, not so much's a snap of static. What's she thinking, I wonder. Maybe she's on her way out to break my arms and legs, like she told me she would if I ever come back. Maybe here's a good time to run for it. But I aim to try just a little harder than all that.

"Are you on drugs?"

"I swear I ain't got a thing in or on me," I says. "On the Bible."

"Hold your head up: I want to see your eyes."

I do it, thinking dry thoughts and *sober, sober.* What difference do it make, I got a mind to ask. But there's another stretch of quiet, seems like she forgot about me.

"I don't want trouble here," she says.

I thought to tell her I ain't brought none with me, until it struck me it follows me wherever I go, so's it's sure to follow me here.

"Where are you staying right now?" she asks.

"Around," I says, but what I mean's on the street and she knows it.

"If I let you in here . . ."

Without I can help it I shift my feet a measure and hold my hand up to the door, then worry I maybe wrecked things by showing I's excited too soon, on account of here she stopped and didn't go on for a few seconds like she changed her mind in the middle of a thought. I know what I look like to her: I seen it myself so many times from the other side, black-and-white john on the monitor all anxious to get in, pushing at the door before he even give his name. This time it's me—dot of a thing on a small TV, practically on my hands and knees.

The door buzzes, and I breathe a sigh of relief. There is a God and his name's Madam. But she ain't letting me in just yet. She's sent some boy, some new boy out to check my bag, digs through my things, comes across Pa's flask. I grab it out of his hand and hold it up like to swing it at him. "Don't you never touch that," I says. Then I unscrew the cap, turn the thing over and shake it a few times. "See?" I says. "Empty. Just for show."

He took me straight back to the phone room, felt like I's back home in a way. But right when I got to the door, I stopped. Put my ear close and tried to listen what's in there, was it safe. Maybe I been tricked; maybe she let me in so's she could break me in two like a wishbone, make a wish I'd go away. She said she would, as much's promised. But I couldn't hear nothing much, just chairs scooted across the floor, shoes walking one side to the other, the hum of shooting the shit, and the boy she sent out to check my bag and bring me in's looking at me funny. So I put my hands on and pushed through.

And there she was, looked just like she done the day I left for cigarettes and sodas or so I said. Same Madam—bossy as anybody's got the right to be—sitting the way she always done; head cocked, eyes drilled straight into you enough you got to look away. This time I looked back, stared right at the old girl, I weren't afraid; until I remembered how high I was from scoring some no-good crap out on the street before I headed over, and here I'd told her I weren't on a thing. I looked down at my feet.

"You're lucky I let you in. What are you here for—want your job? I can't give it to you. I can't have people here who leave without notice. I need people I can depend on."

I shrugged my shoulders, thought, *You and me both.*

"If you're here for work I can't give it to you. I can't give you a place to stay. I can't give you money, because I can look into your eyes and see what you'd use it for. I can't do much of anything for you."

Then everybody's dead quiet like maybe she's going to hit me after all.

"Are you hungry?"

Right there she hit the spot. It was something, at least. After that she had some of the boys call up a restaurant nearby, and they ordered all sort of things—chicken almond and this and that sauce over beef and lamb and sweet and sour, eggrolls, on and on down the menu. When a Chinaman showed up black and white on the monitor carrying a bag of food, one of the boys gone to pay for it, and we had us one hell of a meal: everybody talking at once, the phone's ringing, a thousand stories a thousand different ways, johns coming and going and everybody's on the same side.

Then, the Madam yelled at every mother's son of us to clear out the evidence, yelled some more and louder when we sat around like she meant later. I got up too but she told me stay right where I was. When they's done she told the boys "now get out of here," except for one what she asked to stay and hold fort at the monitors while me and her gone somewheres else to talk.

I followed her up the stairs and into the Captain's Room, one she used to interview new guys in. To somebody what don't know better—it looks chichi, got the rust colors on the walls, model ships and boats, shutters on the windows, material slung up all over the place and knotted fancy, got the oil painting of Captain I'm-Going-to-Steer-This-Ship-Aright Somebody-or-other, and not your average paint-by-numbers; all of it enough to make you seasick. But get up close or stay awhile and you see ain't none of it for real. Them shutters is lean to: touch and it's geronimo. All the material's stapled to the wall underneath the folds. Open the closet it's junk stacked to the ceiling. It's pretty, all right. To look at.

The Madam pointed with her eyes to the bed, meaning she wanted I should sit there. She herself took a wide chair off in the corner so's she could face me when she give me page, chapter, and verse. It was a few minutes of neither one of us said nothing—her thinking and staring at me hard like she didn't know where to start but I best not interrupt her, and me knowing better, thinking *Don't nod out don't nod out*. Then she's breathe in, roll the eyes, and:

"What the hell are you doing? You're killing yourself, right? I mean, surely you know this. You aren't a rocket scientist, no doubt, but it doesn't take one. Wandering around—is that what you're calling it. I call it the walking dead. Am I missing something? Is there something here for you I'm missing? Starvation? Homelessness? Tricking for drugs? You look like shit. You look a breath away from six feet under."

"Where else?" I asked her. "You make it sound like the whole world's mine for the asking, step out the door and wham. I ain't got *nobody*."

"And the options are better here?"

"They's no worse," I said. "You don't understand. This was my last stop."

She shook her head like she run out of patience and I thought maybe here it come, now I's out the door again. But she pulled it back in and started over.

"You better stop feeling sorry for yourself: It'll kill you. There are kids your age all over the city. Okay? Times Square practically spits them out daily. I mean, what—there's the daddy bars, plenty of older men to take you under their wings and ask for all kinds of things in return, most of which you're unable to give after they've extinguished your resources and what little capacity you came to them with, and frankly you yourself, you in particular, don't have much to offer them from the get-go. The strip joints, the dance places, make a buck, maybe a few, tips and shit wages and something extra on the side if you can rig it at the tables. And not like here; management could care less what happens to you, tonight or after. If you fall down dead on the dance floor, no sooner has their janitor swept you up and emptied his dustpan of you out back than someone else is geared up in G-string, one foot on stage ready to lift himself up and go. Now how long can someone like you do that kind of work, if you can at all? I mean, these are your options. I'm assuming, from the looks of it, you've tried a few of them. And blew them, like you blew this. And to deal with it you've kept yourself lights out, am I wrong? And now you're here, right? Because why? Because you've run out? Of what? Energy or junk? What else are you thinking you might do here, the state you're in? I don't know what you're on, but it's slapping you silly. You don't break that kind of habit under your circumstances. You don't break it unless you get the hell out of here. You came to the wrong place. You can't handle this shit."

I knowed it was bad to cut in once she's on this kind of telling-to, but I figured she needed to know how "I ain't got nobody. What do you want I should do—go back to Nebraska, sit out in the cornfields waiting for something to go down or run me over?"

"No father and what—your mother's still living, isn't she? So go to her. I know you have problems with her. But what've you done—run away, stolen maybe, lied? All that can be apologized for. I'm not saying things will be better. They almost never are. That's not what I'm asking you to look for. It's just—you're going to have to change something, and it's not happening here."

"Change *what*?" and despite myself my voice was raised, out come all the rage I been saving up on the street. Weren't until a few minutes later I could finish myself. First it was bawling out in the quiet of the room, the captain looking out of his picture at me all *tsk tsk*. "I done changed everything I know to. When they told me to and if I could it was a done deal. Don't matter to me: I ain't particular about none of it—this or that, don't matter. But they kept asking, change and change and again, point I didn't know no more what they wanted different and they didn't neither; said they wouldn't never know what to do with me, wouldn't nobody. Then it was just they like to hate me cause I couldn't just change on my own. But it weren't I's stubborn; Just I give up's all."

Madam gone quiet, looked at me like if she stared hard enough she'd come up with the answers. Let the room get took over by the sounds from outside, sound of my future, like that said it better than she could. We sat there start and stop, me with the tears, coming out so hard I thought maybe my whole body'd empty out, thought maybe that's all I been carrying around with me all this time, why I felt so lousy.

"Listen," she finally says, "Do you *want* to kick?"

"Yeah," I said in a voice seemed too twisted to be my own, cause it was true. Maybe if I got somebody looking out for me, somebody I could count on, I could handle a dope habit but I's all on my own and it just weren't working out.

"What if you had a way to go home, a way to get back to Nebraska? Would you try it one more time with your mother, even if it's just to

123

know for sure, for good? Maybe all the time you've been gone, maybe that's changed her. I don't know. People change. It's not a promise, but I'm asking would you give it a try. If your mother was willing to work all this out, whatever your differences she was willing, would you consider staying there, cleaning up?"

I nodded yes, not on account of I believed her but just cause I's so happy for somebody, anybody, to look at me and give me the answers, even if they's the wrong ones. Just cause I wanted to nod out the sound of my future. She told me stay where I was, and she left the room, left me to myself, but I's bad company—what with the crying, done took over every bone. In back of it all I thought about how she weren't maybe like what she wanted everybody to think, or anyways that weren't all there been to her. Maybe the stories we heard was true, more or less but anyhow—more to it. Them stories about her throwing furniture, breaking boys' bones, slapping them in the face—no lie, I heard them—but always in the stories it was her shoving and bruising them and still they loved her, pledged their eternal allegiance and come right on back for more. And now I seen they couldn't of come back if she ain't let them in. I wanted to kick, to straighten things out, just to make her proud.

Later she come back and took her seat again, after handing me a box of snot-stuffers.

"I'm sending one of the boys to Penn Station to pick you up a ticket. Look at me: I want to make sure you understand this. I'm not asking you much, nothing I know you can't give. That ticket is non-refundable; can't be cashed in for anything but the ride. You'll need a little extra cash for whatever you're on; I'll get it to you. I don't want you kicking altogether on the train. But you take it before you board and not an ounce of it goes to Nebraska with you. You leave tomorrow morning. I'll give you some cash for when you get to Nebraska, too, but it won't be in your hand until you're on the train. Tonight you can stay here, in your old room, but no drugs in the house. None. So if you're not set for the evening you better take care of it somewhere else, and be back here early enough I know you're not dicking me around."

Then as if all that wasn't serious enough she screws up her eyes and leans out of her chair towards me.

"Look," she says. "I want you to know what you're in for. You're stuck on that train for two or three days, okay? You think you feel bad now, you just wait. Wait until you're trapped in that sleeping car curled up on the bed. I mean, I can't even tell you what you're in for. How long have you been using?"

"Since I been here," I said. "Since the start. A little at first, you know, without it's a problem, then more."

"Shooting?"

"Sniffing."

"Lucky you," she says. "But get ready. Listen, you have nothing to prove. Okay? This isn't about proving anything to anybody; otherwise you're just setting yourself up for failure. It's about you turning things around, even if your mother turns you away. Understand?"

I nodded, but it weren't really sinking in.

"You're going to be very sick. You're going to think it'll never stop. It gets worse before it gets better. These are clichés but not exaggerations. You'll want to die, you might want to get off the train. God help you if you do. Maybe you can sit it out. Because if you can sit it out, you've made it through the worst, and, knowing that—I mean you'll be able to get through almost anything, you're unstoppable. I'll get you up in the morning and have someone take you down to the station and see you off. And when you make it there you go to your mom's, you try again. Don't wreck your chances before you even get your foot in the door. And if you can, you call me, collect if you have to, but only if you have to, and not if you're still on the dope."

I practically spit out I agreed to it, all of it, before she called on the intercom down to one of the boys, told him come get me and take me up to my old digs.

THREE

It's like this.

You's caught up in everything, starts and stops for the longest time, every thought you got's towards figuring it all out and putting it together. And then things trick you—just when you think it won't never let up, you find it's slowing down a little; comes to a crawl.

If you's smart you know it's just building up steam, ready to spin out again, and so fast this time you couldn't never step out, so fast it whips you senseless. But I ain't never been so smart.

Awhile ago, I met this guy out by the courtyard, finally somebody what knows a thing or two, or anyways he'll do. Talked for a while there next to the fountainbed I been calling home then headed to his van just a ways down the street where he said he got some pot we could share. Turns out this was strong stuff, good for a city ain't got much by way of—city where nobody tokes, everybody glares at you like you's giving them cancer when you light up. We got the inside of the van full up of smoke, sat there in the haze, first talking awhile but then we's each of us quiet, off in our own world which was just fine since all I been able to hear the past few days was the rattling of my insides crying out for dope. The peace and quiet give me a chance to sort things out since the hospital.

Until blabbermouth fell in love with the sound of his own voice.

"Look at the sky," my new so-called friend—little mama's boy—says out of nowheres. "Look how blue it's got," and through the small window of the van, through a crack in the curtains over it I seen blue like what's on a map of the ocean, like all them I seen in my grandma's *National Geographics:* deep powder and good news, all's settled blue. Big old pack of lies. Both of us stared at it, eyes heavy thinking blue thoughts. Don't know what was his and don't much care too hard but as for me it was Red's face; them pretty eyes, red hair cut short along the neck and then it's lay longer, straight over the forehead. Seen his face, look he got last time we's together, in the parking lot, when I seen him through the car window. That look what says get lost.

"What if we were trapped in this van, like it was a box we couldn't get out of, and the blue out there's the space we're falling in?"

I wanted he should shut up now, him and all his hippy-dippy talk like the world's just one big tie-dyed T-shirt. I's busy thinking, on account of some of us don't got Mom and Pop waiting in a cozy home to go back to in our little van, garage door opens like magic the second we pull up in the driveway. But now he'd said it my mind grabbed on to it like I ain't already got enough in there.

"Ain't so bad, being in a box," I said without bothering to look at him. You wouldn't have to trap *me* there. Box is better than wide-open outside, all stations go and where to, where next from where you is? Most times that's been it for me here in Colorado Springs and near everywheres else: Like the trick where doors is all around you and behind one or the other or could be any number of them's what you's looking for but what if you get your hands on the wrong one, and find you's like back on your way to the dope or something? What if you start out on the wrong foot, get through the door and on your way and before you know what's where, you got to turn around and find your way back to where you started from, if you can tell yourself its worth bothering. What if it's just that and that alone, all over again? Or you only got the one chance and you blow it on the wrong door—gets slammed in your face?

No: Closed in's better, what with four walls you can reach, and leastways you can breathe, long as you take it slow, not like outside, where you can fill up all that space with your breath and still it's greedy for more. I knowed that from practice. But So-called Friend wouldn't know the first thing about none of that. So-called gone on about blue and some other stuff I didn't hear so good, things like, "What if we was the only people here, just us and nobody else outside," "What if we had to go out to find food and fend for ourselves," and so many other what if whatnots I tuned him out, him and the la-la land he been living in. What if, my ass.

127

Instead I's thinking about Red, last-ditch Red and that's why I's here, seen his face through the glass, wouldn't go away; got to the point I wanted to reach out and touch him. But I knowed better than that by now. Second I reached out he'd be gone, and there I'd of been, stuck by myself in the wide-open. I coughed myself into a little breathing fit just thinking about it, tasted blood in my mouth mixing with the spit.

So-called asks what's wrong. Oh nothing, I tell him, it's just I been getting dizzy here but it's about under control. You should see a doctor, he says, on account of I probably got altitude sickness—no duh—and that can be serious—big surprise. Then he hands me the pipe.

"I'm done with doctors," I said. "They never help. Tell you what's wrong and how to fix it like if you had the money to do the things they say, you'd be there in the first place. I don't need a doctor to tell me I can't breathe—thank you very much—tell me I ain't eating, meanwhile his own stomach's growling in tongues. I don't need no doctor or nobody else telling me take a look at myself. I do just fine."

And So-called laughed like I's telling one long string of jokes and not my life story.

* * *

At Penn Station we walked right past my old street buddies, Mannie's boys, camping just inside the front door like the only shooting gallery. They give me a look like who'd I think I was, then gone back to their business—business I knowed too well: Find The Man and make it quick.

Madam seen me off with one of the guys from the house, stood there like the Queen Bee in the phone room and told him make sure I got to the train, make sure he seen me step on it and slide off with it, slipped him a wad of cash to take care of me one way and another. First we had to stop off and find the connection could fill in for Mannie again, just this one last time. Then my escort and me gone to Howard Johnson, the one I come to when I first got off the boat way back when, so's I could take the stuff. My escort bought a cup of coffee at the counter from the soda jerk while I gone down the stairs to the stinky men's room, done the deed at the sink, front of the mirror at first but then moved to a stall after I made up my mind not to look at myself. *Sniff sniff* and felt the floating come back, that good

128

sinking feeling, started to think forget going back to Nebraska, forget going anywhere, let's get lost. Almost nodded off then and there—probably done, I don't remember—but the boy come downstairs and said get a move on. Come back upstairs and we's out the door, left the coffee on the counter without so much's a sip.

Guy tries to talk to me rest of the way to Penn, silly rabbit. "You picked a fine time," I slurred. "How come you didn't catch me with your questions before I took my junk?" But he was just a College Boy, just started all this, just done it for the money, as if I done it for something else. Or so he said, so he didn't know nothing about dope and peoples what takes it. He wanted to know where I's from—like maybe we'd know each other from somewheres; or something like that I guess. Wanted to know how come the Madam took a liking to me like she done, didn't she never throw nothing my way, what was I gonna do when I got to Nebraska and seen my folks.

"Do your parents know what you do here, and they still say come back?"

Ah now *come on*, I told him; why'd he have to go and get me thinking on that last bit—my folks. Told him I ain't thought about my pa for a long time—"he got the wrong number and died, gone to heaven and weren't nothing I could do about it"—and as far as my ma, well maybe she knowed what it was I done in New York, maybe not. "Either way she don't much care." And just cause I's going back didn't mean she'd have me.

"But why don't you stay here, then, and make more money?"

He just wouldn't shut up.

I's too far gone now to answer him but the junk got me loose at the lips and I made one hell of a go. Talked all the way to 34th Street, blah blah about money and johns and a good night's sleep. Ended up somehow on Walrus and how I left him last time I seen him. "Dead for all I know, but that better be just between you and me." How maybe I cared for Walrus, but how do a body know them things? Maybe I cared but I didn't think he done. How he give me money and food—good food so's my belly was always full—but by that time I's so jacked on dope I weren't so hungry no more anyways.

"Why'd you leave him?" the guy asks, if I's so well fed and took care of, but I couldn't answer cause I never thought of it that way.

I leaned heavy against one of the tile columns inside Penn, tried to stand there propped at first but so heavy I slid down to the floor; guy pulled my scrambag out from underneath me before I sat on it and crushed everything in it. I watched the digital board says what all trains is coming and going and when, lickety-split—the whole big sign one crazy clicking and ticking off, letters turning over on theirselves like everybody, just everybody's, off to somewheres. And wondering why, how come all these peoples going everywheres, how come they can't just stop and stay where they is? Made me uneasy the thought everybody in there was on their way somewheres else, without nobody there or in the whole world could sit still.

I told my escort let me know when **NEBRASKA** ticks itself up in a little conniption fit: Said I didn't want to look at the figures no more.

But that weren't hardly relief, cause even just sitting there watching peoples rush back and forth in front of me, hurry off to one train or another shoving them off to God knows where, gone so fast by me I like to get sick to my stomach, thought, *Slow down. Please, slow it down.* But then the restin' powder cleared that last hurdle and kicked in for good, and done it for me without I got to talk any of them peoples into doing a damn thing. Madam's Yes-man's right next to me, waiting just the same, but once I gone under it was like the two of us was in separate worlds, or anyways waiting for different trains. He give me a look more than a few times like to ask was anybody in there. I give a look right back says your guess's as good as mine.

Some time later a nudge to my shoulder brung me out of I don't know where, and I seen that board, all the information blinking and shrinking over the black screen. Then he's pulling me off the floor before my eyes was even open. "Time to go, it's time." *Well I can't read a one of them but I better trust what he says.* He steered me through all them people, bumping into Samsonite left and right, to a concrete platform what got a train on either side.

"There you go."

"Oh no," I says, my mouth a wad of mush. "No no. Which one's the one? You got to see me right up to the door. Madam said right to the door, otherwise how can I be sure I's going the right way?"

He huffed up like a blowfish. "Well wake up then. I can't be dragging a corpse down the runway." And took me right up to the conductor, pulled out the Madam's wad of bills and shoved it in my pocket.

I barely knowed him, and cared even less, but once I's inside and in my sleeper, nose to the window, I waved good-bye, so's I'd feel like somebody's seeing me off what'd miss me. Pretended he was misty-eyed, waving back. I watched him until the train got so far he was just a speck on the platform. The buildings of the Apple rolled bye-bye, then we got to the dirt mounds what hide on the underbelly edge of the city, where there's all the concrete walls with the graffiti says so-and-so was here, only you can't make it out on account of it's wrote in big fat letters like another language; where there's the piles of blankets and cardboard shacks half falling over, somebody lives there but ain't nobody home. Then full dark into a tunnel, and I knocked out.

When I woke up, it was so dark inside my cabin the only thing I could see's the outside whizzing by, so's I thought I's watching my dreams; them dreams I's always having where I get somewheres to see somebody but they's already gone, or they weren't never there, or they's there but I don't know where to look for them—go to the place I thought they should be and can't find their name on a board of others, can't remember their number, room or phone or whatnot. But these wasn't dreams, these was houses going by. Rows of them little suburb neighborhoods, flittered by like the fields on the way to Buford—one long neighborhood lit up by the glow of streetlights, safe and warm and far away, but all the same so empty. Big wheels left out in the yard, trash set to the curb, not a ghost in sight. Tried to think what I'd got myself into, how maybe I'd got tricked into going back, shooting too fast back into all this by the Madam, just cause she wanted to get rid of me. I started to breathe heavy like I might not make the trip.

Needed more junk; the junk was wearing off. I been tricked. The Madam dangled the junk in front of my face, said go back go back there's a chance in hell for you if you go back. And I took what little dope I needed to get me on the train, thinking all I got to do for free junk's get on, and here the train was—Nowheresville—got me trapped against the window, watching the wreck I's headed for. I thought about Fletcher, quiet Fletcher who wanted me to stay, how last time we talked I thought I knowed you can't never go back, but look at all the going back I tried to do since then. Nebraska wouldn't never work out, specially not now the dope wore off.

But I got money, and four or five ludes I got with the junk. What a relief when it come back to me the Madam give me money. I felt my pocket just to make sure that ain't been a dream too. Then it come to me a train's got bars as much as windows, so I got myself together and left my sleeper, stumbled through as many cars as it took to get to the lounge, pressed the buttons on the doors between them and they rolled aside like presto, like no door you ever seen; heard as I passed from one to the other the sound of outside, of everything rushing past, then through the door to inside and quiet. Past people's faces asleep in their seats, kids crying with their mama's, didn't know where the hell they was. By the time I got that vodka in my hand I needed it more than I could say.

I finished one off at a table in there, swallowed a lude or two to help it go down, turned my back to the window and nodded off, no crappy dreams to speak of. Got woke up later by a man in a uniform snapping his fingers in my face, thought first he was the pigs, come to take me away on account of what I done to Walrus. But once my eyes was bigger I seen he's just the guy what give me my vodka. Asked me did I have a sleeper car somewheres on the train. What's it to you, I says back, like somehow he looked at me and seen I's the kind goes with peoples to rooms. But he just told me I's snoring and since I's sleeping anyways why didn't I go back to my seat. Said it was break of day, and sure enough, I turned to look out the window and seen it was big daylight, steel yards and puffs of steam, sun a bright burst of fire at the horizon like somebody lit a match to it.

By the time I made it back to my sleeper I felt like somebody'd banged on my back, floored me and jumped up and down on it. I's shaking on account of I's trapped who knows where and no dope and I knowed, I just knowed, this weren't but the beginning. Not a few seconds later I got my head halfway into the crapper next to the bed, can't move a muscle except to shake it and ain't like I's the one in charge of that neither. I finally got myself in the bed, freezing cold, shivers, but not without I could take my face out of the john. So cold but seemed like the blanket's crawling with something, critters, and weren't until I just couldn't take the cold no more I ain't cared about the crawlies and got the thing up over me. Kept thinking the drinks I took from the bar might help but ain't got the energy to drink them and didn't think I could keep them down anyways, and couldn't free my face long enough to bother.

The rest of the ride just hell, and course I thought of getting off—

132

getting dope—but where, and how's I supposed to move, get up, walk, look somebody up in some city I ain't never heard of. Leastways here I got somewhere to crash. But in that little sleeper car, don't matter day or night, it was nothing but me getting sick one way or another, smell like I don't know what, and voices; I kept hearing voices. Mostly Ma and Nana, Grandma, but Walrus and Mannie too, and underneath it all Pa's wheezing. We's all trapped in there together. And every once in a while I heard Madam saying this was the worst—after the worst it'd get better, but not before.

* * *

Weren't nobody to pick me up and not much of a station to speak of, just a beat-up wood shack got a window on one side, peep through a small hole to get your ticket, but first you got to find somebody in there. Block or so aways was downtown, if a body can call it that—a row of some of the oldest—and only—buildings around, not but two stories at the most, run along either side of the street facing each other. Mostly it was old men in flannel and fishing caps come in and out the doors, headed off slow as tar for some dusted pickup truck parked a block from the railroad tracks, stared at me like I's the only stranger what rode into town since the last one the sheriff rode out.

I took some of the dough my ride dropped me off at the Memphis Greyhound Station with, gone inside a coffee shop at the far end of all that for a cup and some biscuits near drowned in gravy. Waitress come over to the table looked at me funny like where was my camouflage cap, tackle box, and chaw. But I just stared down into my plate and give her my order, hoping she'd go away, and she done, sent over my food when it was ready. The room was all powder pink and la-di-da, painted like an old lady's bathroom what thinks her shit don't stink, and filled up with old peoples' voices chirping on about the Spring River—how it's so pretty and nothing like it wherever they come from to see it; how peoples raft down it and tump over at the falls without knowing what they's doing; how it's the strongest thing to get sucked up into it, go under and like to not come back up. Somebody told about the time they seen a little girl run across a line of rocks just under the surface, tip top of them falls, hop and skip until all of the sudden she's gone, sunk in just as fast as you please, on

133

account of there been a hole there she ain't seen. They all run right over to get her and seen her standing wide-eyed under the water, in shock like somebody pulled the rug out from under her.

The talk just gone on and on, mostly men's voices telling whatever story, then a woman's says ain't he the cutest, then a man again saying aw shut up already and so on. Then all of the sudden, a younger voice come out of it—clean, quiet, and sure as the Spring River itself, like a sound what's always underneath the rest waiting to be heard, one I been trained to hear all my life—said thank you so much, and I looked up to see whose was it. Seen it was some kid my age talking to the waitress give me a funny look before.

"You staying with the parents up on Tawenow Hill?"

He nodded yes but she didn't give him much more time to answer. "Well, you tell them I said how do. Sometimes I don't think they come off that hill at all. Lens, I remember you this high, Fletcher." She put her hand out flat next to her hip. "Yea high used to come in here with your ma, stretched on your tippy-toes trying to see over the counter. I'd give you a red and white peppermint—red and white peppermint cause that was your favorite since I don't know when. Then this big"—and her hand went up higher—"and bigger and now here y'are. Ya'll grow faster than I can keep up with. Little weeds."

He got the brightest red hair you ever seen, like everyone else is just faking it, and freckles all over everything—got them scattered up and down his arms, over his nose and on his legs. Looked like he just woke up. Here it was noon and him just getting up, got the puffy eyes he's rubbing, lazy slump across the tabletop like ain't got the energy yet to set himself up straight. Maybe that's how come he been so calm and cozy, so like nothing's wrong in the world. Right off I wanted to know where he come from and how to get there. I's so into looking at him I didn't even notice when the waitress walked off; got caught looking when he turned to stare right back at me. I turned as red as he was and got a face full of plate.

Then I looked up and he's gone—looked out the window and couldn't see him nowheres. I tried to make out what was Tawenow out there. All kinds of hills in Buford—Ozarks weren't nothing but, I thought to myself—like the one my grandma lived on. Thought maybe I could stand on hers and see his. But looking around I seen weren't but one was the biggest over all the others, and somehow I knowed that must be it. When the waitress come back to the table with the check and made like to drop it off without getting too close, I asked her where was Tawenow and what about it.

"Well it's where the Diffys live," she says, looking out the window to the big hill covered with trees. She stooped and squinted, raised her eyebrows and pointed. "See at the tip, off to the right side there, the shock of color? That's their house." But I couldn't see it, and all the chatter in the place seemed to make it as hard to see as hear. Waitress stood back up, set one hand on the hip and let the coffeepot she got in the other relax to her side without the heat of it touched her.

"Diffys has always lived there—practically the first ones come to Buford. It was old Mrs. Vella Diffy, Mumma they called her, wife of a Memphis cotton VP, come up here to start a hotel for the springs and summers. Ain't no better place than up the hill, with the Spring River down at the bottom and so high up you can see all of town. Almost everybody goes up there to see things from the gazebo over the cliff, almost everybody. The Diffys don't mind at all. Mrs. Vella come on the train from Memphis every year back when there was one, built a place out of fieldstone and wood with the hotel and a pavilion, tennis courts, an assembly hall. Called it Tawenow Inn, big two-story thing, and all around it scattered across the hill was what they call little honeymoon cottages, little tee-pee cabins; some of them's still there."

"What happened to the rest?" I asked her, and she looked straight at me for the first time, eyes got big like finally she figured me out for a stranger, says:

"It burned down, all but the stone, and most of that crumbled down later on." Relieved, like if it still been around I might go up there and try to break in. "Only thing left was some of the cottages and the house she built for herself on the lip of the hill, hung out over the edge like a diver on the board, but that's gone now too. After the second fire."

"So what's they doing up there if it ain't nothing but a box of matches and a pile of ash?" I says.

Then she tells me how this Fletcher's family built themselves a house on top of where the old one been, after Mumma died, used the same stone the fire left standing; how the place's got enough of the old hotel about it it's like looking at a child and seeing his parents in him; how the Diffys use a couple of them cottages for their family, what's always one or another of them coming up for a visit; how the husband and wife's really "breathing new life back into it" as she says; how Fletcher's from somewheres else—Memphis maybe. Comes in for the summers, just like his grandmama and his daddy done summers before him. There's always some kind of Diffy up on the hill. And that's all I could get out of her.

It was the cheapest breakfast I ever got anywheres: Cost me a couple of quarters and left me with a handful of what my ride in Memphis give me. I left the waitress some of it, even though she weren't but suspicious with me, on account of she did give me some information.

Just out the door, I walked into a cloud of red dust from the Tawenow boy's car pulling up to a curb a ways in front of me.

* * *

So-called asked me once the weed was good and set in was there anywheres in Colorado Springs I wanted to go. By now we's half on and off cushions in the back. I got my head worked out onto the floor and when my eyes was open enough to see much of anything I looked at a string of pom-poms strung up along the roof, made me think of Madam Rosa's cold toes shoved in slippers and Walrus's bedspread what seemed like ages ago. We been sitting there like that for hours, cooped up in the van parked on the curb, to the point weren't no outside to speak of—no Ma or Walrus or nobody else. Nobody and nothing.

Didn't take me but a second, mellow as I was, to figure where he could take me.

My heart got to pounding furious against my chest once we was close by. I think. Got what I got all since I been here—what made me faint and can't breathe, go to the emergency room and all the rest—what my ride called panic attacks. Whatever. All I knowed was it's a rush of something into my chest, felt like I wouldn't be able to hold it in, like I weren't strong enough to handle it without more than the pot and booze, sure it'd tear me apart or send me right back to the dope. *Just get me there, just go,* I's thinking.

We come to a point I recognized from my first day in Colorado Springs, and the feel of seeing the Garden for the first time took over me again, made all the attacks of whatever they was start to slip away. In we gone through the main road where it was tall red walls along the side of the van, like driving through a canyon, and then let onto all the rocks piled high. Sun so hot on everything like to feel you's a steady burning flame. Then the van was stopped and felt like all that outside the windows was rubbing steady up against us, stroking all the crap what gone down the past few years right out of me, like this was a new place and none of it mattered no more, cause hardly no one but me seen it, not even So-called, on account of nobody seen it the same way.

"Want to smoke some more and get out to look around?" he asks.

"I don't know I want to get out into all that," I says, peeking out the window to search out the top of the rocks, but he's already loading up the bowl so I just sat back.

"Indians used to do this here."

I seen Indians sitting in a beat-up van looking through the window at nature like we was, and I must of got a funny look on my face, cause So-called shook his head.

"They smoked pipes," he said, "got crazy high. Then walked up into the Garden."

"And done what?" I says.

"Beats me, but it's true. There's pictures of it."

I thought about the Indians in Memphis—what laid the roads and built mounds and things. Thought how maybe there was pictures but I ain't never seen them, and I hated everybody all at once cause I couldn't, and on account of cause I couldn't see them I couldn't make sure the Indians been there, or couldn't prove it even if I believed it. And I knowed I believed it. I thought it and almost said it, but then I thought better, when I looked over and seen how stupid So-called looked and remembered how often most peoples what looks stupid is just as stupid as they look. It weren't his fault he didn't know nothing, weren't his fault he got it easy and didn't need to know nothing anyways cause he got a warm enough place to stay it didn't matter what happened before. I looked off in another direction where a path cut up through the rock and snaked off out of sight like ain't nobody discovered where it gone yet.

"What's that in there?" I asked, but already my eyes was closing under the heat of the sun and I's so high I didn't care.

"That's more rocks up in there. Trails," he says. "Where the Indians went off to when they smoked their pipes I guess."

He finished a toke and handed me the weed, nodded at me while he held his breath, got this look to his face like he might bust, him and all the colors of his hippy T-shirt. When I took a toke of my own, he let go all his smoke and said through it:

"Wanna go in there?"

But I couldn't get the hang of it—walking—and more'n a couple times I wanted to head back for the van, thinking, *It ain't so far away, not yet.* Spooked me to think I might get lost in the rocks, lose my ride and not know the first thing about where I was. He got his self behind me, so I kept looking back to make sure he's still there. Thought how I couldn't never be happy here, wouldn't never feel it the right way, with him around. But I needed *somebody* there, on account of being there alone scared the shit out of me. It was him kept me going. Him and the ground. Made up of tiny rocks and red dirt, I got to staring at it hard so's I wouldn't have to look nowheres else, figured I could manage that, but all them rocks was so many I seen double after a while, felt like they gone on forever. Like I's on a trail I better not step off of, and couldn't if I tried anyways.

"This here's the Gateway to the Garden of the Gods," he says— sounded like a tour guide the way he knowed the names of every- thing and so pushy with them, like a body don't need a single minute to think to his self. "Red sandstone rising to heights of 300 feet." I just tuned him out so's he weren't but buzz, a warm hum bearing down on me like the sun.

The Gateway was the opening in the rocks I seen from the van, and now we was closer I weren't so sure I didn't want to turn around after all, looked up from the ground and whamo, there she be: Straight through and up ahead, rising up out of the opening was a mountain. "Pikes Peak, elevation 14,110 feet," So-called told me like the only breathing brochure. But all I cared to know was it was a mean-looking thing, all the way up to the clouds. I seen it most of the time I been in town, seen it almost no matter where I gone, but out there it just come off like a wall—just standing there, holding things back. In here it looked too big and all on its own, like it come up out

138

of the ground with a mission and wouldn't stop until it got done, or took everything else back down with it.

"Let's go back to the van," I says.

"You're the one who wanted to come out here," he laughs, and that was a crock. Only reason I wanted out been to get away from him.

"I got to *walk* slow," I said. "Slower than you. Feels like I's out on a ledge. You get up in front of me."

So he crunched past on the gravel saying what a lightweight I was, couldn't handle my weed, said the reason I got altitude sickness was I ain't got it in me to keep both feet on the ground. "Yeah well my fist's flying all over the place too," I says, "so watch out." And that shut him up good. He put his self in front like I told him, where his back blocked out Pikes Peak long as I took care to keep close and not look up too far, and on we gone. Still he was telling me *this is this* and *I know the name of that too,* pointing both directions to show me the sights; yeah, *uh-huh, how bout that* I says whenever I thought his finger gone up or heard he's going off at the mouth, but I mostly got my eyes down on the ground, figuring I may not be able to keep my feet there but damn if I's going to let that stop me from keeping a grip.

Until he stopped altogether, said: "This here's the Siamese Twins."

Which point I looked up dizzy from them pebbles again to see we was on the edge of the Garden, out middle of scrawny little bushes, mountains all around, and right in front of us two towers of rock just the same size and shape or close enough, to the point you'd of thought they sprouted out of the ground from the same seed. They was ring on top of ring, first wide then narrow then wider again, the one not more or less than a yard away from the other, until up top where they reached out sideways in two points like lips puckering up for a kiss, come together like weren't nothing, not even Pikes Peak, been able to get in their way. A pine tree crowned the one on the left who knows how many feet high, like a shock of hair ain't nobody been out here to comb.

"Hey," So-called says, but I couldn't pull my eyes away. Hey and something else, something I ain't paid no attention to, cause by then my mind gone quiet—just the wind blowing a little, whistling between the Siamese Twins. Thinking I don't know what, what seemed like forever.

"Are you listening?"

"Yeah," I says and snapped out of it. "But not to you. I got my head stuck on them two rocks up there. If what you say's true about them Indians come in here, I can see it. What do you got outside of here but telephone poles and wires strung between, cars and roads and skid marks from one city to another to the next, laid one on top of the other so's you can't be sure which come first; tells you nothing. It's enough to make you think life's all about driving around building things and selling them, charging peoples to get in. Then you see something like this, just laid out here for free, not a hand behind it, hid away but bigger than anything and ain't for sale. Seems like maybe everybody all around couldn't help but come in here."

"I asked where you're staying in town," he says, which got me mad on account of weren't nothing left to say and he should of shut up a long time ago.

"I mean, I come in here twice now," I said, staring at them. "Just twice, and I feel like I know things better than I ever done, but couldn't explain if you asked. I mean—all this time, right? Wandering around and I don't know. And nothing, not a thing makes itself knowed. But I just . . . I think I's like this close from figuring it out, you know?"

Okay, says So-called, "but where are you staying until then?"

I told him the usual—nowheres. Said I been staying a while with one guy but we fell out and now I ain't picky. Now I's sleeping in the fountainbed downtown, where he found me.

"Well," he gone on, "what I mean is you can stay with me. Anytime. Cause we click you know? It's not often you get that."

Ain't I got nothing against him, but I couldn't make heads or tails of what he's getting at, and I told him so.

"I appreciate your offer. But I's trying to stare at this rock just now, and really I ain't hurting no more for a place. When I first got here I thought maybe I needed a warm bed or whatnot, but after I spent so much time trying for one, and specially after I finally got it, I seen there's more important things probably, and all along I's just fine where I been, even with the cold and getting colder, the wind and all the rest. You ain't the first tried to offer me a place to stay. Believe me it's just made all kinds of trouble."

Still, he talked me into going over to his house later to at least get something to eat, on account of I might be able to make a bed out of a fountain but not a meal or a bathroom and I needed both like nobody's business, trouble I's having keeping a grip on things, what with the visions of dope swimming in my head.

* * *

I spent a few days with him and near forgot about my grandma altogether.

Sure enough, his parents lived in a big house on Tawenow Hill, just like I heard. Parts was the stone from the old hotel what burned, rest of it was wood walls, from trees his folks cut down somewheres on the property. He told me the Indians owned the hill before him and his family got it. It was just the Indians, and they's the ones first give it the name, told me Tawenow means "among the leaves," and I seen enough how that was true. Even here at the end of summer, what with all the trees pure green, things blooming all over the hill, everywheres was blanket of leaves, crunch dead or dying; patches of it so thick looked like it been there longer than the hotel and the house put together. Told me his ma used some of them rotting leaves to help make her flowers grow.

Front of his place looked out over the Spring River, edge of Tawenow, and I don't know why they called that thing a hill. Weren't nothing sloped about it. Walk to the edge and it's a straight down wall of flint stone into the water. Few places he took me was lookout points he been going to since he's little, spots where the brush been cleared away enough to walk right where the rock folds over, like to fall off. He been doing it so long he weren't even scared of it no more. Told me about a dog he and his folks had once; how the dog run all over the place, got the run of the land, and one day he run his self right off the side of one of them cliffs. They heard yelps and a long steady whimper all day, looked everywheres they could think to, until they thought the worst and gone to the edge of things—seen little Spot or Rover laying down there however many feet down, cozy as a bedbug.

He told me all kinds of things but I didn't tell him the whole truth and nothing but. Told him I come to see my grandma I ain't seen forever. Told him I aimed to stay for good. But I didn't tell him none of the rest, like how I come from Memphis and Nebraska before it, how both of them turned me out, how this here was last ditch. I made it

141

sound like I's anybody else, up here on summer vacation to see my grandma, kind what don't get kicked out. And he bought the load of it, or anyways treated me like anybody else been living in Buford long enough to call it home, like nothing happened before now, or if it done it didn't matter. As far as Fletcher cared, we was starting from scratch: I's whatever I said I was.

Right after we hit it off, downtown Buford, he wanted I should come up to the hill and meet his folks. I said I ain't got no objections to seeing his house and the two of us hanging out, but the folks thing weren't an option. Told him, being's how I just stepped off the bus and got all kinds of travel thoughts on my mind, I needed a minute's rest before getting all that familiar. After all, I said, I ain't even rushing off to my grandma's, and she's the reason I come in the first place. He just smiled—all teeth and his face gone red from I don't know what—and told me I's a strange bird, put his arm around my shoulder and shook me up. We drove to the foot of the hill, where there was stone columns either side of a gravel drive, got a wrought iron sign arched across from one to the other said **TAWENOW HILL**, more or less, on account of some of the letters been knocked off. By vandals, he said, what made me flinch and go sad. "Wasn't me," I said, and he laughed. Then we walked up the steep drive—red gravel, dirt orange-red, from iron, he said. Left the car parked at the entrance, on account of he just washed it and didn't want to get it covered in the dust off the hill.

"Those go to some of the honeymoon cottages," he told me, and pointed down paths what broke off from the main road we's walking. But I couldn't see nothing and didn't care. Whole place—trees and the sun coming through the tops of them, the wind moving things back and forth like weren't nothing it could make up its mind about—it was all too much at once, too much to care about anything else, any other old road and where it gone off to.

Before we got to his house we come to a place where he pointed out a sassafras tree, little twig of a thing growing out slaunchways from the rocky soil off the side of the path. We stopped there so's he could pick some of the roots, shake the dirt off and bring them with us, said he'd make us something powerful strong to drink out of it when we got home. Rest of the way was the red of the dirt and the smell of sassafras, crickets chirping, things scattering through the leaves on the ground somewheres off in the trees. After one last bend in the road, there she was—what used to be the Tawenow Inn, from the backside—big and quiet and snuck up on.

All around the stone base was flowers, and foliage—mostly iris, Fletcher said; died away to the leaves already. There was as many flowers as I ever seen in one place, hugged up thickest at the house but everywheres else too, scattered around. He seen me staring at them, told me they's all his mama's, and before that *her* mama's. You mean she left it to her on purpose, I said, or your ma just snuck in and took them over without she knowed it? He laughed and looked at me funny, said no, weren't nothing secret about it; his grandma planted them iris and things before she died and they just been spreading ever since. His mama watched his grandma grow them all her life, so's she seen how to do it for herself. And I didn't hate him like I done others when they said what they got and how long they got it, on account of he made me feel what's his was mine.

To the left of the house was more honeymoon cottages, all of them what got names. He took me to the closest one, Never Inn, just off where the drive touched the house. Walked me through the ivy growed all around the door and up the sides of the place, pointed out fat leaves come up out of the ivy, said they's lily of the valley and I just missed the most amazing flowers off them, tiny little things cupped like bells—missed them by a few months but there's always something else ready to pop. Then through a screen porch and into a big room got a wood floor and walls with figures painted most places over them. "My aunts painted that one summer way back when," he told me. And weren't only the walls they painted but tables, a mirror, a bathroom off to the side—bright colors and words I couldn't understand.

"French," he said. "If you stay over we'll spend the night in here."

Front of the house was a fountain with lily pads and a Doberman pinscher named Madame what liked to jump around in the water, what was even just then splashing around getting herself wet until we come up on her and she let us pet her. She was big as a house but more friendly, let me rub under her mouth and around the eyes, got a sad look to her face, though I knowed weren't nobody could live on that hill and be sad, so maybe it was just a lazy look said "I's just right and so's everything else in the world."

143

Further up was a big stone patio overlooked the river, but we steered clear of that, on account of maybe his folks was there and I didn't want to see them just yet or ever. Instead we took Madame and gone over to what you call a gazebo, which's Chinese or Japanese for porch with a pointy roof. Like everything else on the hill it looked out over the Spring River, big green thing—"algae," said Fletcher—running crazy down below, got trees all along the sides, peoples rowing canoes back and forth, swimming off docks further away. We took a seat on some chairs was out there and watched all that while we talked. Madame didn't want none of it, I guess, and took off to roam.

"She likes to run around and come back when she feels like it. As long as she knows we're here she's fine." Then he said his grandma's house used to be right here under this gazebo, "until it burned down with everything she owned inside."

The sun had a clear shot at him where he sat. It caught up in his hair and turned it bright red, like flames from the fire he's just then talking about, like they's a memory what stayed with him for everybody to see. His freckles too—got that look like weren't nothing anywheres else in the world as alive and on fire as he was right there and then. And all over the hill it was the same, like it's still on fire too, from the columbine what scattered itself all over in bursts of orange and red.

"All her furniture and quilts and dishes, just everything, all of it ashes. She wasn't with us by then, so her house was all we had of her. Everything the way she left it. Mumma was quite a lady. Quite a character. There was nobody like her. They say the dirt on her hill has got to be the best in Buford, after the ash from as many fires as we've had."

"And you just keep building everything all over again, do you?" I said, and he nodded like weren't never no question about that.

"Course, my grandmother started planting before all the fires. The iris you saw, pinks and all kind of perennial. Most of the iris have been here so long they don't bloom anymore. Mama says they're too cozy and content to work that hard. Ever since we built the house up here she's been separating and transplanting them as best she can; they've come to life all over again. They're not the only things buried here.

"I've found things you wouldn't believe. Old metal hardware from the hotel; doorknobs, hinges. Nails. All kinds of glass melted into shapes you couldn't come up with on your own. Mama tells me not to dig, says I'm as liable to step on a nail as dig one up, but I haven't got hurt yet. I come across lizards and spiders and all kinds of critters digging. I got some in glass up at the house I can show you later. I keep thinking I'll find things guests from the hotel left. I know that's all in there. It's just a matter of time I guess."

He looked like if I ain't been there he might of been off digging now.

"Pretty soon it's dinner: You hungry? I haven't even told my parents you're here."

Which was exactly how I wanted it, but I knowed I got to see them sooner or later, just like my grandma.

"Listen, I just want to sit here and rest for a few more minutes," I said like I got nothing to hide. "Then we can go." Told him I weren't much hungry, even though I's dying for a bite to eat.

And after that it was just them crickets, and all around us, like to form an army and rise up against us they's so loud. We sat and rested, just like I asked, both of us quiet. I thought Grandma thoughts, throwed together and shook up; how she don't even know I's coming and what about it; what if she turns me out. Her too. Maybe Ma knowed I's coming here, maybe she knowed me better than I knowed myself, figured it out herself before I even decided, called up Grandma to break the ice between them and warn her about me, or—worse—come up to tell her face-to-face. "Boy's no good and he's on his way over there."

To get away from them thoughts I stared down into the river, at some kids diving off one of them docks. Jumped into the water, then climbed a ladder back onto the dock and again. And I seen how it was like that there in Buford, at least up on the hill. Everything come and come again. Thought how you couldn't never lose nothing since you's bound to come across it again, digging through the leaves or flowers and the rest of it what's been there forever.

* * *

I didn't have to go down on nobody to get to Colorado Springs.

Instead I turned around and marched right back into the carnie, headed to the first body I seen, said:

"Madam Rosa and the Alligator Boy sent me, said you's to give me something to do so's I can get a ride to Colorado. Go ask them if you don't believe me." Then I stood in his way in case he took me up on it.

Guy looks me over like maybe I's a joke but he needs the help, wouldn't mind taking a rest, tells me I can go help take down the tents. I ain't never done it, I says. So learn, he snaps back.

I watched four or five guys what was taking one of them things down, taking their time at it, kind of stood around quiet like they's at a funeral watching the coffin get put under while the tent's losing air there on the ground, then lazy walking over it to get the kinks out, and start the folding. I fell right in with them and weren't nobody knowed different. Took maybe an hour I guess to get it squared away, which point we lifted the damn thing and carried it to the rig.

Weren't until then nobody asked me what exactly I's doing there. I told them Madam Rosa sent me, said I's to ride one state over to Colorado with them. "That's a laugh," one of them says, and the rest broke out. "Madam don't normally give a fly about tearing down one way or the other." Well we's family, I told them, go way back and I got to get a ride from here to there so she's helping out, come through for me like family do for each other. And I guess when you got family things *is* just all around easier, cause once I told them that they all give me swigs from the booze they's drinking, which kicked my drunk back in nice and good.

After they's done they moved away from the rig a little at a time, strayed off alone or in pairs ribbing each other with bad jokes if you ask me, but I stuck right there by that rig on account of I aimed to get on when the time come and take off with it. It was that or find a john, and I's done with that. I's a free agent now—go where I want, even if figuring how to get there's a problem. I's the kind what leaves without nobody's got the chance to say get lost.

That's when I reached to my back pocket, come to find Red's picture's gone, must of fell out when I's moving the tent. Well I pushed the panic button, didn't know what to do—leave the rig and look for the picture, risk losing my ride, or stay there and forget it, which is to say forget Red, or what he looks like, which was anyhow all I got left of him. Figures he'd leave me altogether, first his body and now the rest when I ain't looking. Thought well maybe Madam Rosa's got an idea where it gone to, maybe she'll come along. Or maybe it's in this very rig, somewheres folded up in that tent, what a laugh, needle in a haystack. Kicked myself cause here's just one picture I try to hold on to, just the one. Can't even keep a hold of a single thing, a single picture. Checked my bag thinking maybe I stuck it in there but no; just everything else but. Tie I got from the dirthead in Memphis, some of Walrus's things, the letter got my Nana's name and address on it. Pa's flask.

You better remember right now what that picture looks like, else you won't be able to see him in your head.

And I come up with of course the red hair, cut short, the red coat what's scuff marks most places, freckles and how, leaning against the bleachers, Ferris wheel behind him and the rest of the midway stretching out like an open road, booths all along the sides what got the stuffed animals. *And what else, think harder,* cause that's the point where I couldn't picture nothing else. *Now they done tore the carnie down I ain't got that to look back to neither, won't never know what none of this looks like again until I track down Red.*

* * *

"What am I supposed to tell them, now they know somebody's over but I haven't introduced you?"

After dinner already and still I didn't want to meet Fletcher's folks. Why'd he have to go and tell them I's out here, I said. They wouldn't of knowed anything without he brung it up.

"But they probably know your grandmother," he said. "There's nothing to be scared of."

"I ain't scared," I lied. "Look. I got some serious business to talk over with my grandma. I got all that on my mind right now and I can't be pushed. So if you keep on about your folks I'll just have to go somewheres else where I can think."

Course there weren't no other place to go except my grandma's, and I weren't ready for that, but I had to bluff him, otherwise he'd of marched me right up to his house.

"All right. I'll go up and tell them you're not feeling good, you're tired and you just wanted to go right to bed. You'll meet them in the morning."

"That's right. In the morning."

"But they're going to wonder why you're not just going straight over to your grandma's if you're so tired. They're going to wonder and what do I say?"

"Tell them you's tired too, and got to go to bed yourself."

He left me on the gazebo and I watched him walk up the lawn to the house, past the fountain it turns out his grandaddy dug, what got the frogs croaking inside, and the sharp plants he showed me earlier, called them Jesus' Candlesticks, got the white bell flowers smelled up near the whole of the hill. Least God's good for something, I said. Then he was up the stone steps, across the porch, disappeared through the door.

Just walked right in, I thought, and then I seen why it was I didn't want to meet his parents, and how come he wouldn't understand. I turned and looked out to the Spring River. Nobody left on the water, all the canoes drug in to the docks, swimmers too—just the water, looked still as the sky, and took up with the same purple and orange. Never know it was moving if somebody didn't tell you. I got the sudden bug to go down into the water, jump in and stay there, moving but not moving, see where it took me. Ain't like a car you got to steer through traffic down a road somebody else laid down. This here's like the Mississippi, set by God know's who, long time ago, goes whichever way it damn well pleases.

Thought about the story I heard on the TV at some bar in Memphis. How a bunch of local yokels built up dams to hold back Ole Miss, built themselves houses along the safe side, and years later the river wouldn't be held back no more, crashed through the dams. Peoples putting up plastic and rocks, making walls trying to keep the water back, save their houses from the flood, but no go. Seen whole buildings floating in the mess, trees snapped out of their roots, all of it gushing back into the pull of the river.

Yes sir, I wanted to jump in a spell.

Then he's back, says well his folks can't make heads or tails of it but they's going on to bed, let's go to Never Inn. But I asked could we walk around the hill first since I ain't done seeing the rest.

"Look," he says, "aren't you hungry yet? My folks'll be asleep in minutes flat, and we can go to the house for a bite. All kinds of food up there. They won't even know we're in. Once they're to bed they're out like lights for good."

So after a few more minutes of looking at the river, and things going darker, we made the walk to the house. If this was anywheres else I wouldn't get in, I thought, as we got to the door. Felt strange, downright wrong to get that far up the porch and close to the house without somebody come out to stop us. But a turn of the knob and we was in. Easy as that.

Cozier than all get out, little glowing lamps spotting the place, lit up old china and wood cabinets and handmade rugs. To the right was a couch and chairs and a table with a big jigsaw puzzle, mostly done set on top.

"Daddy's been working on that for a couple weeks," Fletcher said, and pointed for me to go sit over there, but it didn't feel right.

"I'll just sit here on the floor," I told him, and parked it next to an old cupboard got all kind of family pictures framed and laid out. He gone into the kitchen around the corner to scavenge something for us to eat, and sitting there in somebody else's house, I got queasy. What if his folks got up to use the bathroom or heard a noise and come out and there I was, sitting in the middle of their place. I looked over one of the doorways and seen an old rifle hung there, ready to rip. What kind of man takes kindly to a stranger in his digs, eats him out of house and home? Got so nervous I's praying I wouldn't be left alone much longer.

Soon he come back with the scraps from his folk's dinner; got pork and potatoes and beans. Some pecan pie, made from nuts his ma picked herself off the hill. *Well ain't this just too much*, I's thinking. Once we got the pie, and my stomach was feeling like a regular Joe's again, I asked did his folks got any firewater for dessert. "*Firewater*," he said, "what on earth do you want that for?" Just cause, I told him. Just cause. "Can't you please?"

He said his folks weren't much on moonshine but he'd see what he could find, come back after a spell with a bottle of fancy liquor, sweet as he was. Sat watching me with that pretty smile on, his face red like he his self been drinking some, said, "You're something else," and "easy, now," when he seen I might of done the whole bottle in one gulp.

Then he opened the cupboard door and pulled out two big photo albums, asked did I want to look at some pictures while we's sitting there. Two of the biggest books of photos I ever seen, thick as phone books, stuffed with pictures of his kin. There was first off black and whites of his ma and pa getting married—Ma dressed in everything white running down the stairs of some church got her arms throwed up in the air—her and his pa in the church, flowers everywheres like somebody brung some from Tawenow. By now I seen these peoples liked a whole lot of flowers and got plenty of room for them.

Then one kid born—little baby in blankets—then another, and another.

"That's me," he said, pointing to the picture, laid his finger across it so's I seen it up against his fat baby hand.

Then a slew more of him: Easter Sundays with baskets and candy; him in his bathrobe by the Christmas tree; birthdays in front of birthday cakes. He been the best-looking flash of white gold hair and freckles you ever seen, running all over the pictures getting his self into trouble. Told me the things he done, like painting the folk's car when they left the housepaint out, throwing his peanut butter and jelly sandwiches under the couch or behind the TV when he's done with them, started the dinner table on fire; near drove everybody crazy but he turned out all right. All of him, right there, stuck into this book so's it was the story of his life, as easy to read as any other picture book—all the parts filled in, still a mystery but everything a body needed to put it together weren't going nowheres.

And when we's done we sat there quiet with the books closed, listening to the crickets you couldn't barely hear now the doors was closed on them. But nothing, no door or window or house locked tight could keep out the sound of the train what passed every other hour, run along the bottom of the hill and sounded a horn what seemed to shake the whole place and made Madame howl bloody murder.

"Let's go to Never Inn," Fletcher said the next time we heard that train. I nodded my head, after I asked could we bring some more of them bottles of sweet stuff with us in case I got thirsty again.

That's where we done it—inside Never Inn—with the crickets and moon coming through the windows, barely lit up the paintings on the walls, smell of grass and river everywheres at once made me feel we's right out in the open of it. Was two beds in there but before neither one of us laid in them we pushed them together. Pushed them close to make one bed then got in it. I laid on my back staring into the dark, the ceiling I guess but in my head it weren't. I seen stars. Then his hand on my arm—touched me then left it there. I been with johns so's I knowed this was how things got started with people what felt funny about starting them, but with him I took over and it was all right, on account of I felt as funny as he done. I took his hand, put it in mine. Brung it to my face where I touched his fingers to my cheek. In the dark they's first his baby fingers then back and then again. Then I kissed them, and he was over and he kissed me.

I think it was the best couple days of my life, them I spent on Tawenow, and I never did have to meet his folks, on account of he got sick of asking me and just plum give up. It was just like the two of us owned the hill.

Days it was on the Spring River, current moved so fast like to pull you away without you's anchored to something. He said there been a couple times the family dock got tore loose from storms wearing down the ropes, like the flood a few years back what almost washed away all of downtown, left a ring of mud and slime around all the buildings. Diffy somebody or other gone to the bank of the river, walked down the steep wood steps his grandaddy built, and nothing—just the wide open yawn of the river. Dock ended up downstream God knows where; floated in the night and whatever in its way got going with it.

Said there's snakes what lived inside the dock, between the Styrofoam keeps it afloat and the water there's pockets of air and that's where they called home. Said every once in a while a girlie come screaming up the hill, bloody murder, running like a scalded dog, towel barely held up, couldn't breathe she got the vapors so hard. Some girlie, seen a moccasin and thought it was Satan. But we never seen one the days we's down there—girl or snake neither one.

With us it was just lazy floating on the water, dock turning slow circles around the cord what tied it to the riverbed. He laid on the bench bolted to the dock, but that was too high up for me so I took the floor. Come out of the ice-cold water hair wet and matted to my head, laid flat on my stomach with my eyes closed. Whenever I opened them the dock done turned and I's somewheres else. And when my hair caked dry I braved into the cold of the water again.

Laying there he told me stories, things about his family. How when his ma met his pa they's just teenagers and today they was still together, and all they been through between. He got two brothers and a sister, all of them sturdy like him—got the squinty eyes from their ma and the squat legs from Pa. The brothers was one older and one younger, like bookends one either side of him far's looks and the way they seen things gone. They was the tightest, them three.

The sister said she loved him, anytime he seen her anymore it was I love you and blah blah like so much she couldn't really mean it, or didn't mean it but wanted to, or didn't want to but knowed she should so she tried to make everybody else think otherwise. He never told her he gone with boys but she could probably figure, what with he never once dated a girl, always with a boy on the hill, and just he's all around different. She give him looks when she weren't telling him how much she loved him, and when she weren't doing neither, she told him how he should be living his life different than what he was.

She herself was married, got two kids. Weren't long ago her husband took up with another woman or two, at least two's what they knowed about. But nobody talked about any of that on account of his sister's feelings might get hurt. Besides, the husband ain't never done it before and promised he wouldn't never again, so what was there to talk about anyways is what I guess they all said. He told me how his sister wouldn't let none of her kids talk to him, cause of the way he was—whatever that means. What's the way you was, I asked, since I thought he's the best person I ever met and couldn't see why anybody'd steal him from anybody else.

Sometimes while he's talking I squinted out the sun to look at him over me on the bench. Got pink and purple shorts what couldn't of gone over well with the sister. But really he weren't at all what you'd think of when you think percy-pants like he made out his sister said. He got the freckles up and down every inch of his hide, tough skin— specially at the fingers where they's chapped and split and squared, the red hair he didn't take no care in particular about combing; them legs what looked like they could stop a truck short without it knowed what hit it. Weren't nothing girlie about him.

That's why at night we'd end up with the beds pushed together, him telling more of his stories in the dark until his lips was on mine, like the story been about them getting closer. Feeling his skin pitch-black with the crickets busy, point where whenever I thought about his skin the sound of crickets was part of it. In the dark I measured up the way his skin felt to the way I seen it on the dock. To the touch it weren't rough at all, but soft, so much it was like touching somewhere what never gets touched and ain't supposed to. In the light everything about him was brittle, crisp and wiry. Not so at Never Inn nighttime.

Got to be he was one person I seen days, another at night; that's how come I kept on at him about telling me more stories, so I could put the two together. And when he seen I's interested, he asked did I want to watch some home movies they got in storage. One night we drug out the projector and all the cans of film, made a screen out of the cabin door, and he flickered to life, little squat of a boy, all fiery white hair and speed—a shot of light across things like he his self was lighting up the picture. Him getting into everything, his ma or pa or brothers pulling him out, his sister shaking her head somewheres in the corner about it all. Too much for words: I just sat with my mouth wide.

Between the film melting and jumping out of whack it was him time and again, his whole childhood right inside the cabin with us. I never seen so much of one person put together right before my eyes, and I told him as much, though he didn't know how that could be. Then he give me a funny look, started asking me all the questions: where you from, why, what for, and all the rest. But I had to stop him before he got started, on account of I weren't about to go there.

We was on the gazebo looking through old books from his folk's house when I come across it, and it like to take my breath away. "That's her!" I says, and sure enough it was.

Out falls some picture of "Lady J"—my grandma in the flesh. And on this very spot, since as Fletcher told me, "She's sitting on Mumma's porch," what used to be but weren't no more. Smile on her face like life's good and the Spring River aflow behind her, rocking in a chair what been his grandma's too, and look to the side of the picture it says in tiny print that there's taken by my grandaddy.

"My grandaddy took pictures," I says. "She's smiling at him."

Fletcher knowed all about Lady J—said she was legendary in them parts, what with she holed up in her house like to never come out and all she done to make the town of Buford what it was. Said she's in real estate, sold most of the houses in the area. A tough loner, he said, just like I thought, which is how come we's a perfect match. Told me a few stories about her he couldn't say was true or false, about her making friends and enemies and got a sharp tongue could cut through bullshit, weren't nothing she couldn't do on her own or so she come across like. All I could think was how me and Fletcher's connected before we ever met; all that time ago my grandma been sitting on his gazebo.

Later he left me there to go up to the house—with the locusts crazy singing, the river setting stiller now everybody was letting off her. I stared straight into the sun thinking *I won't go blind*, until I could see my grandma in my head, not just the way she was in the picture, but like I knowed her all my life and come every summer like Fletcher and his family and every other regular person done.

Then I put myself in my mind with her, set us together on the gazebo. Two chairs and her in one of them, set right next to me. Looking out on to the river and thinking about everything all at once and all of it made sense. *How come I can't do the same with Ma or Pa or nobody else,* I got to thinking. Maybe it was Buford, where things was away from everything, or up here on a hill covered by trees or who knows.

I looked down at her hands and seen they's a china doll's like they always been, soft and milky as anything's got a right to be, wondered was they soft as Fletcher's.

When he come back, I's ready as I's going to get's what I told him. He looked at me like I must be the strangest thing he ever knowed. Whole time I been up there him asking how come you don't go over to her hill? I couldn't never think what to tell him and still he didn't much care. No matter what I told him we ended up nights with the beds pushed together, and when I's hungry he fed me until I couldn't think of another bite. Give me everything I wanted no matter where I come from or who'd have me.

The drive over was backtrack on the roads I come down on the bus, roads what veered sharp and single lanes like no turning around, nothing off to the sides but treetops, red dirt and rock. Round one bend was trees took over in vine. "Kudzu," says Fletcher. "It comes all the way up to the road and might just cross it if not for steady traffic." True enough, the trees was so choked with it they looked like big animals you couldn't put a name on, covered in blankets and stooped over the road.

"I ain't told you but I come all this way to settle for good."

"So we'll see each other all summer," he said, and smiled ahead. "On one hill or the other."

Driving crunch across my grandma's gravel road brung back the only memory I got of her, the only ride I ever made to her house I can remember. And just like that I's nervous; struck me she didn't know I's coming, that just cause I been talking it over with her in my head didn't mean she got wind of it. I tried to ready myself for the worst but there was too much excitement run through me.

Then we come upon the house and I got Fletcher to stop the car for a spot. The place still got the stone base, but the wood siding been worn down good from weather. It was just a big fort in the middle of a high grassy field—crickets mad chirping or whatever it is they do. *All the bugs what must be in them weeds,* I's thinking, trying to figure was they saying come on in or beware turn back and go away. Along the drive was wrought iron patio furniture and glider swings rusted out, sat crooked off to the side. Got some plant pots scattered around, some trash too; nothing to say nobody lived here no more. Over the top of the hill we seen the view of the lake, must of been the one my grandaddy helped dig, curved around the land the house sat on until it disappeared into the trees of her property.

"Lake Vagabond," says Fletcher, only it didn't look a thing like I pictured it. The two was miles away different, and I got the worst feeling in my stomach. This here weren't nothing but grown over with weeds. "They let the grass grow back over."

I thought I didn't want to go nowheres. Wanted to stay with Fletcher on Tawenow, set up house in Never Inn, where I's so well fed, got good company, folks ain't nowheres to be seen, train come by like clockwork. Got a bad feeling about my grandma's, bad enough now I seen it I couldn't hide it no more. But Fletcher got his own family, and I got mine, even if they didn't want me. My only shot at one was the other.

We pulled up to her carport and I thought well this is it, even as Fletcher got out his side like going to visit just anybody. I waited in my seat long as I could get away with, until he realized I weren't following him and come back to the car and over to my side. I rolled down the window and give him a look he probably couldn't read.

"You coming?" he laughs.

"Ever feel like maybe you just need a second to rest up before you set out to do something?" I says.

"You have to do that a lot. Are you sure your grandma's expecting you? How long's it been since you saw her."

"Look," I says, "I know you mean well but them's questions you need to lay off of, on account of right this minute my stomach's got a lot of work cut out for it."

I wanted to tell him more, but couldn't talk and rest up at the same time. So he stood there—leaned against the side of the car—put his hand through the window and onto my shoulder like to say whatever I needed to hear. And the door opened, here come an old woman I ain't never seen out my grandma's house, woman what can't barely walk, or she's lopsided or something I can't at all figure. She got the meanest look on her face, and clutching at her shirt trying to keep it closed. I's embarrassed, thinking well why don't she just button the damn thing, when I seen she ain't exactly got what you'd call fingers, but gnarled things what swelled and gone off in different directions like they's all got a mind of their own, like to pull the rest of her hand along with them.

Weren't until she was near up to the car I could take my eyes off them. Closer she come, the better look I got; trapped thinking, *I know who this is, please don't let it be her*. When I pulled my eyes to her face I seen she was all pinched there—looked to me then Fletcher then back again like we ain't seen her yet so she didn't need to get friendly.

"Lady J, I'm Vella Diffy's grandson, from Tawenow Hill," says Fletcher, stuck out his hand to shake hers until he seen that was a bad idea and pulled it back like he never done it.

And like it was that easy to turn off, her face gone friendly.

Now they both looked to me, and I knowed either I better say something quick or count on wrecking everything for good.

* * *

True enough, So-called's folks was in the other room the whole time we's there. We gone in and said our hellos, barely got a look from a one of them, then off to the kitchen where we raided the fridge. That thing was crammed full of every kind of vittle, got meats and vegetables and sodas—all the food groups—plus bottles of vino stuffed in wherever they fit. He rifled through the loot like it weren't but trash, throwed one thing then another at me to take back with us to the van.

Shhh, he says as we gone out the front door, squeak and creak over the step. I don't know what he cared. His folks got the TV turned up so loud we'd of had to park a squad car in the dining room, siren going, to get their attention. And still we'd of had to snap our fingers in front of their faces.

While he unloaded the groceries from my arms, I looked up at his house, lit up with a lamp on just about every clear spot of brick. Little wreath on the door for no special reason, bird bath squat in the middle of the front yard, dry as a bone now it gone so cold. Through the windows of the garage I seen two cars—flashy new things, looked like—one what got a bumper sticker said **Proud Mother of a Very Special Boy.** I looked at him and didn't see's how there's nothing so all fired highfalutin.

Anyways, if he was so special why was they inside like they couldn't care neither way.

In the van it was yak yak and popping open potato chip bags and cans of whatnots. I thought I made it clear on the way over I needed my shut-eye, but here he was, trying to get me to eat near everything we brung out, pushing it in my face like I's some kind of fiend for it. One point I grabbed his hand, held it away from my face, told him he better put all them snacks away less he wanted to sleep with them outside the van. Ha ha he says like I's kidding, until I took one of them bags and pounded every last chip flat, which point he got rid of the smile, just sat there trying to figure what next to keep me wide awake.

It was like this kid never been alone for a minute in his whole life, like once his folks gone in the other room and left him to his self—never to return—he took off right away to hunt down somebody else would sit and listen to every story he got to tell, took longer to tell it

157

than live it. Don't see why he couldn't sit still and shut up, what with all the quality ganja he got at his disposal. Anybody else'd be happy to go off into nowhere special hanging on the tip of one of them joints.

I rolled over and played dead and even then he gone on, I guess thinking maybe I'd pop up and give him the go ahead. I tried to sleep, figuring, well I told him that's what I wanted, but the only reason I told him that was so's he'd shut it up. I found out in no time I weren't sleepy at all, not with the first chance to think in days. No, with all the quiet it all started coming back to me. For the first time in don't know how long I could see Red clear as day in my head, like it was yesterday and I ain't never lost the picture. What's more I gone from him to Ma to Nana and on down the line without a one of them was hard to make out. Every one of them, clear as day. Even when big mouth started snoring like to shake the van off its wheels I gone on, sharp and bright as day. Thought how I didn't get into Nana's house, or Ma's—how maybe I got back into the Madam's but only to get put out again when it come down to it.

I looked up to his house. All lights; like a truck stop blaring Come On In! Parents wax figures on the sofa chairs, high on TV. Thought, *Well now, there's a thought and ain't no knock-knock to it.*

* * *

My first mistake was I couldn't do nothing right with her. In front of Fletcher, she said she's glad to see me, but then he was gone and she didn't want I should do whatever I done the way I done it. Wanted me there but she didn't, on account of she couldn't do next to nothing with her hands the shape they's in. But she didn't want nobody to do it for her, she wanted her own hands back, only she wouldn't say that. You just seen it in the way she looked. She'd got to the point she could do all kinds of things on her own you wouldn't of never guessed. But still there was always something—always something she come up against and weren't no way to get around it without somebody else got a hand in it. Place was falling apart—grass out of control and everything lean-to. But she just sat there at the kitchen table without she once looked through the window what seen out across her property, I guess on account of looking meant seeing she couldn't do nothing about it. Here it's late summer, the air starting to cool, finally, after the worst weather the Mississippi ever seen, cool breeze coming up the hill and stirring around in her trees, and she wouldn't so much's open a window, any more'n she cracked a smile.

I was all questions, wanted to know how come we ain't seen each other more than we done. How come weren't nobody but me knowed or cared where I been, what was a family doing acting the way we was? She just sat and sucked her cigarettes, squinted through the smoke. Got this way of lighting them, what with the crooked fingers; held the lighter sideways, used one of them thumbs to flick like it weren't but a means to an end. I figured maybe she's shocked to see me after all that time, so shocked she couldn't think of nothing to say. Or maybe she's just happy we's finally together. Never occurred to me to think any different, even if I should of after all I been through.

Course I scoped the place out every chance I got—tried to see now where would I be shacking up, which room did I like best, where was something and how about everything else. Whenever she gone to the bathroom or seen to somebody on the phone I's off and running through them rooms. *She lives all alone here in this house*, I thought. Just like Nana, only she can see straight and knows my name. Ain't seen me but once and knows my name. I looked in kitchen drawers, where I come across stacks of papers might of meant something if I had the time to go through them, without worrying she's coming back any minute; seen one was full of pictures, long skinny drawer full of them single file—got them separated by cards with scratchy handwriting said **Grandkids, Edna, Millie**, and others I ain't never heard of—not a mention of grandaddy and ain't a picture of him neither. She kept all them drawers cracked open so's she could get in them easy I guess, but it didn't look like she been in any of them for a while. They got that look says they's frozen that way; petrified wood.

I couldn't get a good look around much anywheres else on account of she ain't ever left the room long enough. But it didn't seem like she never left that kitchen table much anyways, not unless she got called off by Mother Nature; seemed like that kitchen table was it. Going in her bedroom weren't an option, but I seen it whenever I passed from the kitchen to wherevers else, when Mother Nature give *me* a call. Through a slit in the door I seen stacks of boxes along the walls like she just moved in, a pile of coins on a dresser, fishing tackle on the windowsill, a couple of shotguns propped next to the headboard.

159

Aside from them stuffed and stuck in that drawer there weren't a picture in the whole house. When I asked her where was the charcoal pictures of Ma and Aunt Edna and Millie I seen one time, in frames what made them official, she sucked cigarette like to take in the whole room, said:

"I took them down to paint the walls."

What *she* wanted to know was how'd I meet Fletcher. Was we friends long and did I know his family. I told her I met him on my way to see her but we hit it off so fast you'd of thought we knowed each other longer. Said we gone down to the Spring River a couple times and planned to some more. Said as soon as I's settled the two of us'd be into some kind of trouble and wouldn't be her or nobody else could tear us apart or get us off the river, said we might just end up growing fins. She looked at me like maybe she knowed about Never Inn and pushing the beds together, like she might of said something to match the sour look on her face if she ain't got to be civil on account of the Diffys was her neighbors after all.

"Peoples always drowning on the river," she says. "Don't know what they're doing. Get drunk and don't know how to steer a key through a keyhole. Canoes tump and they go down."

Well I might not know about it but Fletcher sure did, I said, since he been here and on the river all his life, could practically jump into it from Tawenow Hill. "Fletcher'll do to ride the river with," I laughed.

But I didn't care about any of that. I wanted to know all there was to know, the sooner I got started the better. "After all, so much time's been wasted," I told her.

"Speak for yourself," she said.

But I kept at her, asked everything I could think of—barely let her rest or things go quiet long enough for her to change the subject. If we was going to make this work I got to make sense of it all, know it like she knowed it, straight from her own mouth. Already I seen from the look of things how wrong I been; about the state she was in, the house and lake, her hands and everything else. I needed her to tell me, so's it'd be in my mind without it could slip away. House was near falling down, and she couldn't do nothing but sit there and watch; if she told me what needed fixing, what gone wrong, I could start to build things up again.

How come you's in pain, I wanted to know, and how do you get around. How long's it been since you seen Ma or Edna, did she know anything about my pa. Some of it she wouldn't say—just stared at me like you would somebody's trying to sell you something you already got rid of. But what she would say I ate up.

Like what was there *to* know about my pa except for how he treated Ma. What was there to know but he run ragged the patience of near everyone around him, and by the time they's worn out he was too, ended up sick, beat from drink and smokes or so the doctors said, but look at her, she told me: She smoked herself, and *she* weren't sick in bed. No, weren't nothing to know about Pa except he was a book you could judge by the cover and even that you didn't need to read but the once. He gone sick cause the way a body lives inside is what happens sooner or later to it on the outside. Disgraceful, the way he done your mama, she said, but as usual how's I to know what that meant without she told me the rest. Said Pa run around but worse than that he just weren't never there, weren't what a man in a marriage should be. And Grandaddy's to blame for that, on account of the kind of example he set for Ma to look for; and maybe even Grandma, she herself said, cause she waited so long to give him his scram papers.

But you's sick too, I wanted to tell her. Look at yourself. Pa ain't the only one. And if he got sick on account of what a body dones what it becomes then what's with you? But I's in her house, after all; never stopped to think she'd side with Ma, of all peoples. Ma: Go figure. When Ma's the one what kicked me out, told me I ain't her son no more, and whatever Pa done to her—way back when—Ma made up for in the end. Locked him in that room's what, talked to him like he's not worth talking *to,* practically spit on him with every P and Q. I seen right off that things was backwards at Grandma's; not just the way things was but the way she seen them too.

She told me she got rheumatism, near ate up her joints, but not cause of nothing she done; she ain't had nothing to do with it, cause why would somebody go and do that to themselves, she said. Said one day she was fine, next she knows she can't move her hands. "Sure there was signs, but I went on with things like I always done." She weren't about to let a little pain stop her, "never done before." Kept on keeping on and on. Don't wait for nobody to do nothing cause there

161

ain't time to waste, she said. How was she to know? How was she to know things wouldn't stay the way they was. Kicked out Grandaddy and weren't nothing could stop her, then one day she's at the lake, practically *her* lake for all the say she had in building it, at *her* dock, with friends she made without his help cause she done fine that way thank you very much without him, him and his friends might of dug the lake down there but it was her helped sell all the property around it and fill it up with peoples. One day with *her* friends she's fishing like on any other day off, tries to throw the line and her hand gone numb with pain like you can't know. Said it made her so mad she couldn't see straight.

I knowed the rest, I think, on account of I heard Edna talk about it one day, only Edna said Grandma got so upset she throwed the fishing pole to the ground and run off crying all the way back to the house, and ain't nobody, not a one of them, seen her cry before. Or after. Who's to say which was which, whether it was Grandma cried like Edna said or she's just angry like she said herself? But all the stories I ever heard about her, even Fletcher's, was practically the same: always alone and upset one way or another, all fired up crazy mad. Or around peoples she put a face on for. From the look of things, whatever happened, whichever way, she run all the way to the house and ain't practically been out ever since, practically slammed the door on her hands.

Edna and Ma always talking about how Grandma ain't got time for them after a while, what with all the visitors and business friends she got some land to sell; and Fletcher saying practically the same, that she holed up in the house and got took over by legend. After the girls was growed up anyways, older with kids of their own and Grandaddy was out of the house, throwed out on his back end. Ma and her sisters weren't throwed out but they might as well of been, on account of they ain't talked to Grandma much since then. Only thing Grandma said to me about them was they all wanted her things and she weren't going to leave a will, she'd just let them fight over it for all she cared.

Then she'd get on how Grandaddy tried to come back to Buford however many years later, must of been years ago but she told it like it was as fresh in her mind as yesterday. "Come back here after the younger one dumped him, crawling back like the little crawly thing he is, and everybody feeling sorry for him," got her face all scrunched up like a crybaby with a grudge.

"Took up with one of the ladies he run around with in the old days, one of two-hundred-and-forty'leven in town he been friendly with. Lived out in back of her place. Wanted to set up a studio—just like he had here—only he weren't stupid enough to think I'd let him step through this door, so he looked for a space downtown. Well he couldn't find nothing; of course not. Not by then, because I'll tell you. He was the same as ever, but not where it counts, and you could of spent twenty days or years downtown and wouldn't of found one little lady down there would of wanted to have him take her picture. And even if he could of—sweet-talked the same way he always done, and he could of got those pretty ladies to give him a snap—where do you think he'd of got the money, after he wasted his whole life chasing and spending on any perfumed two-legged? Come back here without a cent, s-c-e-n-t, to his name. And if there's anything worse than a pathetic young man without a means it's an old one. So he had to pack it up and head out of here, tail between his legs, for once. And I never heard hide nor hair of again."

Course two peoples can only sit at a table staring at each other so long before what goes without saying gets brung up. Grandma wanted to know the story. What happened with me; she heard my ma and I ain't been the best of friends, heard I's roaming around Memphis and God knows where else. Don't a young man my age work—don't he look out for his self? Well of course I done, I lied. On account of I may be an idiot but my mama didn't raise no fool. Told her the first thing what come to my head—said I worked at a bar and not for peanuts, made me a pretty penny, working my way up. Yes sir, ma'am, you can bet on one thing and that's I got a head on my shoulders, I told her. Yes, she said, I can see that, but do it got anything in it, cause if it don't you might as well sell it and make some money off it. I got money and a place to live, a future, I said. Then why you here, she asks. Why, Grandma, what do you mean? I's here to see you of course.

Every time I looked out the window I seen there was the yard needed cutting, or something else needed done. But I been going for so long, and here finally I got somewheres to stop. Felt like I better rest for a while—just a spell. Once I got me some rest I'd show

Grandma what a help I could be, how I's different from Grandaddy and anyways he been dead for a long time, and maybe I's a lot like Pa but Pa ain't been as bad as she thought; how she wouldn't have to worry no more about her hands or the pain or not being able to do things herself cause I got two of my own and after all I been through I didn't keep them to myself. Might not have much to offer, like she seemed to think, but I weren't stingy with it.

*　*　*

Getting out the van weren't no easy play—took waiting until So-called was sure asleep, then a climb across him and slide the door open without he woke up—and I's flat-out drunk. Midnight and all the lights full blast, sound of crickets what don't seem right out here in the middle of suburban nowheres. Like there shouldn't be nothing but houses all look the same and the concrete what takes you from one to the other. When we drove into his what-you-call subdivision, every three houses was the same except for maybe a garage switched around to make you think things was different.

"They use one blueprint over and over," he said, all proud, like that been a good idea. All I could think was what happens if you's coming home late and can't figure which's yours, what street leads where, and so many dead ends what just circle right back into theirselves you might as well hand out keys to all your neighbors. Course, maybe that's how come all the lights—so's you couldn't miss the place.

I gone in the way we come out and twice as quiet, first off didn't hear no TV, so that was off. They's already upstairs in bed's what I fig-ured, and sure enough the first floor was dark all over. Whole outside lit up but in there you couldn't see your hand in front of your face. Top of the stairs there was a light, but I held off on account of I wanted to see the downstairs now that Mom and Pop Android wasn't around.

Turned a light on just off the entry, suddenly the living room's all mirrors and there's me all over the room. This here's one of them rooms they don't use, saved for something or other what never comes around nohow, got the mirrors I guess to make it look bigger—big empty nothing. Everything crystal and white and plastic over the seat cushions, plastic mat for where you's supposed to walk when you got to walk through but you ain't supposed to officially been in there.

Not a speck of dirt but smelled like a dog took the worst kind of piss wherever he damn well pleased and come back like to say And another thing. Pictures of So-called—Special Boy and Proud Parents—hugs and bright eyes and glows where smiles should be.

I gone over to a chest got a bowl of pine cones painted gold on top. Next to the bowl they got this vase, clay or something, peoples painted every which way on it like it come out of a caveman's digs, picked up the lid and there's still a price tag on it. Such a big number you got to figure that's how come they left it on. I looked in there and seen there was something glass, caught the light and made daggers out of it. Reached my hand down and come out with it and what do you know—a rock, the good kind, the color red. *Like blood*, I thought. Like somebody died and here's what they coughed up, little bloody gem of a heart. I put it in my pocket, on account of they didn't probably need it if here it was, thrown in a jar what still got the tag on. If it turned out it was worth something I could hawk it.

The place reminded me so much of the living room at the Madam's that before I left I's looking up around the corners of the walls for cameras just in case, looking at the mirrors thinking well who's behind there. Then it was lights off and through the kitchen I already seen enough of, though I stopped quick to lift another bottle of wine from the fridge—one somebody already been working on— took it into the TV room with me. I turned the light on and seen it was messy just like his folks left it, *TV Guide* and slippers on the floor next to Daddy Bear's chair, knitting next to Mama B's.

What's a guy like So-called got for a room's what come to me.

So I took for the stairs and gone easy up them, sidestepped the creaks. Top landing was pictures all along the hall what gone to doors either side. Enough pictures of Special Boy to make you sick. Sure they think he's special: They ain't never got out the TV room and seen nobody else.

Weren't but one door open, and I knowed it was his.

* * *

Before long I got the lay of Lady J's place figured out, and then I's looking all around.

On account of she wouldn't tell me nothing, or let me do nothing either. Been there three days and two nights and here going on another and she wouldn't let me lift a finger, wouldn't let me out of her sight. She wouldn't take her eyes off me when they's open, so I waited until she gone to bed at night and closed them, laid her head down next to them shotguns. Then I snuck out of the room I been staying in, back of the house—one she practically walked me back to come nighty-night time like to make sure I got in bed and shut my eyes too, like she's locking me in there for safekeeping. It was dark and musty in there, smelled like nobody, not even Grandma, been back there before she opened the door and put me in. Just a bed and a dresser, window what been boarded up to tack on a garage. It was off a big room got all kind of boxes in it, boxes I ain't got time or the guts to look through, on account of she might come in any second and there I'd be, middle of things got my hands dirty, digging around.

Course, the room with the boxes ain't been used in years, ain't that just the way; got boxes stacked on top of boxes, and up above's the highest ceiling you ever seen, on account of this been a two-story room, and when I looked up I seen why. Overhead was a balcony, weren't but two feet wide of walking space on a landing, only thing holding anything back from falling off's a flat piece of pine tacked up for a railing. Landing got a bookcase along it, full of some books but more than anything it was *National Geographics*—big yellow blocks of color on the shelves. And at the end of the landing's a door peeking open just the littlest bit. If I could get up to that balcony and through that door I could look around all I wanted, in private, stuff the bed with blankets so's nobody'd ever know I's missing.

But where was the stairs; I couldn't see them nowheres. Like I say, ain't that just the way. How to get through the damn door if a body can't get to it in the first place? I looked all around the room, through boxes stacked waist-high, and higher, believe you me, so high in so many places they cut parts of the room off from others. There was paths cut through them but just barely, like somebody started to find their way through but figured they already seen all there was to see back here and let the boxes stack back up like grass growed over a footpath. I walked behind one wall of boxes come up to my head, and found a couch, and on top of that couch was them black and white pictures of my ma and her sisters, way I remembered them.

Got the gold frames around them, only those was mostly dull

from dust. Even the pictures theirselves got a good layer over them. I got up as close as I could, several feet away held back by the boxes and other things in the way, stared at them like they got something to tell me, seen Ma in the middle, fresh-scrubbed, tiny little thing. Edna and Millie. But they made me sad, sitting back here like dirty secrets, like maybe there was something about them a body shouldn't see, after all, and that's why they's back here like this covered in everything. If I could of took them—if they was small enough I could of fit them in my bag—I'd of done it. But they was too big, specially all together, and seemed to me like the three of them should *stay* together, even if nobody cared they's here.

Finally I found the stairs, gone up steep behind one of them walls of boxes, far corner of the room, wall I thought been the wall of the room itself. Them stairs stood between the two like it was all they could do not to let theirselves get squeezed out. They's a straight shot to the landing, and now I knowed where they was I gone back to the room to make a body on the bed, took blankets off the foot of the mattress, quilts out of the top shelf of the closet, poked and slapped them until I got them the way I wanted, then put the bedspread over loose to look like a body. When I got to the door, I turned quick trying to see it like somebody'd maybe walked into the room for the first time, and the thought hit me it looked like Pa on his back, head stacked up, and it was all I could do to take my eyes off it.

Gone up them steps as quiet and slow as you please. All along the wall there's animal heads, deer and boar I guess and whatnot. All of them got these wide eyes, saddest you ever seen—the memory of the bullet. I would of pet them on account of even if they's dead and it wouldn't of made them feel any better it would of done for me, but I couldn't feel sure they's dead after all, and I's scared if I reached my hand out maybe I'd get bit. Worst was up at the top, almost throwed me off the landing, straight through the flimsy pine beam; across the way was another ledge I ain't seen from the ground, got a coyote on it baring his fangs, hair standing on end, back of his neck and tail. I thought for sure I's a goner and froze like they says to do when you seen a snake, but that coyote weren't but stuffed, might of been ready to attack but wouldn't never get the chance.

I walked along the landing and pushed the door open oh so slow. Felt along the wall inside for a switch thinking, *What kind of animal's*

167

in here? Found it and flick, everything lights up; just a big room with more boxes and some chiffarobes, got a plywood floor and muslin walls, bunch of silver air ducts. But I ain't got nothing against boxes, it's just I need some privacy to get a good look in them I ain't supposed to look in, so right off I gone to the nearest ones and started poking through. First one I come to was old bottles—so many shapes and sizes and weren't none of them good for nothing up here stored away. I would of give up on them but got to make sure there weren't nothing else at the bottom of the box, so I dug through to the end, and found more bottles.

Up here was a lot of them framed pictures, got my ma or Edna or whoever else staring at me every time I turned around. Even when I seen they's just pictures I found I's explaining myself, explaining why I's sneaking around up here in my own grandma's house. *Cause I got to,* I told myself. *What do you expect? How else 'm I supposed to figure it all out? Ain't like the rest of you, what don't seem to care not to know, or knows but don't care to talk about it. You'd do the same if you was me,* I said to myself, even though I knowed the only ones done the same as me wasn't around no more to look at or get looked at by. What with Pa dead, and Grandaddy run off with his tail between his legs to join him.

Mostly it was just dishes and clothes, souvenirs; found a menu in one of the suitcases was up there; menu from when Elvis sung in Las Vegas I guess it said on the back, some hotel. Course it made me think about the man what give me a ride to the Greyhound. Then a loud noise near shook me out of my pants, like somebody running a car into a wall, sent my heart racing—still racing, even after I figured out it been the air kicking in through the ducts. Looked over that way and seen there was something—some box tops or other—peeking out from the other side, sandwiched between the ducts and the wall. I climbed over the things in my way until I got to them, seen they's boxes full of pictures and negatives and slides.

I pulled them boxes out from behind there and don't you know near every picture my grandaddy ever took was inside. Pictures of Ma and Grandma and the rest of them: at Christmas all dressed up like elves; roasting barbeque over a grill in the yard; birthdays holding up the cake, their faces lit up by the candles; dressed in blue and white check dresses on the way to their first day of school like it said on the back; Grandma out in the woods holding wildflowers in her hands; and every kind of flower by itself close up like to study. I held some of them slides up to the light and they come to life full color like whole worlds on the tip of a matchstick.

One stack was aerial shots of Buford, took before Lake Vagabond got anything to do with it and after, I guess to map things out: roads snake in and out and trees what took it from there, the river, strong as ever and can't nothing stop it Spring River. Then come all the pictures of the women folk, not Grandma holding the flowers no more but pretty stranger girls, like the flowers been snatched out of Grandma's hands and put in theirs. Girls on rafts in the water, playing at the falls in their bathing suits, dipping their hands in to get a grab of the river. I felt bad for Grandma; so bad I's ashamed I ever been on the river somehow.

At the very bottom was pictures of my ma and pa. Ma got a baby in her arms and I seen it was me.

It weren't possible to get a good look at all of it up there, stooped over the way I been, bad light and all the framed pictures staring at me, telling me I should leave well enough alone. So I picked one of them boxes and started out with it—aimed to take it downstairs and hide it in the closet of my room. Shut the light on my way through the door and got across the landing to the top of the stairs before I seen Grandma sitting down there in a rocking chair, shotgun laid across her lap and propped on the armrests.

* * *

All over his room's pictures, posters of vans, like the one he got but not nearly, souped up and ready to go. Kind what's got the camper on top, little hoity-toity house on wheels. Along one wall he got models on a shelf, of cars like the ones in the pictures, sitting up there pointed towards the middle of things like they's going somewheres. None of that was anything to me neither way.

I gone to his window, looked down to the driveway at his van and thought about him sleeping inside. So he's got what he wanted, I thought. He's in that van and don't never have to come out, even at his own place.

For a while I stared at the setup—the way the streets been laid perfect, squares and crisscross straight up and down, all fit together so's nobody'd ever have to feel they's lost. Driveways single file. Practically all them houses the same color if they wasn't the same everything else to boot. I felt froze that way, on account of I seen enough by now to know weren't none of it real. I felt like nothing, a blur, and had to pull myself out of it.

Broke away to the bed—had a seat. Cozy. Seen he got more pillows than a body could do with, bed fixed straight like it ain't ever got used. And I hated him more than ever, or at least finally figured out why. Here he was, got all this—I mean, anything he thought he might try out was his for the whim—and he's out there wasting it, motherfucker. Here he's got these folks don't care what he do, folks straight out of a kit. He could parade through the place with a marching band and fireworks, could raise all kind of stink and they wouldn't know the difference. Instead, he's sleeping out in the van like he got it rough, taking his food out there like he got to eat on the lamb.

So I stood up and took a good long piss on that bed.

In his closet he got all kinds of junk hid. Best was the plastic Toys "R" Us bag full of mags, pictures of guys and girls going at it like there been more than money involved. These was like I can't tell you how many peoples I knowed before. I seen the looks on their faces and they might as well of been just about anybody I run with in New York City. Mouth drooling, eyes wide, seems they's hungry for love and the one they's with, when really anybody's met a one of them knows it ain't love they's looking for, ain't hardly, least not in front of a flashbulb. No matter where a body goes—from Colorado to New York City to Tennessee—it's just peoples staring at pictures of other peoples like this, pretending they know them, when if they seen them for real they wouldn't let them through the front door, wouldn't want nothing to do with them peoples unless they got as much say over them that way, in the flesh, as they done with the pictures.

I throwed those aside and dug deeper. Mostly it was just clothes what still got the price tags on. I took the ones I thought I could use and slung them over my shoulder so's to take them down to my bag and change them for the old ones I got from Walrus or whoever else. Found a camera and took that too. Polaroid with film left in it and a cord around so I slung it over my neck. Take some godamn pictures of my own for a change.

But nothing else was anything I ain't seen before, and it bored me.

I's glad I ain't got things like this, things what never get used and even when they done they's kept like new. I closed the door and gone to a desk what got a clip-on lamp give it a glow. On top's stacks of shit he dropped off, I guess from when he come up to the room to pretend like he lived in it, in between making like he didn't. I gone through some of it: postcards from aunts and uncles, *wish you was here*, here and there, only—duh—by the time he got it they ain't even been there no more; report card from school, got the Wite-Out set next to it like he been trying to change the grades but give up when he seen he couldn't, or figured his folks wouldn't never ask to see it nohow.

Then I seen the picture of Red. The one I lost, or so I thought at first, until I seen it weren't black and white but color, took somewheres before or after we met in Nebraska. Hair weren't red no more but blond, and even his clothes wasn't the same. Before, it was the scuffed jeans and the red coat, looked like it been around more than he done. Here he got on hippy-dippy threads; Mr. Beaded Necklace, tie-dye T-shirt and all the rest, like So-called got his hands on him and give peace a chance. It weren't the Red I knowed. He done just what I thought—gone to another place and slap-wham he's a different person altogether. I studied the space around him, tried to figure where he been when it got took. But weren't a thing in focus but his self. He could of been anywheres.

Grabbed that thing and tore out, swift down the stairs two at a time, run through the front door without I remembered I got the bottle of wine in my hand or them clothes on my person. Bottle hit the wall as I gone through, sent itself crashing on the entryway floor— bloodred streaks across the white marble and the clothes what fell too. *If that don't wake them zombies upstairs nothing will.* Only thing that kept the camera from flying was the cord choking my neck. I took it and hid it under my shirt, so's I'd at least get that out of the deal.

He was still sound asleep in the van, sucking his thumb like Little Boy Blue, when I shoved the door open, stood there screaming at him to wake the hell up. Yelling at the top of my lungs how all along he knowed Red and ain't told me, and here he seen I's looking for him.

"Don't you know how crazy I been to find this asshole?"

And I got to put up with the slow waking up, rubbing his eyes like the sun's shining through lace curtains and it's a brand-new day. "Just get your ass up, wake the shit up. Look here."

I shoved the picture not two inches away from his eyes.

"What's into you?" he says, so groggy you'd think he ain't never woke up without his breakfast set out on the table.

"You lied to me, said you didn't know Red, didn't say a damn thing. What—he tell you not to say something to me? That it?"

He tried to take the picture from me to look at it better but I wouldn't let go. I weren't about to lose another one. I figured he or somebody else got it coming to me. Instead, he brung my hand lower, finally took his eyes off me like it been all he could do to tear them away. Studied it a few seconds, then this look come over him what got him pinched between the eyes.

"*Who's* red?"

And that done it.

"Don't try to back out now I got the picture right in front of you. You know exactly who Red is, he's right there," and I shook myself free from his grip, danced the picture around in front of him like he already seen it and knowed damn well what it looked like.

"That's *Robert*," he says. "Robert . . . Quinn, or Gwynn or something."

"It's Red and you know it."

"Look. His name's Robert and I barely know him. Not Red—not that *I* know of. Maybe he used to be Red."

"Damn right he used to be."

Then it hit me, how Shorty, the guy in the tent, didn't know Red neither, least not by that name. Hit me maybe I's the one didn't nobody know.

"Can you take me to him—this what's his name?"

The front door swung open and out come the man of the house, got his hands on a gun the size of cop shows, pointing it at me, says get away from his son—porch lights start popping on one after another all up and down the street.

* * *

"You don't need that thing with me, Grandma," I says.

She got the shotgun trained between my eyes, picked it up and took aim the minute she seen me come through the attic door. Couldn't barely hold it like anybody else would; got to set it up on her wrist, pencil in the trigger like a lever. Course I could of run halfways around the room before she got a bullet squeezed out but I didn't want to hurt her feelings. I wanted on her good side.

"I ain't as much your grandma as you like to think you's my grandson," she says, which stumped me.

"Sure I is. I's in the pictures." And I nodded to the box in my hands like to say so.

"I been on the phone with your ma," she says, and course I's worried this been coming from the minute I got to her house. Only a matter of time before Ma told her what she told the rest.

"She says you do this everywhere you go, sneak around rifling through people's things. Take what you want and don't care who misses it. Says you'd steal the dimes off a dead man's eyes. You go put that back where you took it from, and show me what's in your pockets."

I set the box down, showed her there weren't nothing in my pockets but my own hands turning them out, but she ain't put the gun down. "There's that box and a couple more full of pictures up there," I says. "Must of been lost. Got shoved up under the ducts. All Grandaddy's pictures. Edna says he asked about them until the day he died, said—"

"Edna should keep her mouth shut and tend to her own knittin'. Those pictures got nothing to do with me."

"Sure they do. You's all over them, almost every one. And Ma. Edna and Aunt Millie too. Bunch of peoples I don't recognize but we's all there. I's just bringing them down now we know where they is."

"Only thing I'm bringing them down for's to burn them. And you shouldn't be sticking your hands in things ain't yours. You know what they do to peoples for looking the wrong way up here? Take them places they don't want to go, and nobody asks questions, and I got a mind to teach you a lesson."

But I couldn't figure it out. "That what all this here's about? Fact I gone up in your attic? I know it's wrong. It's wrong but I ain't really done nothing up there. I mean, I don't know nothing about so many things seems like I should. Grandaddy—but not just Grandaddy, everybody else too. I only know what I been told, and all I ever been told was tend to my own knittin'."

"Ain't nothing to know," she says, and I could tell the gun's getting heavy. Her hands was shaking but she wouldn't bring it down an inch.

"I promise I won't never go up there again."

"No. You won't. See them magazines?"

She raised the gun a whit to point out the *National Geographics* behind me on the bookshelves of the landing. I seen them, but they didn't mean nothing to me. I nodded anyways.

"You like to look so much, start looking through those. Keep looking, until you find a place you aim to go. Long as it ain't too far your mama and I'll give you the money and get you on your way. You just make sure it's far enough."

"I don't want to go nowheres," I says. "I's fine right here: You and me."

"You is but I ain't," she says.

"But I know if you'd just settle down and hear me out you'd see how much we got in common. I don't care about Grandaddy, if that's what this is about. I don't care about them pictures. I won't never bring that up again. I been just as screwed over as you. We got that in common."

"I don't know what's got you screwed in the head, boy. We ain't nothing alike, except for the one of us has some girl in him shouldn't. Nobody in this family but you goes off like that, takes money from men, and you a man yourself on top of it all. You think nobody knows what goes on with you? You think you can just traipse through these parts like a tomcat without a worry to what it makes the rest of us look like?"

"I guess I ain't never thought about nothing I done made nobody else look like anything in particular."

"None of us can say who come out of us or not, but that don't mean we have to take on the burden of a no-good for life. You's just like him—ain't you?—go off with whoever whenever. Spitting image, come back thinking you can sweet-talk everybody when you see how rough things is out there. Now I want you to go through them picture books and find a place."

* * *

It was so late at night that So-called said we wouldn't be able to find Red, or Whatsisname, until morning. Just fine by me, I says, we'll sit and wait.

We drove all the way back into town, past the dark of those damn mountains I seen just about enough of for the past however many days, point I thought I's about to heave myself dizzy. Talked all the way, Mr. Questions. Wanted to know how come Whatsisname weren't Whatsisname but Red.

"You and me both," I says.

Wanted to know how I knowed Red, and why I's so crazy looking for him. "You queer or something?" he says. I sure as hell is, I told him, "but don't flatter yourself. If it made a damn difference to you you'd of knowed it by now, so close your damn trap and I'll tell you to open it when I got some good use to put it to." He shifted in the driver's seat a whit and kept looking at me in the rearview mirror, like I might have me more than one name myself. But I wouldn't tell him nothing, not just on account of it weren't none of his business but I needed to think, and now I's so worked up it was harder than ever to breathe. Instead I looked straight ahead at the road racing against us into the lights of the van, listened to the putter of the engine like somewheres in it was the way we were.

Seen Red's face in the road, no clearer than it ever been since I lost the picture—fading in and out, eyes staring hard like the last time I seen him. At least that I remembered. I got the new picture but that weren't Red, not really, so I wouldn't look at it unless I had to; even so, the black and white, the picture I always seen, was blurring at the face, and now I seen the color one, him with the blond hair, I's filling it in without I could help it.

He didn't want to see me again, and now here I was and weren't a thing he could do about it.

A pair of headlights broke into the rearview from behind us, clouded Red's picture all the more. Who the fuck else come out this time of night, I's thinking, until my eyes adjusted enough I could block them out, and I seen Red again. Just the two of us cars out on the road, drove into town, "ghost town," I says. Like the nights I slept in the fountainbed. "Ain't a soul around," after the other car turned a corner quiet and disappeared, and So-called started asking questions again. I told him pull over, I got to think.

"You've been thinking ever since I met you," he says. "Haven't you thought it all through yet?"

"You think I know anymore'n you do?"

He parked and started rolling a joint.

"No you don't," I says. "No sir. I need to keep clear for this. Let's go get some wine."

"But you already drank all the bottles we got out of the fridge," he says, starts whining like I's his mommy telling him I ain't got him what he wanted for Christmas. "How much more can you drink? We could go back to sleep; We got until morning. I'm not even sure he'll be in tomorrow. He might have a night shift."

"So where's it at?" I says.

And he pointed across the street and down a ways, said:

"He works in the restaurant down there. Busboy."

"*Busboy*," I practically squealed. "All this time I been wasting and he's right down the street under my nose scrubbing plates! Right down the goddamn street. And I's wasting all this time with *you*."

"Not a dishwasher. A *busboy*," he said, and he started rolling his joint again, talking under his breath about how if it wasn't for him I wouldn't never of found Red, right down the street or no. And he got a point there.

We gone to get a bottle of wine at a liquor store what was just about to close. I talked So-called into spotting for it on account of he been right, if it weren't for him we wouldn't neither of us be in this mess. Then we sat in the van, me drinking the bottle to myself. I let him have his joint, long as he cracked the driver's window so's I wouldn't get a contact high.

"You're high enough to last three days already," he says, but he ain't never seen me on dope.

I watched the street like it was a movie where something's set to happen, thought *When the sun comes up I'll see it on them buildings, and then it's just a matter of time*. Weren't a sound or stir but for once in a long while when a car—maybe the one from back on the highway but I couldn't tell—come through like waiting for something of its own. "See it's not altogether a ghost town," So-called says and laughs, like I's so stupid I figured we's the only ones in the world.

Idiot: I just said it felt like it.

When I seen the sun wouldn't be coming up for a while and it was safe to think some other things into order, I leaned back and thought about the joke called my life, knowed it's supposed to start where the seed hits the chicken or the egg or whatnot, but like everything else it weren't that way with me. I should of gone with Pa's what, ain't none of this would of happened; should of gone through with the thing of trying to do like he done, whatever it was, then none of this here would of happened. But who's got all that time to sit around waiting for it on a bed?

Instead I let him slip away, get put in the ground, and I's stuck with Ma, who couldn't figure what to do with me. Sends me—what—to Nana, who don't know no better. From there to Mojo's, then streets of Memphis, hello life on the street. Turning tricks, for I don't know what: Never thought about it. Too busy thinking about the rest. Stealing too: Somehow Ma and Nana and the rest looked at me and knowed I's a thief even before I done. Tried to tell me all that time but I didn't believe it until I seen it for myself, I wouldn't shut my mouth long enough to hear it's what they says, and then I knowed why my hands was always moving towards other people's things weren't mine. Maybe if I'd of stayed with them I'd of got the help I needed to stop before I started. Grandma in Buford, that been the only answer I knowed, long time ago when I thought I could go back. So I done all I could to get there, saved my money the only way I knowed how, turning a big enough trick to pay for things in one shot. Gone across the bridge on the bus, met the Tawenow boy. Fletcher: Oh yeah, him.

Weren't no good the last time we talked. But I didn't even cry on my way out of there, like it weren't the hell it was. Thought I's a man that way, thought I's bucking up, wouldn't leave or come back bawling neither way like Grandma said my kind done. She said I ain't never growed up, and I aimed to prove her wrong. Get on with things—get on with it even if I couldn't get it together. No more Buford; no going back.

Draw a number, she said, pick a city, and I figured New York's the place, on account of it weren't too wide across and looked like it's just blocks stacked together, easy enough. Seen a map and a article in one of them magazines said how New York City's where all the Problem Kids goes, just like what they all said I was, so how come I ain't never heard of it. *No wonder*, I thought. *I been in the wrong place all this time. If you's going to make a living with Good Old Boys you got to go where the bucks is.*

So Grandma figured out how to get me there and drove me to the station, had to steer the wheel with the palms of her hands on account of the shape the fingers was in. Only way she could close the door on her side of the car was to gun the motor then slam on the brakes, so's the force swung the door shut without she got to move a muscle she ain't got in the first place. Talked the whole way there, things I could of done without, then dropped me off and said good luck.

I wanted to ask her for a few bucks to get me through the trip, case I needed something to eat or some smokes, but then it struck me she weren't like a trick I could haggle with. So I's practically broke when I got off the bus and Hello New York. Hello Madam and the House, guys my age and even there I couldn't make it work. It was then I started to figure out I ain't meant to live in a house like regular peoples does. But I shacked up with Walrus like to give it one more try and boy was that a mistake. So I left him, and ended up on the street, trying to make that work around the Deuce, Mannie or no. Done the junk from one place to the other, and more of it as I gone along, then right back to Walrus's, like everywheres else, I gone back. Wondered now, was he dead on the bedspread like I left him, or maybe he got up and found him another boy like he said he would. Plenty of boys what needs a home, he said. Then right back to the Madam's door. And she talked this idiot into going to Nebraska again, though now I seen it weren't but to get me off her hands.

Big zero in Nebraska, and here's where it gets me every time, when I make it thinking that far: Seems like I gone back so much things turn into a big circle of a blur, fold back in on theirselves like to tell the story all over again the same way but more even more confused.

Well, I might go back to a lot of things, but I's damned if I's going back to dope.

I looked out on the street, seen the sun's about coming up. Thought, *Thank God I ain't got to think about none of that no more, now I found Whatsisname.*

* * *

I didn't get much sleep that last night in Buford, sat up eyes-wide in the back room after Grandma walked me there and shut me in. She still got the gun, but down to her side so's at least I didn't feel like it might of gone off if I said the wrong thing. Weren't I thought she's outside the door or nothing's how come I stayed up, just I sat there thinking over things—what's the plan, so to speak, for the rest of my life.

New York City.

I asked her could I look through them magazines before we left and get me all the ones said anything about the place—what the people's like lives there, weather, anything. All I knowed about it was there was Broadway, Times Square, Statue of Liberty, I don't know. And she let me take the few what said something. Got me a map to keep and some articles what talked about Broadway since way back, like I cared, but still there was some good pictures.

So I got them spread out on the bed with me, got to staring at them, then my mind gone off thinking, then stare again, trying to figure what would them pictures look like with me in them. But even though I knowed what I looked like I couldn't see me there, or anybody looked like me. Maybe I ain't supposed to go there's what I got to thinking, worrying about's what. But Grandma and Ma and everybody else said I's flighty, and I wanted to prove I got stick-to-it-iveness.

Must of drifted off sitting up, sometime later when the quiet of the room swallowed up my thoughts. Woke up with them pictures bent around my legs and licked to me in places from nightsweat. I peeked through the curtains next to the bed to see was the sun out, and sure enough it was waking up just like me, seen it come through the cracks of the board held the garage at bay. Thought about going outside, say good-bye to Lady J's property, kiss the air or what so long. Thought, *Well, maybe not, on account of she might be out there waiting with the gun.* That's just the kind of thing I guess she'd expect I might do. But I ain't never really got to know the place enough to say hello or see you later neither one anyways.

Sitting in there dressed and ready to go without I could leave to get Grandma and tell her come on, I realized I didn't like her much. Didn't like her and didn't have to, not if she didn't like me. I could think anything I wanted about her, and everybody else, cause if nobody'd put me up I didn't owe them nothing. And if I didn't care what she thought, and as long's she weren't standing outside the door with that gun, there weren't nothing to keep me from seeing her property one last time. I didn't have to make up a reason to do it; didn't need no reason at all. Reason was I felt like it.

So at the door I knocked quiet, two times, and called her name. Figured if she ain't here to keep me in or out she can kiss my ass, and she weren't. I opened it a creak and seen the room outside was just as quiet and empty, so I gone in, moved towards the door let onto the outside. Some chest of drawers in the corner caught my eye, on account of I realized she already thought I's a thief so why didn't I take something to remember her by. I pulled them drawers open slow as I could—seen the top ones was linens, frilly doilies she probably ain't never used, but why would I want a thing like that.

The middle drawers was the jackpot, got mostly junk but a dig underneath turned up a long box got a man's watch inside. I left the box but took the watch. Since it got a stretch band I thought to put it around my ankle, under my sock. I knowed damn well the old lady'd check me before we gone, strip search if she could. It rubbed against my pants on my way to the door and I smiled on account of I knowed I's the only one could feel it, not stupid peoples think they know so much.

Not two feet outside my shoes was covered with wet from the grass. Great: *Now she'll know I been sneaking around.* But I weren't sneaking, cause I didn't care who knowed. Anyways, she done said as much about me already so what I got to prove. I walked all the way to the field out back of her house, where the land come up on a mound for what used to be a pond, got pine trees all the way around, just this perfect circle dish of land what used to be full of water. Now dried up, empty bowl with flakes of dirt crusted up in the bottom—big surprise. And all the way around the property there, a barbed wire fence strung along rotted wood posts. Used to be they got a Shetland pony what all the girls, three sisters, got to ride, got the fence to keep him in. Pony got sold to somebody or other what turned it to glue, nearly broke them girls' hearts even though they didn't find out about it until later when the truth slipped out and by that time they couldn't remember the pony enough to make sure he ever really been there, and ain't got no heart left anyways.

Here they was trying to forget all this—the pony and the pond, Grandaddy's pictures, Grandaddy his self. All of them so busy trying to forget so's soon enough it was like them things never happened. I ain't seen none of it, only halfways heard it here and there when things slipped out. I stored it and took it out once in a while to put pieces together. But I ain't never seen a whit of it, not one. Them trying to hide it away, and when I dig it out and keep for my own what anyways nobody else wants, they said I's a thief. Well; so be it.

So be it.

I gone back inside, opened the drawer and was just putting that watch back in its box when I hear my grandma's voice.

"Never stop, do you? And you'll go crying to somebody sure enough how you've been turned out I bet. Turned out for no reason, poor you."

She was standing in the doorway, old thing, without she got the gun up and pointed but don't you know it was right there at her side. *Who's the sneak,* I thought. *Everytime I turn around she's slinked up out of nowheres.*

She drove me downtown, past the kudzu covered trees again, the log cabin off to the side of the road what said Pie Lady sold pies there. *Peoples who live here sees this stuff every day,* I thought, *pass by it every day of their lives.* Some parts the road curved so fast like to throw the car off the pavement and over the side rail without a warning. I tried to count how many peoples I thought got killed that way, instead of looking at things I wouldn't never see again anyhow.

And not a word from her, not even to tell me more about my nature, way she put it. So I got to thinking what she'd say if she *was* talking.

I's no good. *Cause I ain't the way she and everybody else is, don't like girls, even though she herself don't like girls neither, ain't got the patience for them, or so Aunt Millie says, just boys, like me but not. I steal from peoples I shouldn't steal from, meaning I guess her and Ma and Nana, peoples wouldn't give me nothing even if I asked, cause if I asked I's greedy. I get nothing cause I take things, but if I left things alone I'd still be a thief; I tried it that way before. I's a thief cause I's born that way. I's a thief before I figured it out. And now I'd figured it out weren't nothing I could do about it but go away.*

She got out her pack of cigarettes, kept her eye on the road. Put the cigarette in her mouth but couldn't find the lighter. Sat there with that thing hanging off her lips for I don't know how long without I could stand it no more, so I asked did she want me to find her lighter for her, and she mumbled the go ahead like she didn't much care neither way. Don't know how she'd of found the thing, shoved into the bottom like it was, got her hands on the wheel. I fixed her cigarette in her mouth and one in mine, lit the things ladies' first—got girl in me or no—and started to put the things what falled out of her purse back in; still, no word from her. I studied the lines on her face, so deep and gone from her forehead to her chin, thought under there somewhere's the Lady J become my grandma.

When she seen I's staring at her she snapped I should mind my own business, and started telling me everything she could think of, which I been trying to get her to do all weekend, but now she's saying it like she's spitting on me. Told me my Nana's got what's called Alzheimers, what'd I think of *that;* said she's forgot everything, including her own kids, said they got to take her out of her house on account of she'd started burning things, they's afraid the whole thing'd come down. She said things trigger it—what Nana got—and if anything been a trigger it was me and the way I run out on her, sneaked around her house then run away and all over town.

Then she told me how she talked to Ma on the phone last night while I's snooping around upstairs; how she ain't talked to Ma forever but maybe she should of, on account of then she might of knowed about me before I showed up, and what the one knowed could of warned the other. Said Ma's the one what told her about Nana misremembering, even though I's the one told Ma before anybody else done—way back when I's living with her and she's always talking to herself, couldn't find her necklace or her own backside. But it was Ma knowed it, found out not from me but cause of me, cause of when I run out Nana gone off.

Then Ma started crying to Grandma's what Grandma said, crying on the phone cause maybe it been her fault I turned out the way I done, on account of when I's a baby and she's home alone with me, I cried and cried, wouldn't stop and Pa nowheres in sight. Shh, she said, it's all right. Shhh. But I wouldn't, kept on wailing, and she ain't knowed what else to do, so she put her hand over my mouth. Just to get me to keep quiet a little's all, my grandma says, looks at me like anybody would of done it in her shoes and I should try to say something bad about it after all I myself done in my own damn shoes, I's one to talk. Just to keep me quiet but even that didn't work, course that got me crying harder, so she kept her hand there until I's fast asleep, passed out cold. And that shut me up good. Done it just the once, until I cried again later and made her do it again.

"You ain't never knowed when to shut your mouth," my grandma says. "And ain't nobody's fault but your own. Can't go on blaming us and everybody else. Time to grow up and get on with things."

At the bus station she seemed nervous, looked around the car, asked me did I get everything. "I only got the one bag," I says, confused, on account of she made it sound like she give me something to take with me. "Same bag I always got." And when I closed the door and I's walking away she said good-bye, stern like I should know better than to act like I's happy to hear it. I turned and didn't bother watching her drive off. Just heard the wheels crunching on the gravel, the engine pick up as it shot onto the main road. No use trying to look at what weren't never there.

She'd handed me the money for the bus when we's getting in the car at the house, said if I spent it on anything else don't bother coming back trying to get more; didn't leave me a lick more than the cost of the ride, I's lucky to get that. She said I better not spend it unless I got some other way to get out of town, on account of if she caught word or sight of me there it wouldn't be pretty, and wouldn't nobody know she got a thing to do with it, or blame her once she told them why. Might as well not try to do what I done other places, she said, on account of there weren't peoples like that in Buford.

Weren't until I's staring at the few spare coins of change in my hand I remembered Fletcher and it come to me I weren't just leaving my grandma but him too.

I looked up to Tawenow Hill, thought how it was just a few yards away to the stone arch what let onto the property. Looked up and seen the flash of his folk's house hanging off the cliff, thought, *I can see it now; I been up there and I can see it.* Thought how it looked like it's about to fall off, but that cliff's a stone more solid than most of the houses I been in. And thought I could get there too. But I already got my ticket; weren't no time to trek up and back, and Fletcher wouldn't of knowed how to say good-bye face to face any better'n me. Instead I thought to call his house with one of them quarters.

Looked him up in the little book what got everybody's name in Buford—dialed Diffy 2468, and there come his ma on the phone I guess. I asked for her boy, and wondered if she could tell from my voice I's a thief and a never-was, like Grandma said everybody else could. I didn't want to get him into any trouble.

"Fletcher here," he says, and I couldn't talk at first.

"It's me," I finally spit out.

He asked how things was going at my grandma's, and I said fine, I got to leave. What was I talking about, he says, and didn't I want to stay with him for a while?

"No. I can't; I got to go."

"Go *where*? Come to the river. I'm leaving in a few minutes for the dock."

It struck me I ain't never been the one had to say good-bye before. I didn't want to say it like it been said to me, on account of I knowed how bad that felt. So I says "Listen: I don't want you to never think I'll forget you, cause I won't. I couldn't I don't think, even if I wanted to and I don't. I'll remember Never Inn, them photo books, the home movies, the dock. I won't forget—"

"What happened?" he says, like I weren't making sense.

But I knowed even though it might not make sense now it would later when he thought back on it, since things in his life seemed to go in a order where he could do that kind of thing.

"I can't stay like I wanted. I's off to New York City instead. I finally figured it out," I lied. "All along I's supposed to be there. That's where my kind goes, and so I's on my way. You ever been?"

"I can't go to *New York City*," he said. "And neither can you."

"I ain't asking you, much's I wish I could. I know you don't belong nowheres but here, but I can't say the same for myself. I just figured a different place'd be better. No hard feelings. For a minute I thought maybe that changed, but it's about the only thing what stays the same—so what can you do? I been reading a lot about New York City. Says peoples like me goes there every day. Says we step off the bus, train, boat or tops of buildings every minute. I can't remember the numbers: I won't be lonely I don't guess. But I appreciate all you done. I ain't never had a better time in my life I don't think. If it was up to me I'd spend the rest of it on the Spring River with you, let it take me and you both wherever."

"Look," he says, "stay where you are, you're talking crazy. Where are you? I want to come get you."

I almost told him—almost let him. Cause I wanted him to. But what would the two of us done in Buford without my grandma on our side? And if I managed to get her and Ma and Nana and who knows else against me, wouldn't be long to work over him neither.

"I'm on my way's where. So just listen. I ain't got long to talk. Just know I won't forget, all right? I might put it out of my head, I might have to—I give you that. But I won't throw you out for good. You'll always be there. All I got to think's red hair and freckles, and all the rest we done at Never Inn'll come back to me and can't nobody take it away. Okay?"

He said okay but he didn't sound sure. So I said it again, told him how pretty I thought he was, prettier than anybody, whereas I's what my grandma says they call disaffected.

"God, don't say that," he says, and he tried to argue with me. Said *his* door was always open, *he* always got the latch string out for me. Said I got just as much place to be in Buford as he done or anybody else.

Yeah, right, I thought. *That's how come I got a bus ticket in my hand and a sore ass from looking for a place to spend the rest of my life all night, and if a toady frog had wings he wouldn't bump his ass.* But I kept my mouth shut: He meant better than anybody I ever knowed.

"No, it's true and so what," I says. "There's disaffecteds like crazy in New York City's what I read. All over. They go there so's they won't be no more. Now just remember: You's thought about." And I hung up.

On the bus I closed my eyes and got the sleep I ain't got the night before. Whenever I come to, somewheres down the road, I forced them closed again like there's no tomorrow, until I's out. Told myself I's putting it all behind me and tried to picture the future.

FOUR

For a minute I come to without my eyes was open, and all I seen was the black of my lids. I thought maybe I gone blind, and then it was *where'm I at anyways?* Coming so slow out of sleep I couldn't figure what city I's in.

New York? Memphis? Had I got to the train station yet, and where was I going in the first place? Maybe I's in the car with Grandma, or I's at Graceland. But none of this could be right, I finally figured out, on account of I already knowed what come next with all that.

When I realized I's in the van, and got a sense of the sun blaring through the windshield over my face, warming me awake, I shot up like a lightning bolt thinking *Dammnit, God dammit what time is it!?* Just knowing I missed Red. I swung my head back and forth looking around the van for my ride, sure he must of left me there, elsewise he wouldn't never of let me fall asleep. But there he was in the deepest darkest corner, wedged into them damn pillow cushions ready for mummy-hood.

"Wake up, asshole," I yelled, but wished I ain't said it. I wanted to get Red on my own. Just me and him.

After a few seconds of waiting to see did I wake him up, I crept out, slid the door and left it wide open to get back at him for letting me knock out. I didn't even know what time it was—forgot to look at the clock in the van and didn't aim to go back in case it was later than I thought. The sun got that burn to it what could go either way; could be it's afternoon, midday, final peak before twilight; got the shadows laid sharp from the curbs of the buildings, cast out long and lean over the sidewalks and into the streets. Peoples walking around looked tuckered out, beat down but that could just as easy be from

186

starting a long day as finishing one. I just knowed I missed Red already.

Then I seen the car pull up in front of the restaurant, shiny antique sports car, fins on it what rose up from the back like a shark gliding along the surface of water. And out comes Red, or Whatsisname, dressed in his hippy clothes like he been hanging out with Mother Earth feeding the masses. Got on pants what flared at the bottom, sandals, a shirt loose enough to be a tent somebody pitched on his chest. But his hair's the clincher; not red no more at all, but blond, longer. He was a totally different person now and I knowed right off I better watch myself, on account of he couldn't be trusted no more'n nobody else.

I stood in the shadows of a building what got a big sign hung off the front, said in bright green letters **ENERGY,** cartoon sparks popping out the sides. Customers whipped out the door in front of me with their buys; door got a string of bells tied to it, so's every time somebody come out there's ringing and the sound they made wrinkling their paper bags. All the noise made me feel like I's in another place from Red, where he couldn't see me and things was altogether different here than where he was—all quiet glide, smooth shiny car and such.

I watched the flicker of him go to the back of the swanky car, pop the trunk and pull things out. I couldn't so much tell what they was, though some of it looked like band instruments. I thought I seen the shape of a guitar in the bundle, stuck between different sized bags. For a while he stood there staring into the trunk like he's forgetting something, like he got all the time in the world to think about it now. Stood there staring first into that trunk then up ahead at the street, and when it seemed like he decided he'd pulled out all he aimed to and he's making a move to shut the trunk, I broke out from the shadows and started towards him.

As he come around the side of his car, he recognized somebody in a group of men I ain't noticed out of the crowd before, and his face screwed into sudden anger. He's ready to fight before them folks got within ten feet of him, but it took me a little longer to figure out who they was. Weren't until I myself was fifteen feet away I seen one of them men's the guy what drug Red off from the carnie not too long ago—good old Mr. Shorty. Maybe Red looked like somebody else, but Shorty looked exactly the same—same old suit and tie and a hat to match tipped over the forehead, little shit. Got that cocky grin to him like he could handle you no matter who you thought you was. Whereas Red looked meaner'n I ever thought he could. Again I pulled off into the shadows to see what's going down.

Shorty got two others with him, all three's dressed for business. Two with him's taller and the both of them twice his bulk. They all three stopped in front of Whatsisname and formed a circle around him with Shorty in the middle, face-to-face with Red. And before a one of them got a chance to speak Red's tearing into them. I couldn't hear much of what he said, just bits and pieces—"I done that already," and "Deal's a deal." Shorty looked aside to one of his guys, and without he got to say a word the guy's moving to Red's car, got his hand out from his hip a little, walking along the driver's side up close, got his hand fisted and leading the way against the smooth yellow paint job. Red watched only until the guy's halfway down the length before he turned back to Shorty and the other one and started in again even louder, so loud this time I heard near every word.

"You said if I did my part of the deal and kept my mouth shut I could go on my way. Why the hell'd you stay out here? Why don't you go back? I ain't gonna tell anybody else anything. My mouth's shut."

Then Shorty's talking, but being he's as calm as Red's upset he was quiet and I couldn't hear nothing.

"No I didn't," said Red, defensive now, voice rising like there's a girl in there somewhere. "Nobody knows. They think I moved here from Denver, the ones who bother asking. Nobody cares where I come from. Nobody's asking. Look, it's gonna be this way for a while, I'm breaking in these shoes. But I've done this before. I mean, this is what I do. Did. This is what I did. I'm better at it than anybody else. One step ahead."

Then Shorty raised his voice enough, just enough I could hear him, and what he said didn't send shivers down me until after he done saying it and all the fury gone out of Red's face, turned to fear like he'd just woke from a bad dream.

"Good. Because it can all be taken away as easily as it was given. And if nobody cares where you came from, they won't notice when you disappear."

* * *

I hung outside the restaurant for the longest time, tried to come off like I weren't looking through the window, but with so much glare on the glass I had to stare hard.

I gone over to the curb where the car was parked, looked inside trying to figure if anything looked like the Red I thought I'd knowed. The seats was bright vinyl, cream color without a tear or scratch, like this old car been sitting somewheres in a garage since whenever it was made, ain't been driven nowheres but right into Red's hands. Hanging on the rearview mirror's a rubber toy, got string tied around its neck to keep it dangled. Just a stupid kid's toy with a idiot grin painted across its face, eyes wide with brain-dead glee.

Stuffed down into the cushions between the rests for back and ass was some piece of paper, looked like it been kept in somebody's pocket through a wash or storm, folded in half a few and beat dull, but something wrote on it: where the corners bent back enough I seen there's definitely something wrote on it. The ink weren't but bleed mostly, but holding all that blur together was the thin hard scrawl of handwriting. I come in closer to the window, put my hand to the glass around my face to stop out the light coming up from the pavement. I can't say whether I might of broke through that window to get at that piece of paper, on account of I's sure it could tell me all I needed to know.

"What the hell you think you're doing?"

And I recognized that sound anywheres. Call him Red or Ricky Rocket: the name and everything else about him might of changed beyond you could recognize him, but weren't nothing to change about the way he talked. It was that same sweet voice told me to get lost back at the carnie.

I took my hand down from the window and seen him there, got the sun in his eyes and squinting mean, but more'n one thing ain't changed and that's he looked like he got other things on his mind. I pulled away from the car and turned slow's I could to face him, watched as his face showed he's recognizing me.

His face gone from squint to eyes wide enough to take in a train wreck, and as soon as they got to the point where they looked like they couldn't get no bigger he was at me, gripping my arms hard, fingers digging through my shirt enough I thought he'd poke a hole in my chest I ain't needed there. The force sent us both against the car, rocked it on its wheels from the impact of my back hitting the passenger door. Red didn't let that stop him from trying to push me further; even though I weren't going anywheres but flat against the window he kept moving into me, got into my face and looking wild around the street like checking for anybody might of come with me before he come back like in for the kill.

"Who are you with?" he almost yelled, and he shook me.

"Nobody," I says, "I swear. Believe you me."

"How long you been following me? How long!?"

"Just . . . I left the day after you done. I been here almost's long as you, right down the street practically the whole time but—"

"Who you with? You better tell me, cause no matter who it is I got nothing to lose. Don't think I won't do you damage before they can get to you." He kept shaking me, thudding me each time against the car, looking around like whoever he thought I come with was nearby, and then I remembered the van.

"I come with this guy says he knows you, says you's Rick, or Richard? I don't know. Lay off."

But he wouldn't and I realized I didn't much care.

"Where—? Who is he? What's his name?"

"I don't know who he is. I mean I met him around, you know? I been hanging out with him a few days, in and outside his van. Until he said he knows you and I got him to bring me here."

"Make sense," he said. "Make some sense. Why'd you come here? Who are you?"

"You met me in Omaha, remember?"

I said it like to bring him to his senses but it only got the hairs on his back up higher. Without he let go of his grip on me he shoved me aside enough to see into the car. He looked in as hard as I done before he caught me, then he come back and pulled me to face him again.

"Look, asshole. What are you looking for? You better start talking. Enough with the one word answers. I ain't scared of you, any of you. I know exactly what I'm doing, and it won't be good for you if you don't tell me who you really are and the guy's name you's with."

"My name's Earl, same's I told you at the fair. I ain't got *nobody*. All right? NOBODY. Guy with the van give me some weed and a ride around and not a whole hell of a lot else but grief. I don't know his name cause I don't want to. I never bothered to get it. If you want it you can go over to where his van's parked up the street," and I pointed to the thing, still sitting a block or two away. Red looked at it like it was a trap, then back quick to me, sure I's up to something.

"No friends, no money, no cigs. Nothing. Okay? So don't get your head neck-deep up my ass looking for things ain't there. I ain't the one with the flashy car, ain't the one traded in everything for a new load of crap, clothes and car and everything else. Mr. Guitar like I's Peter Paul and Mary. Ain't the one lied about who I is. I told you from the get go. Told you I ain't got a thing; told you more'n I ever told nobody else, and beats me why cause here you's living high on the hog like somebody else not a week later, just goes to show if something's worth keeping it's worth keeping to yourself."

I gone limp in his grip to show him I weren't going to give him the satisfaction of putting up a fight to make his slinging me around legit, and he loosened his grip a little, even if he didn't move back enough to let me get much of anywheres I might of got the mind to.

"So why you here then?" he says. Asks me this like he wants to believe me but it don't make sense without that piece of the puzzle put in—got this sound in his voice like nothing I could tell him'd convince him anyways.

But I took in a deep store of air and tried. "You told me not to follow you. Remember that? Why else would you say it unless you thought I might be crazy enough to do it? So how come it surprises you now I done? I want to stay with you, whatever that means. Whatever it's like. I ain't never stayed with nobody just cause I wanted to so I ain't got the first idea how it goes or what come next. But I ain't got nothing to lose neither, and anything else I ever wanted I either got by now and seen it's a crock of shit or I ain't and know I never will. Never. So I's free. You know? Free. Whoopee, I got the power. I can do whatever I want. Not a thing to stop me, cause nobody cares what I do, long as it's get lost. And what I want, only thing's, to be right here. I don't know nothing about you. Didn't think I needed to. Now I see maybe that was wrongheaded, on account of you ain't the person I been following. You traded in the way you was for all this stuff."

I stamped the car door behind me with my open palm, which point Red crossed his arms, sneered his self into a smile what said it was too late for nothing I got to say to be good news. And even though I knowed I's supposed to get as scared off from studying him

191

as he wanted me to be, even though I's kind of squirming on account of I wanted him to let off, I stared at his hair, the sunlight wrapped around the locks rough from stripping the color off, and I thought red, black or blond, he was one of the the prettiest accidents ever.

"Did you ever stop to think that having nothing's not how everybody wants to live?" he says. "Some of us want oh just a little something; a place to stay, a street people knows to find me on. *Car*. For a long time I had all kinds of people could give me a car and some of them did. Gave me all kinds of things, things I said I wanted and things they just thought a guy like me should have, but no matter what it was, didn't matter how big or how small, it was tied to a string that led right back to whoever it come from. Just when I thought I knew what it meant for it to be mine . . . yank."

He shot his hand back, drew it up into a fist like he's set to throw a punch. Then his hand and arm both gone slack against his side.

"It don't mean nothing anyway. I'm a goner. Only reason I gone hog wild on all this shit was they offered and I probably knew better, knew deep down it wouldn't last for long whatever it was, so I took it and how."

"You got to tell me once and for all who all these peoples is," I said. "I seen that guy, that shorty dickhead and his buddies. What's going on? I know you's in trouble. I know they's after you, right? Can't do nothing about it unless you tell me."

He laughed, looked set to cry, and accidentally spit at me all at once, rolled his eyes, said.

"Oh, Mr. Bigshot; Mr. Romance. You can't do nothing about it either way. And where do you get all this inside information on me? Guy with the van, or what?"

"Madam Rosa. Remember her?"

"Madam *whosa*?"

"The lady reads heads. At the carnie. I gone to her after you left, later that night when I's looking for somebody what knowed something about you. I gone to the Gator Boy first—yeah, I met him all right. Big crock he turned out to be, but he sent me to her. She wouldn't tell me much, don't worry, just said you's in trouble, you's being followed."

"Yeah. By you. Some mind reader. Look, you freak me out, okay?

You freak me the fuck out following me all the way here. Don't even have a life of your own."

I guess it was supposed to hurt my feelings but it didn't on acount of I ain't got a lot of things and shame's just one of them.

"Don't look like you got much of one neither," I says, then we stood there staring at each other for the longest time.

"You got somewhere to shack up?" Red finally says.

"Don't worry about me."

"I *ain't* worried about you, retard. I got to find somewhere to go, lay low. Feels like everybody can see me. They're probably watching me right now, wondering who you are. Jacks'll recognize your ass from the fair, thanks to the scene you made of yourself that day. And he's gonna think what I thought, you're up to something, only he'll think I'm part of it too."

"Who's Jacks?"

He been looking around for the last few minutes, studying the scene and every person in it hard like they's a wolf in sheep's clothing. I looked too now; seen how if a body got paranoid enough nothing looked like what it was. Through the windows of shops might be going on what always gone on, or something different, play put on for show, parked cars maybe not parked at all but planted like decoys, to scope out. The worst thing was once you started looking at the peoples they started looking back, and sideways, so's you couldn't be sure whether they's up to no good or just as freaked out by you as you was them.

*   *   *

He drove us in that yellow car to a burger joint a few blocks over, sat us in a booth back in the corner where we could see the rest of the place—who come in and who sat a spell. When we'd parked outside he brung me over to the driver's side, showed me where there's a killer scratch run the length of the body, and I knowed right off that's what Shorty's man done, shook my head like to say he who give it take it away. Now in the booth he bought the two of us coffee and some fries, lit us up some cigarettes while we waited, asked me did I know who Shorty—who ain't really Shorty but Jacks—was, by looking at him.

"I'd know that face anywheres," I told him.

"No," says Red. "Do you know what line of *work* he's in?"

Told me it was the business of breaking people's bones and making sure they stayed that way; kind of guy whose way of cutting you slack's to get it all over with at once, cause usually he draws it out good and long—so's you feel it, so's you can concentrate on what he's trying to say to you.

"But why? What's he want to say to you?"

Red rolls his eyes. "I'm just gonna level with you," he says. "Just gonna lay it out cause whether you know or not, once they seen you with me they'll figure you do. See the thing about us is they know we ain't got nobody looking after us. See? Like you told me, you ain't got family, and neither do I. Not a soul would do a double take if we was there one minute and gone the next. Expendable. They liked somebody like me in the first place for that very reason—we run around on a different level than most. People see us but they don't, we can fall into the cracks. We do most of the time anyway, cause it's easier for people not to see us, so when these guys need somebody to do their shit, they got a perfect setup in us. You remember anything I told you before, back in Nebraska that day?"

"Yeah," I says. "About Boystown, how the hawks come in there to get the ones like you, how one of them come in there and took you away, to his place, right? And set you up there."

"It's more than that. They got a whole operation. Most of the guys who come in are down and out to start with. They got men working there who take the boys into their trust, okay, get to know them on such a personal level they figure which ones is ideal for them, which ones is prime candidates. These is boys that keep to themselves. Not the loud troublemakers who say one thing in one direction then rat on everybody in the other. Not the loose cannons. They want the quiet, to themselves boys: the ones that open up to all their attention.

"Talk to them quiet ones over a long period of time, sometimes months. Have to make sure it's a 'safe investment,' make sure they got these boys under their finger. Once they think they do, they set him up with a hawk. But these ain't just any hawks. These is the biggest wigs of Lincoln and Omaha. You got high-ups in police force, state university, guy whose family owns as many restaurants and hotels as you got hairs on your head. The list goes on and on. See, Boystown ain't the only place they work, either. That's just how they got me, how they get *some*. But they look everywhere. They work the streets and the clubs, the juvenile system too. They even got it set up cross-country; into California, D.C. Flying boys back and forth like they's trading cards.

"When they get a boy 'placed' is what they call it, into one of them hawk's nests, that ain't the end of it; just the beginning. They start using a lot of them to carry—middlemen. Sounds crazy I know."

But it didn't. I heard from some of the guys in the house and some who worked for Mannie how they done the same thing some-wheres or other before. Heard about the preacher man hung out around the Deuce, what took them in under his robes, got every-body on his side and can't nobody see just what kind of religion he got going on under there. Heard about pick-ups and drop-offs, only God and the preacher man knows what. Cause nobody looks twice at a kid like that.

Something caught Red's eye at the front door: His eyes lit up and he got quiet, like whoever it was could hear us from all the way across the room. He didn't say nothing more until the waitress brung over our fries, and that was just to ask me should he order some more, after he seen how crazy mad I dug into the basket. I got embarrassed, set myself back for a breather. But he said go on, said he knowed what it's like, how I probably ain't ate in days. Which weren't true. I had my fill the night before in the guy's van. But nothing since then, and for days I been feeling like I got a lot of catching up to do.

"Here's where it gets complicated. I moved up in the ranks. I started out as one of them boys, nested in a downtown penthouse, Omaha. Not bad, better than Boystown. For a few months. Didn't have to do a thing but sit around and sex as usual. But that was noth-ing. Then the hawk I'm shacked up with comes to me one day and says he knows of a way I can make some pocket money. Now, I been spoiled, idiot enough to start thinking, against my better judgment, that I was set for the long haul. All of the sudden he's coming to me telling me—what—I have to get a job. Anybody who's been in those shoes knows that's the way you read that. I figure I get a job or it's back to Boystown, and even figure if the job turns out to be so bad I'll just screw things up so they *will* want me back at Boystown off their hands. I didn't know that once I was in it there wasn't no going back to Boystown or anywhere else.

"So I start flying all over. Mostly D.C. at first, met boys like me there at parties where politicos and well-to-dos hobnobbed like a bunch of schoolgirls. Except these is some of the richest men in the world, buddies with the President, Big Man, so on and so forth. All I know is I get handed a bag in one town and carry it by jet to another. Best thing's I get away from my hawk, get some fresh air. Meet new people, even though most of them's people I wouldn't care to know anywhere else. The boys I meet's just like me only they got so much drugs and booze in them they's talking to you through closed eyes. Zombies. All done the same thing I did, one way or another. Like I said there's different levels. I moved up cause I was one of those quiet ones they take a liking to, even after all I seen. Others weren't as good at wearing different hats, didn't have the background I did, turning tricks, first in my foster home then out on the street. Before I learned anything else in life it was you's whoever the one you's with wants you to be, and so good at it they would never know you's not who you say you is."

"Yeah," I says, "I took that class too."

"D.C.'s where I met Jacks. Found out later he been watching me the whole time. See, they's all watching you, sitting on a roost deciding what they want but you's so caught up in everything, the clothes and digs and money, flying on private jets, you don't notice. Jacks comes over to me at a party one night says he's heard a lot about me. Says he's impressed. I know he ain't got a thing to be impressed by, cause I just do what I'm told. Later I figured out that's what impressed him. He says he wants to get to know me better. I say, 'Well have you met my friend?' Trying to give him the picture I's hitched. But they's all friends, and I find that out too, soon enough. Find out the only thing matters to them is you's only what you are when you're with them, that's the only time exists to be concerned about. When you's with one you belong to him and when you get passed along well you's somebody else's. But nothing more, and they can all work that out between themselves without having to talk to you about it.

"Jacks starts flying to Omaha, takes me out to dinner, buys me all kinds of things. Funny thing is they never buy you a car, not 'til now when you need it and they can take it away just when you'll miss it most. They don't want to give you something to get away in, unless you's like I am now and you got nowhere to go. I should have remembered that, but back then I didn't need a car. I was geting so much stuff I never had before. I can't tell you; I mean, so much that I couldn't use it all, and the more I had I couldn't use the more I asked for. I wanted to see what it's like to have too much. And don't think I didn't know there was payback. I was raised on payback and don't expect nothing else. If I made any mistakes it was I'd never run up the kind of tab I got with them, never knew that kind of interest and that ain't my fault.

"More they gave me, the more I was in it. I owed them, and there was no going back. So, when they come to me said there was jobs to be done . . ."

He gone quiet and I seen that whatever he done—whatever job they give him—was still with him, whether he wanted or not. I knowed all about that, doing what you didn't think you could, not cause it was something you wanted to but on account of it's a trade-off. You got yours and now you got to give back. Ain't nothing's for free.

"Whatever you done," I says: "Whatever it is—"

"Shut up," he spits at me. "Running bags was the easiest. They got plenty of guys could do that. That's almost entry-level. I supervised that shit. What they really needed—the shortage is in combing the streets, bringing the new ones in. Taking them under your wing they call it. *Big-brothering,* if you can believe it."

At first I didn't know just what he's talking about. So he brung other guys in and so what. They'd of been turning tricks where he got them from anyways. He done them a favor setting them up with penthouses and steady gigs. But that weren't what he brung these ones in for, and he couldn't look at me while he told me what they done with them.

"Look," he says, mad at me I thought but then I seen it's his self. "Everybody's got their own thing. As many people's there are. Right? There's as many trips. It's just some things is harder to carry out than others. You can't do just anything with anybody, no matter what kind of money you got. There's the matter of finding the boy that suits your taste, then making sure he's the right material, a good investment. This is the way they talk about these things. Some have to be able to disappear, not just into another level of things but altogether. I mean they never say that, you see, but it's understood. You just understand a thing like that—same way you understand that the only way to make sure you's not as expendable is you's useful."

I got an idea where he's going with this. On Forty-deuce you heard some of them talk about easy money, once what used to be easy ain't so easy to come by no more. Talk about it for a while, how it's looking better and better, how some guys want them to come make a movie, turn a big-time, one-shot trick. They's thinking about it for a long time out there, you see it working out on their faces, next thing they's gone and ain't nobody knows where, or got the time to worry about it. The rest's just whispers, don't get talked about out loud on account of even the guys out on the streets got things they's better off not seeing.

"What are we talking about here?" I says.

"Snuff, mostly. Some people will tell you satanism. Like rituals and shit but I ain't never seen that. It ain't that simple, that easy. This is flying somebody out to make a movie, drug them up on the way over so they don't know where they's going, how they got there in case they find their way back which ain't likely but you take precautions on your investments. It's easy enough to drug them up because mostly they been working on a habit for a while anyway. These are guys who had habits out on the streets, even in their foster homes. They never really stopped. Drugs was the carrot the hawks used to lead them in to begin with. See?

"They have to be drugged up, so they have what's called endurance, so they can go through with it, which ain't really their choice by then anyway but some conditions make for better movies than others—cinematic, they say. Somebody who don't poop out the first time the thing goes in, don't blank out, go limp. They need somebody drugged enough, used to enough they's able to sit it out, take it all and still be a pretty picture. They have to want another fix, or death or whatever, enough they's willing to go through to see what they think they need on the other side."

"But why," I says. "How come they need you?"

Don't be thick, Red tells me, says I know damn well why: why they want him, why they want to do it.

"They needed me for the same reason you think you do; cause you think we's the same, right? Think we got something, and so did all the boys I got off the street. They trusted me, or wanted to. Simple as that."

"But how come they do it, them men? What for? So they get off on the boys and they want to see them hurt but then they's dead and what's to see no more? What's to get out of it after there ain't nothing to get nothing out from?"

"Think of it this way," Red says, like he been thinking about it so long he made it into a science. "What if they just want to do it cause they can? What else they gonna do they ain't already? Think about it like that. So some kid dies. So what. There's others where that one came from. Try again. Try something new, or something you already did you can't get enough of. Means nothing. There is no why. Why's for people who got to ask it. It's not they set out to do it. You got it wrong if that's the way you's seeing it. What I'm saying is they want these guys for whatever, okay? No limits. They don't know exactly *what* they want to do until they get there and kind of get into it. So it ain't like they exactly set out that way. It's more like they don't have to worry if whatever they do ends up there. You see? So what they want's for it to make no difference. Just in case."

I stared at what was left of the fries in the basket, mess of catsup and greasy waste, and got sick thinking about them kids. Got sick on account of what they got done to them, but sick too cause once they's gone there weren't nobody to figure it all out. The only ones what could make any sense of it was too busy doing it all over again to somebody else. I thought about money and not having none, and what having it done to peoples who ain't used to it, how maybe I could take Red somewheres neither one of us'd ever have to worry about it again, wouldn't have to ask nobody for a thing, do nothing in return. Couldn't nobody take away from us the right to figure it out. Then I thought how much shit it been to figure things out, how mostly it seemed like you never could. Maybe it was pointless after all.

"You helped—when they done this stuff."

"Once I was in it, I did whatever I was told, right up until now."

Then it hit me: What's to say Red weren't doing with me what he done with them others. What if he done a number on me to get me hooked, *made* me follow him here, just to turn me over to Jacks and the car scratchers. How's I so stupid I thought I knowed him, even after he kept telling me he's somebody else? I could feel the french fries in my stomach, felt my gut twist into pain like from slow poison what just now took hold.

"What do you want with me?" I says.

"What the hell are you talking about?"

"Talking about dragging me here, to Colorado, telling me to get lost so's I'd tag along. Giving me all this talk so's I'll think you's safe now to go with."

"You're crazy. Look, I ain't gonna lie. You're exactly the type. You fit what they look for, to a T. But I don't think you really want me to tell you."

"You's just saying that cause you think I'll make you now."

"Fuck it," says Red, "Number one, you ain't got a lick of sense in your head and nobody to tell you better, otherwise you wouldn't of come here. Two, you got a dope habit—"

"I ain't used in more'n a week."

"Exactly. It's written all over your face. Three, you don't care what happens to you. You fit the profile, sure enough. Besides all that, you probably got something."

"Like what?"

"Like AIDS, fathead. Tell me you ever been tested. Tell me you know just what to do to get it. Tell me you've always been safe doing what you do."

Course I gone through the roof, but what could I say? True enough—all he said was spot on. And I thought about it wherever I been, somewheres always in the back of my head—voice what said *you got it, you got it, if anybody's got it you got it.* But things was too busy finding a place to sleep, finding a john, turning tricks; hell, I don't know. Ain't time to think about something like that. He was right. I didn't even know where to go to find out for sure, didn't even want to know half the time, not from no damn doctor. If I got it I got it, and I got it, so what do you do.

"Look," says Red. "If you think I can drag you into this, you's a little late. I'm pullin' out. I done everything I could to get rid of you. All I'm saying is you wouldn't hardly need my help anyway, and that's something maybe you should start thinking about, instead of me."

"How you know when you got it?"

"Got what," he says. "What they want?"

No: AIDS, I says. Got AIDS.

200

"Myself, I do know. I got it. You, on the other hand, maybe, maybe not. You get tested. It ain't over 'til it is. They draw blood, keep it a few days, let you know. Worst couple days of your life, every time you do it. Getting it's almost a relief. Don't have to worry no more. Or that's what you think at first anyway."

"But . . . so then you's dying. Right? Dying anyways. So why do they care, Jacks and them, what happens to you if they can save their-selves the trouble?"

"You remember everything I said, up 'til now?"

I nodded.

"That's how come. I ain't going nowhere too fast. There's a lot can be said between now and then."

"But why'd they set you up here in the first place? How come they didn't just rub you out if they done it with others, back in Nebraska?"

"I'm stupid, like you. That's all."

"But that's what they do, kill peoples, watch them die. So what's one more?"

"Like I said, I ain't going nowhere too soon. It ain't much trouble to kick off a few kids, not when it's a pleasure. But nursing me through, no way. Money for pills and time they ain't got any interest in wasting. Point is: I knew this was coming. I knew the time was coming they'd get rid of me. Wouldn't care what happened to me no more. So I told them I wanted to cut a deal. I thought I had it all worked out. Found a new way to make myself useful. But they got more brainpower on their side, even if you wouldn't know it by look-ing at them. Well, maybe not brainpower but money. They got a lot of that, and they want to keep it, so it makes them smart in a way. Smart enough not to care about nobody and let that get in the way."

From the look on his face I seen it weren't nothing I wanted to know about. Somebody got traded in for something, and Red's the one made the bargain. I seen enough of playing the cards you got to recognize a poker face like he got on. Some kid: He promised them some kid they couldn't pass up. I tried to picture what kid, whose. And like he knowed what I's thinking Red finished my thoughts.

"The ones from good homes is the ones they want, but they can never get their hands on those. The ones from families whose parents pay attention to them, don't beat them, take good care of them. I mean, come on, they're like perfect creatures to them in a way. Cause those never see it coming. They never seen anything you and me seen, don't know the things people do where we come from. When things go down, the look on their faces. It's strictly for connoisseurs. Pure. That's what they covet—that's what I brung them. But not until they set me up here."

I knowed it, but I didn't want him to tell me, and now he done. I expected he'd bow his head in shame, turn his eyes from me at least. Instead he got this look to him what dared me to say something bad of him.

"Like I say, what makes you think all of us wants nothing like you seem to? I ain't got long and I want a little something. I brought them what they want, and now I's out of it. Or thought I was."

I stared at the table, pattern of boomerangs tangled together in bright green. I couldn't look at Red, couldn't now I knowed he good as killed somebody. Took somebody out of the home he ain't never had. I hated them much as he done, as much of the time; for what they got, cause they didn't deserve it. Fact they's so perfect made me hate them even more. Do somebody have to be that perfect, is that how come I ain't got what they got? Kicked myself how many times cause I didn't know how to make myself perfect like they was so's I could get me some. Kicked myself cause I got to learn it—lessons, examples, whatever—whereas they's just born with it. In my head I seen them fall off high places, seen the railing snap and down they come.

I seen their fingers break, their hair fall out, crying their throats hoarse without nobody'd come to check on them, bleeding for the first time and nobody around to tell them blood clots. They got hit by cars, left home alone, and always the worst, getting kicked out for good. But when I come to that in my head I seen that I couldn't never wish the things what happened to me on nobody else. Them things was all in my head, wanting them to happen and feeling bad for it both. And stayed there.

Then I thought about Walrus, and how I left him, maybe for dead. I done what I needed to, to get out of something I's stuck in, and here I was, still living with myself when God knows what become of him. Who's I to say?

"Couple of new kids gone to a senator in Nebraska, told him the deal—not really much of it but more'n he'd ever heard or thought

202

happens. Heats on everybody, but I don't know what they's so scared about.

"Won't nothing happen to them. I mean it never does. That's what we's for. Already one of them's left town, took his money and bought a plane ticket out. Police chief's transferred somewhere else. But now they's worried about me out here. Loose ends. Saying bullshit about I's ratting, can't be trusted. Funny, they trusted me enough for eight years. I'm a liability, so they's watching me close, too close; don't know what they got planned. Just know they're back up on the roost checking me out. The deal was a car, a stash, a new name. New everything. Did you notice? I'm somebody else. My name's Richard now. I'm Rich, I got money—some joke, huh?—a place of my own to live. A job. Two parents, back in Idaho, call me all the time to check up on me. Can't seem to let me grow up. I come from a big family where everybody gets together every holiday; they always done it that way. Room so crowded you can't get to your own plate. I'm learning how to play the goddamn guitar, cause I got pretty songs to sing. Nobody'd ever guess where they come from."

And I thought of that too, whenever I let myself sneak it in. What it'd be like if I's somebody else, not just cause I used a different name in whatever room with whatever john and they wanted me to be whatever they got in their head, not just cause I's in a new place and wanted to make like I weren't living with the same old shit. That was just survival, that; kind of thing where maybe they believe but you ain't got a quiet enough place to go back to so's you believe yourself. Whenever I could, I thought about *really*—no lie—being somebody else. And sometimes that somebody else was somebody I knowed, like Fletcher. Somebody I thought maybe was everything I'd want to be if I could name the rules.

Before it was anybody, it was my pa. I seen that now. But he died, and it was either follow him or find somebody else. So I found Fletcher, or he found me. And when I had to leave him too, I found Red. Only I been so busy looking for Red I almost didn't recognize him on account of he's just as set as I been on being somebody else.

"You don't like me now, huh? Well don't say I didn't try to scare you off good."

I looked at him without I said nothing. Just looked at his hair, them eyes, so damn blue. How his skin looked like it been through something but ain't told him about it yet.

"I don't hate you. Maybe I's wrong for feeling the way I done before, I mean without even barely knowing who you was: I can see that. But I don't hate you either, and I can't do nothing about it."

For the first time ever he give me the kind of look I like to tell myself I followed him for. Clear eyes and straight ahead at me, couldn't nothing be read into it, and didn't make no sense, but hit; made contact and locked. Kind of look you can't help but want to put thoughts over and explain.

"I worked on this guy, Rich, I can't say how long. Before eight years ago when I met Jacks and the others. Before anything else I remember, before I had a name for him, knew what he looked like: He was there. This idea in my head. Got bigger as time went on. And I thought now I could be him, right? Thought nobody could stop me.

"They sure as hell did. I was so stupid, thinking I could trust them any more'n I trusted myself."

* * *

We gone back to where the van been and it was still there. So-called still sleeping inside, dead to the world like ain't nothing to worry about but sweet dreams. He already knowed Rich on account of they met at the courtyard just like him and me done. When we woke him up he thought we come to all of us hang out, like if I got a choice I'd of spent our time with him. But we needed a ride and probably more, so I let him think whatever he wanted.

"Take us anywheres but your folk's house," I said after we's on the road. So he took us to the Garden of the Gods.

Red and me's sitting in the back while he drove, and he kept asking why didn't one of us come up front with him; how come we's hiding in the back. I told him we got a lot to discuss, since it been so long we ain't seen each other. Told him Red and me was practically brothers. Ain't got the same Ma or Pa or even growed up nearby, but like all them other things what can't be explained, we got a connection and this here's the first chance we got to plug it in again.

When we pulled into the place it was like I seen it before, only now it was earlier in the day there was peoples climbing all over the rocks, got the colored stripe ropes strung out. Looked like an invasion. Me and Red watched them together without saying nothing for a few minutes, watched how slow it was they got from one place to the next, so's it looked like they wasn't even moving. It seemed pointless, watching that kind of thing, on account of you wouldn't never get the sense you seen the move from bottom to top; still, the two of us couldn't take our eyes off.

Until old Big Mouth up front started banging his jaws, hopping across the van so's it shook, asking what was we going to do now, like boy oh boy. I turned around set to knock him and good, but Red's hand come up to stop me, pulled mine back down, and he looked at me like to say we needed this idiot more than we needed quiet. So I bit my tongue and held my hands to my side, stewed even as a few minutes later Big Mouth started reading off the names of all them cliffs in the garden, like even though I heard it a dozen times maybe Red ain't. He didn't get sidetracked a whit when he set to rolling a joint. Just kept on with them names, every so often put his head up to nod this way or that, then back to the task at hand. I been around him long enough to know he could roll a joint in his sleep.

"Indians used to do this here," he said, nodding to his handiwork, and he started in all over again about brave Chief So-and-so way back when. Like he knowed everything.

But turns out Red's the one done. Red tells him how the whole reason the Indian ain't around still doing it's cause whitey come and kicked him out. Our honky forefathers come in and thought it's such a neat place they acted like they's the one's created it. Only thing in their way was them Indians, so they done what anybody else would of done, or anyways what anybody ever since has, what we call relocated, which's just a nice way of saying forced them out. We stole their place from them and called it our own, and the only time we let them back in since was to put them on show where they got to play by our rules, look pretty or get lost.

"Ain't neither of you seen it?" asks Red, "The Petrified Indian? What a fucking joke. He been on display at the Trading Company up the road for years." And where the Indian left his mark on the rocks we crossed it out and scratched our own names in. "They's still there too," pointing outside the window somewheres. "At least a dozen of them. It don't matter. It all goes around and around. They come in and found it, then we come in and done the same. But in the end it'll get took back the same way it was given. The ground'll split and suck it back in just like it spit it out. It'll write its own damn story."

Course I couldn't let him go on no more, on account of he could of been talking about me and I's ashamed, the way I come into the Garden and wanted to take it over, set up camp and make it mine like it been waiting all my life for me to come in and leave my mark. I weren't no better, no different.

"We got to get out of here," I told Red under my breath, but he weren't the only one heard it.

"Get out?!" says Big Mouth. "Last time you dragged me here I couldn't get you to leave the van. Now we haven't even smoked the weed and you want out."

"I ain't talking about the van."

And Red give me another look like don't tell the idiot no more than he needed to know.

But I couldn't keep quiet. I didn't like the idea we's stuck with only Big Mouth and no way out. I come all this way to find Red and now I got him and seen what kind of trouble he's in there weren't no way I could sit still.

"If we keep moving around in the same places they's going to catch sight of us," I says.

"Shh," from Red, who didn't take his eyes off the rocks.

"But we got to keep moving cause we got nowheres to go. And if you don't shut up we won't have that either. We got all kinds of peoples after us."

"Pff," goes Big Mouth without he looked up from rolling the joint. "Yeah right."

I didn't smoke none of it but still I guess I got some contact high secondhand, all that exhale trapped in the van like we was. Red smoked a little his self which I couldn't figure on account of it seemed like we needed clear heads. Pretty soon the two of them was just laid back and out but not me: I's sitting there trying to figure what we got to do next. Then it come to me. The only problem with the van was the guy driving it. If we got rid of him we'd be made.

So when they's both so knocked out they couldn't hear me snap my fingers in front of their faces, I started dragging So-called to the side door of the van, got the thing slid open with one hand while I got his legs in the other, and just a rumble out of him, like tossing in his sleep. Hardest part was bringing him out to the ground, a step down from the van; I took his head and arms first so's there wouldn't be no thud when he touched the dirt and stones what's out there.

Drug him a few yards from the van, took his jacket from back inside and wadded it under his head. His eyes opened a peep and for a second I thought for sure I's cooked. But soon as they's open they was closed again, brung on by a lazy grin what come over his face.

"Mmm," he whispered. "What're you doing?"

"Just making sure you's cozy," I told him.

"Where are we?" he said.

"Keep your eyes closed and it'll come to you," I says. "The Indians used to do this here."

"Okay, Chief," and the grin got bigger before it gone out altogether, gone off to wherever he been inside his head.

I walked backwards to the van to make sure he didn't wake up. And once I's inside I sat at the wheel, big circle of a thing, thinking, *This thing'll take me wherever I think we should go, all I got to do is turn it.* Looked to Red, asleep in the back, then back out the window to Big Mouth, snoozing ditto. To one or the other of them then out to the Garden, the rock climbers slow moving across the rocks—damn invaders. Started the van and drove it toward the Gateway what got the afternoon sun behind it, bright red doorway to wherever. Big Mouth got smaller and smaller in the rearview until he weren't but nothing compared to the rest of the place, just a little piece of not much, like everything else but the rocks in the Garden and Pikes Peak beyond.

Just out the other side of the Gateway I stopped the van, had myself a think about where we's going to head. Looked down the road a stretch to the left and right. *Where to, where to?* Then I seen the car. First I thought it was just one like any other. Then it hit me it might be the one I seen when me and Big Mouth was driving into town earlier that morning, only other one out on the road when we was, kept snaking in and out of the buildings downtown, cat and mouse. *There's all kinds of cars,* I thought, *and lots of them look the same.* Could be anybody. Could be nobody.

When it got closer I seen there was three men inside, got the three profiles made dark from the sun behind the car—two tall heads on either side, little Shorty peahead in the middle. As they coasted past the van and through the Gateway I got a good look from high up where I's sitting, seen them staring hard ahead like they's done wasting time. Same look the Madam give when a boy crossed her wrong, only she ain't a hawk.

How they know we's here? I's thinking.

If they followed us they'd of seen the van right off and pulled over, and if they didn't follow us how'd they find out where we gone when we ain't told no one? Then I thought of So-called strung out across the gravel back there, easiest one to ask a question—you'd have to be an idiot *not* to ask him what he's doing there like that—what with everybody else in the Garden up on the rocks. They'd think he's Red, the way they's both tie-dyed and hippied out, way they both looked like any other boy in Colorado Springs, and even when they seen he ain't they'd think he must know him and they'd start grilling him. He'd tell them about we took off in his van and what the van looked like, and we'd be as good as goners. I floored the pedal without I even decided left or right and it showed. The van lurched forward like a wad of spit before I got hold of the wheel and decided which way.

And the start shook Red awake. I watched him in the rearview as he come to his senses, or what little the pot left him with. Nodded his head like trying to lose his high, then a look around the inside of the van trying to figure why it felt like he's moving but everything looked so still. Got that look on his face like everybody'd left him, until he looked up front and seen me at the wheel.

"What's happening?" Voice come out as hazy as he looked, barely there like he ain't figured for sure how to use it just yet.

"I had to leave him. I had to. We wouldn't never of got to where we needed, let alone fast enough, without I done it."

He stared at me for the longest time.

"What are you talking about?"

"I left him back there, in the Garden, laid out and he'll be just fine. He's as snug as a body gets so don't worry. And now we got to get on the move, and all I's saying is: weren't no way with him wondering why and what for."

Then what I done must of hit him full cause he jumped up, so fast the sight of it in the rearview made me jump, and he stomped over to the passenger seat, sat sideways with his hands on his knees, fingers spread tight over the pants there, shook his head again, said he thought maybe he's more stoned than he felt like.

"I heard you wrong, right?"

"Look," I says, "we ain't got time to argue. I seen Jacks and his guys come in when we's driving out of there."

And then Red's legs started tapping like crazy, sent his fingers scampering across his knees and back over theirselves, muttering, shit shit. Shit.

For a while we was clear, weren't so much as a person or a pebble neither one on the road behind us. Couple times I thought maybe the rearview mirror lied like everything else, so I turned around just to make sure. If there'd been anywheres to turn I guess Red would of give me directions, but since there was just the one road, what didn't let off nowheres but onto a skinny shoulder of dusty gravel, weren't nothing he could do with all that energy but put it into shaking his knees.

"Look," he says, "I don't know what you're thinking, but I'm not going anywhere. I mean, you can leave, you know? But I can't go with you. I'm staying here. You're just making it worse. Really."

Up ahead like a single dot on a blank page was the turn-off what would take us back towards town, but no sooner'd we seen it than another dot, some car what with our luck couldn't be nobody but Jacks, showed up on the rearview.

"Speed up," says Red, like he's crying look out.

"And get us pulled over so we's like sitting ducks? No sir."

"That's the best possible thing could happen to us at this point," he says. So I stepped on it, but weren't much to step on. That van was older than the both of us put together, just a box of tin with some wheels throwed into the deal. It gone a little faster, a little, but mostly it just puttered louder than ever.

"We's going to have to pull over," I says, "but it ain't going be the cops. We'll be lucky if we can make it over to the shoulder in this hippy trap."

But Red weren't listening, got his head turned, eyes peeled on the road behind us. Nearly off his seat, but finally he got up altogether and gone to the back window, where he kneeled off to the side watching the car. Didn't take his eyes off for a second, like he knowed it'd catch up with us, like he knowed and there weren't nothing he could do about it.

I looked in the rearview myself, and sure enough the car'd got bigger, and sure enough it was Jacks. Shit shit shit, and step on it, says Red, come back to the passenger seat like to say it's hopeless, only I can't step on it anymore'n I's doing. Worst kind of feeling, seeing that car make on us, getting closer and we couldn't get away, feeling like we's trapped in that van even as it's moving, trapped and they's gaining and there ain't nothing we can do. Maybe we'll make it to the turn-off, I says. Maybe we'll make it into town and then they won't be able to do nothing, not with all them peoples around. Bullshit, says Red, don't make a difference neither way, and he starts laughing like to prove it. Before long that car was right on us, disappeared from the mirror and shows back up right alongside, so we's looking down into it, and seen Shorty's motioning we better move over.

What'm I supposed to do, I's asking Red, but he's looking straight ahead, won't look at Shorty on the one side or me on the other. Then he must of decided there weren't nothing else straight ahead neither, on account of he turned to me finally, says pull over. *Pull over*, I says. You crazy? No, he says, but this is. Do it. So I done.

Slowed it down and brung the thing to the side of the road, sat there with the engine going, watched Shorty and his men park. Looked at Red and hated things—hated things on account of I couldn't know what's about to go down. I started out of my seat but he puts his hand up, says whoa. Rolls down his window, and Shorty walks up to it, got the two man-towers right behind him to make sure I guess Red knows they's there, like after all this who could forget.

"I want a minute with the kid," Red says, and I look around the van trying to figure out who he's talking about.

"Who's your friend?" says Shorty, nodding his head towards me.

Nobody, says Red. "He ain't a friend. Just give me a minute with him and I'll get out and explain."

"We don't really owe you any favors at this point," says Shorty. Says they don't got to let him do nothing, specially after this kind of scene, where he's trying to make some kind of run for it, ditching them at the restaurant where he said he'd meet them after he got off work. But then he tells him he's got exactly two seconds and make it quick. And Red rolls up the window, turns to me.

"You know I got to go with them," he says. "Don't worry about it. You just go back."

"Get off it," I says. "Go back where?"

This ain't an option, he says. He's got to go with them. But I'll be okay.

Don't do nothing stupid, he says. On account of now ain't the time and these ain't the ones to do it with. Pulls the handle and he's out the door, shuts it, goes to them three, they's all standing at Shorty's car. I's turned around in the seat watching out the window, got the sun coming through makes all kind of play on the glass.

Fucker said I weren't nobody.

I flung open the door and charged towards them, said hold it right there. Shorty turns and looks at me, them two guys puts their hands to the chest of their suitcoats like they got an itch there they's getting ready to scratch. Shorty holds out his hands to them like to say don't scratch just yet. "Listen," I says when I get to them, "I want him to come with me." I gone over and stood by Red, even though he looked at me like I's about to know the meaning of a fist in the face.

"Jared," Shorty says to Red. "Isn't this the kid from Omaha? Do you want to tell me why he's now in Colorado Springs, starting trouble? Do you want to tell me why I should believe you when you tell me you haven't been making contacts?"

Red looks down at the ground. "Look," he says. "He's nobody— knows nothing. He's got a family back in Omaha and he's just on vacation, they sent him here over school break, that's why he talked to me at the fair, found out where I's going and said he's going to; but that's it. I shouldn't of told him that much—shouldn't of even told him where I's going. It just slipped out and he kind of followed me."

"Slipped out," Shorty said, and let it hang in the air like it was something for all of them to think about.

Red looks at me, look says Godammit get the fuck out of here, what do it take with you. I looked right back at him and then at Shorty and I says, "I is *too* his friend. I just want that out, so everybody remembers. We's friends."

"We all feel so much better you've told us," said Shorty. "Now that's settled, we have to be going."

"Wait," I says. "I want a picture. I want one of you to take a picture for me."

Red rolled his eyes, turns towards the car, puts his arms on the hood and his face in his hands.

"Jared," Shorty says, "this kid's now asking for a picture. Why is this kid asking for a picture?"

"Cause I want one," I says. "I's standing right here, even if you don't see me, so why don't you just aim anything you got to say to me this way. I want a picture cause I do, that's all."

Now *Shorty's* rolling his eyes. "Jared, please say good-bye to this kid and let him get back to his vacation, or we'll have to be changing his plans."

Red spins around, got a worried look on his face says I ain't going to get a picture. Forget it. I looked in his eyes and seen—what? I don't know. Him staring at me, the puzzle of somebody else.

"I got to get something," I says.

"Jared, this boy's now going into the van to get something," says Shorty, which point I said thanks for telling him but Red's got eyes of his own. Them two others got an itch again, held their hands there while Shorty said, "We'll just wait and see, boys." I gone to the van slow so's not to shake up nobody. Searched all over looking for the thing, finally found it, my scram-bag, under one of them pillows in the back. Dug through looking for it, past Nana's letters, Alligator Boy squinting at me, tie from the man in Memphis; and there it was, Pa's flask. I unscrewed the cap, brung it to my nose for a smell, back floats all kinds of things.

Here, I says, holding it out by the car, for Red to come get it. "I want you should have this. And I got a camera too."

Red come over slow and put his hand on the flask to take it.

"This is yours," I said before I'd let it go. "I give it to you for free, cause I like you—just cause. First it belonged to my Pa, then me, and now it's yours."

Then while Shorty and them other two's standing there with their mouths wide open I got Red close to me and held So-called's Polaroid out front of us, pushed the button and the flash blinded our eyes.

Colorado Springs

I been sitting in the Garden of the Gods for the longest time. Wondering what I'll do now.

I give So-called's picture back to him. Jared or Richard or Red, blond hair. On account of I got my own. That and his camera, said I's sorry I took it, or thanks for letting me borrow it or whatever. Stared at my picture so hard, thinking I can't tell you what—thinking it's mine. Ours. We's a little blurry in it; just a little, like a memory. Red's freckles is just shading across his cheeks.

When I took the van back to So-called I asked could I have the red gem I got out of his folk's house, told him I'd understand if he's upset I took it, said I don't know why I done.

"Keep it," he says like he ain't recognized it. "I didn't even know we had it anyway."

So I's looking through it as the sun's going down, around the Garden at the way it cuts everything into pieces, broken red pieces and every one so perfect, makes a strange order out of things. Looking at the picture through it—me and Red a thousand times, turn it and we's a circle.

Circle, yeah. So what. So okay. So things is a circle. So maybe there's sense in that. I mean if you stand in the middle then you can see it all at once, you know? There's power in that. Cause if you's in the middle you own it in a way. You's the center.

It ain't a matter of going back. I don't think so now. I think it's a matter of going around. Like Red says, around and around. It just goes. Ain't anybody holds the key, not really, and that's where you get the power I guess. We's all of us in there, we's all of us equal, so small ain't none of us can play God. Ma and Aunt Edna, Grandma, Nana.

Pa, God rest his soul. God or whoever. Rest his soul. I's still figuring it out.

I don't know. Maybe I'll call Madam. Things ain't turned out the way we planned, but what's new? She said I could, call; if I ain't back on dope, and I ain't. I sure as hell ain't. Maybe I'll track down Fletcher. He said I could too. They's good peoples. Point is I can do whatever I want. I know at least two folks who wouldn't mind helping me, and I figure that's enough for now. Maybe it's more'n I thought I got.

There's always So-called, who ain't really that bad. He said I can stay with him until I figure out what I aim to do, said he'd come pick me up when it gets dark, on account of I told him I need some time to myself. Told him I's really sorry I pissed on his bed, on account of I know he might not understand any better than me why I done it.

When I brung the van back earlier I asked did he want to look for the names scratched on the rocks with me, see the writing on the walls for ourselves, and he said yes. So we smoked some weed and set to it, tried to remember where was it Red been pointing when he told us about them. We searched all through . . . in circles—the Tower of Babel, Balanced Rock, Montezuma's Temple, the Three Graces, and back to the good old Siamese Twins can't nobody but the way things is come between. Seen signs off the paths said **This land reclaimed** and laughed, on account of we both knowed it'd take it all back for itself when it damn well pleased, like Red says. Finally found them names, north side of the Gateway Rock. Crude *Wm Hartley, A C Wright* carved several inches apart. *1858.* Them and a bunch of scratches we couldn't make heads or tails of.

"They were looking for gold," says So-called.

Which point I got sad a little and rubbed his head hard, give him a noogie.

"That's no excuse. Who ain't?"

214

Thanks to the following:

Lady J; Sue Stein, for wondering where I'd be in ten years, when the rest of them had my grim plot firmly etched in stone; my parents, for giving me my freedom, however inadvertently; Jeanne; Dennis Cooper; Ira Silverberg; Keith Kahla, Teresa Theophano, and all unseen hands involved in the production of this book; and most of all Bill Castle, the best home a body could want.